FLINTLOCK:
KILL OR DIE

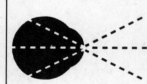 This Large Print Book carries the
Seal of Approval of N.A.V.H.

FLINTLOCK: KILL OR DIE

WILLIAM W. JOHNSTONE
WITH J.A. JOHNSTONE

THORNDIKE PRESS

A part of Gale, Cengage Learning

 GALE
CENGAGE Learning·

Farmington Hills, Mich • San Francisco • New York • Waterville, Maine
Meriden, Conn • Mason, Ohio • Chicago

GALE
CENGAGE Learning®

LIBRARY OF CONGRESS CATALOGING-IN-PUBLICATION DATA

Names: Johnstone, William W, author. | Johnstone, J. A., author.
Title: Flintlock : kill or die / by William W. Johnstone with J. A. Johnstone.
Description: Large print edition. | Waterville, Maine : Thorndike Press, 2016. | © 2015 | Series: Flintlock ; #3 | Series: Thorndike Press large print western
Identifiers: LCCN 2015041223| ISBN 9781410487100 (hardcover) | ISBN 1410487105 (hardcover)
Subjects: LCSH: Large type books. | GSAFD: Western stories.
Classification: LCC PS3560.O415 F596 2016 | DDC 813/.54—dc23
LC record available at http://lccn.loc.gov/2015041223

Published in 2016 by arrangement with Pinnacle Books, an imprint of Kensington Publishing Corp.

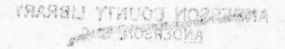

Printed in the United States of America
1 2 3 4 5 6 7 20 19 18 17 16

FLINTLOCK: KILL OR DIE

CHAPTER ONE

A Mexican Mona Lisa with a come-hither smile was Sam Flintlock's undoing. In fact she damn near got him killed, a source of irritation that would trouble him for days.

The girl held open the blanket that served as a door to the cantina, stood to one side and beckoned to him. Now a man of Flintlock's experience should have heeded the warning signs. A woman who wore a red, clinging dress, yes, cut up to *there,* that barely covered her breasts, a tightly laced corset and high-heeled ankle boots was obviously up to no good. But the beautiful femme fatale wore an eye patch of scarlet leather adorned with a thin pocket watch . . . and Flintlock was fascinated.

How readily he ignored the two expensive horses standing hipshot at the hitching rail, one of them bearing an elaborately engraved silver saddle with the initials *AP* on the back of the cantle. A man of the West like Flintlock should have wondered if those initials could possibly be those of Alphonse Plume, the Nacogdoches draw fighter.

But the smiling seductress showed a deal of tanned thigh under fishnet stockings and black garters and Flintlock threw caution to the winds. He advanced on the girl with a smile on his homely face and a song in his heart.

It was a bad move and one he'd very soon regret.

After the heat and searing brightness of the southeast Texas day the cantina was cool and dark, lit by oil lamps. The odor of peppers and ancient human sweat hung in the air. The girl took Flintlock's hand in hers and led the way to a table. Her one good eye stared into Sam's pair of good ones, flicking between the two, and she said, "Buy poor little Conchita a drink, big boy?" She smelled musky, like desert flowers.

"Sure," Flintlock said. "Name your pizen, little gal."

Conchita lifted her head and yelled, in a now brassy voice, "Carlos. Tequila."

Carlos, a fat, oily little cuss who looked like he'd put the grease in *greaser*, brought a bottle and two glasses. He gave Flintlock a pitying glance and said, "Are you hungry, señor? I have hard-boiled eggs and cheese.

Do you like cheese?"

"He's not hungry, Carlos," Conchita said. "At least not for food." She smiled and rested her little chin on the palm of her hand, and the dozen or so silver bracelets on her arm chimed. "You're very handsome, señor," she said. "We will enjoy ourselves tonight, I think."

Flintlock knew he was anything but handsome, and the thunderbird tattooed across his throat added nothing to his appearance, but he still didn't smell a rat. Even when one of the two Americanos who sat back in the gloom got up and crossed the floor, his big-roweled Texas spurs jingling, he didn't notice, or care. The man opened the curtain, glanced outside and then returned. He whispered something to his companion and the man nodded.

Had Flintlock's head not been filled with the glorious scent of Conchita and his mind dwelling on mattress time he might have put two and two together and realized that the man had looked outside to check on Flintlock's horse, to see if it was worth killing him for. It was a brown horse and Sam had paid a hundred dollars for it. On the frontier a man's life was worth a whole lot less than that.

Conchita set down her glass of tequila,

bade Flintlock to drink up, then waved a hand in front of her face. "I'm so hot," she said. The lashes of her good eye fluttered and she smiled. "You'll have to help me out of my corset tonight . . . what is your name?"

"Flintlock, but you can call me Sam."

"Sam is such a beautiful name," Conchita said.

"Yeah, I'm right partial to it my ownself. How does that there corset work?"

"It laces up the back. See?"

"Oh yeah, I see it. I'll have that off'n you in a trice, little lady."

"Bad boy," Conchita said, smiling. "We'll have fun, huh?"

Flintlock drained his glass. "Depend on it."

Then a man's voice, loud, commanding and belligerent.

"There's a woman in this here cantina cheating on me," he said. "I won't mention any names, but if she don't get up and come over here quick I'll take my fist and close her other eye."

Conchita's anger flared. She jumped to her feet, flipped her eye patch onto her forehead and placed her little fists on her hips. "Alphonse Plume, you don't own me!" she said. "I can entertain any gentleman I want."

Flintlock saw that Conchita's eye under the patch was every bit as healthy as the other, but that didn't bother him much. Women wore some strange fashions. But the name Alphonse Plume did. He was a top-name hired gun and a man to be reckoned with.

Plume rose to his feet, grinning. Even in the broadcloth and frilled-shirt finery of the frontier gambler/gunman he looked half man, half gorilla. He was a foot taller than Flintlock and at least fifty pounds heavier. Plume had mean eyes and the talk was he'd killed eight men in gunfights. Looking at him and the two ivory-handled Colts on his hips Flintlock had no reason to doubt that figure. The man next to him was also in broadcloth, not quite as brawny as Plume, but he looked just as mean.

Plume crossed the floor, grabbed Conchita by the arm and said, "Get to your room and wait for me there."

"I will not," the girl said, her generous breasts heaving. "I don't need to do anything you tell me."

"You always have when I've been paying you," Plume said. He had big teeth. Yellowish white, like walrus ivory. "Now do as you're told."

"I will not," Conchita said, breaking free

of his hand. His grip left red welts on her arm. "You don't own me."

"Yeah," Plume said, "you told me that already." He grabbed the girl again and cocked his fist. "You want to wear two eye patches?"

Flintlock got to his feet. His Colt was shoved into his waistband, his usual mode of carry. "Let the girl be," he said. "She wants nothing to do with you, at least for today."

Plume was surprised. He looked Flintlock over from the crown of his battered hat, his sweat-stained buckskin shirt, shabby pants and scuffed boots. His gaze lingered on the Colt for just a moment, then he said, "What the hell are you?"

"Nobody. A peace-loving man is what I am. Flintlock's the name and I always say, Flintlock by name, Flintlock by nature."

"What the hell is that supposed to mean?" Plume said.

"I have no idea," Flintlock said. He reached into his pants pocket and palmed a silver dollar.

Plume pushed the girl away from him and she fell heavily against a table.

"I want no trouble," Carlos said. "I run a respectable establishment here."

"You run a damned brothel," Plume said.

12

"So shut your trap." He glared at Flintlock. "Some men need cut down to size, mister, and you're one of them."

"Like the man said, I want no shooting scrape," Flintlock said.

"Maybe so," Plume said. "But you got one."

"You're hunting trouble," Flintlock said.

"No kidding," Plume said. "But you're not going to give me much trouble, saddle tramp. It's just been a while since I killed a man and I'm overdue." He nodded to Conchita. "And I enjoy a woman after I kill somebody. So you see how it is with me."

"I see how it is with you, but I'm not buying into it," Flintlock said. He flipped the dollar at Plume. The gunman reacted for just a split second, his eyes flicking to the coin. It was all the edge Flintlock needed. He drew from the waistband and fired. Hit hard at a range of less than five feet, Plume went down.

The second gunman was much faster than Flintlock on the draw and shoot. His right hand blurred as he went for his gun. But Flintlock's Colt was in his fist and he had the drop. He fired before the man cleared leather. The gunman staggered back a step, his revolver coming up. Flintlock shot again, a hit. His second bullet missed, but it wasn't

13

needed. The gunman crashed onto his back and lay still.

His ears ringing, gun smoke drifting around him, Sam Flintlock looked down at the havoc he'd wrought. Two young men dead in the time it took for the watch in his pocket to tick off five seconds.

Conchita was the first to recover. She let out a wail of anguish, flung herself on Plume's bloody body and covered his face in kisses. Then, her pretty face twisted in a mask of fury, she turned to Flintlock and said, "You murdered him, you no-good son of a bitch."

The man called Carlos was at Flintlock's shoulder. "You better run, señor," he said.

Deafened by the roar of his guns, Flintlock said, "Huh?"

Carlos raised his voice. "They were Brewster Ritter's hired men. He'll come after you."

"You're already a walking dead man," Conchita said. "Get out of here and die somewhere else."

"They didn't give me much choice," Flintlock said.

"Brewster Ritter isn't going to give a damn about that," Carlos said. "He's a hard-driven man, señor, and nobody kills two of his men and gets away with it."

Conchita's anger mangled her accent. "You feelthy peeg, Reeter will keel you so slowly you'll scream for days."

Flintlock shoved his gun back into his waistband. "I guess I'm not wanted around here, huh?" he said.

Carlos shook his head. "No, señor, stay if you wish and drink tequila. But where there are two of Ritter's pistoleros ten more will be close by."

Flintlock, not liking what he heard, thought it through. Then he said, "How much for the drinks?"

"On the house, señor. Now leave before it's too late."

The writing was on the wall and Flintlock saw it clear. A single chair stood under a window opposite and above it in black paint were scrawled the words:

RUBE HOOPER, CRIPPLE, WAS HUNG IN THIS CHAIR. AUG 4, 1867. RIP

Flintlock, all his attention focused on Conchita, had not noticed the writing before. Now he took it as a bad omen. "Well, I'm outta here," he said.

"A very wise choice, señor," Carlos said.

As he walked to the door Flintlock heard Conchita spit in his direction.

15

CHAPTER TWO

Sam Flintlock rode in the direction of the cypress swamps that bordered the Sabine River, his horse plodding without sound across yielding, sandy soil. Piney woods lay to the north but around Flintlock was a land of gulf prairies and saltwater marshes that attracted birds of all kinds. He saw gulls, terns, sandpiper and snipe and woodcock, but none of the alligators that he'd been warned about. The day was hot and humid and draped over Flintlock like a blanket soaked in warm water.

Old Barnabas sat on a lightning-blasted tree trunk. A great iron gear wheel as wide across as he was tall stood between his feet. The old mountain man, dead these twenty years, glared at Flintlock and said, "I never reckoned on raising up an idiot, but I surely did."

"What are you doing here, Barnabas?" Flintlock said, drawing rein. "I don't need you around."

"You got to start thinking with your brain, boy, instead of that thing that hangs below your navel," Barnabas said. "Why did you follow the girl into the cantina and almost get yourself shot?"

"Like you said, I didn't let my brain do the thinking."

"That's because you're an idiot. I raised up an idiot."

"What you doing with the big wheel?" Flintlock said.

"Cleaning it up for you-know-who. He says it's time Hell joined the industrial age and now we got iron foundries all over the place, great roaring, sooty, scarlet places they are too. There's always molten iron and steel splashing and sparking out of cauldrons as big around as train tunnels and tens of thousands of the sweating damned shoveling coal, tending to the furnaces and the steam engines. Clanking, clanking and hissing goes on all the time, deafening everybody." Barnabas slapped the huge wheel. "This is for a steam crane."

"What do you do with all that iron and steel?" Flintlock said, interested despite himself.

"You're an idiot, boy. What did I tell you afore? You remember nothing."

17

"I recollect you told me that the walls around Hell are a thousand feet tall and glow white," Flintlock said.

"That's right and they're white because they're white hot. You any idea how many times walls like that need repair? Plenty of times, I can tell you that. In the olden days Ol' Scratch tossed melted iron against a damaged wall and hoped it stuck. Now we use boilerplate that's riveted in place. It's a great advance in engineering."

"And what do you do, Barnabas?" Flintlock said.

"I'm a trusty, so I drive a steam crane. Good job if you can keep the gears and cogwheels free of soot. And the tears of the damned can cause rust. That's always a problem."

"What's with the getup you're wearing?" Flintlock said.

Barnabas wore a black top hat with a pair of goggles parked at the bottom of the crown and a black leather coat done up with a dozen straps and brass buckles. A huge pocket watch on an iron chain hung from his neck.

"This is a crane driver's outfit," he said. For a moment Barnabas's eyes glowed red, then he said, "Now you get into the swamp, boy, and find your ma. Tell her you want

18

her to give you your real name. Flintlock ain't any kind of name for a white man. Where's the Injun?"

"O'Hara? He's around. He comes and goes as he pleases."

"A breed, ain't he?" Barnabas said.

"Yeah, half Irish and half something else."

"He's only half the idiot you are. Now find your ma. Whoever he was, you should have your pa's name."

"I'm headed that way now," Flintlock said. His mustang jerked up its head in alarm as a siren wailed in the distance.

"Break time is over," Barnabas said. He lifted the gear wheel above his head. Flintlock guessed it weighed half a ton. "I remember the olden days when we were summoned back by a blast on a hunting horn. Times change, I guess."

Then he was gone. A marsh wren landed on the trunk where Barnabas had sat, ruffled its feathers and fluttered away in alarm.

That night Flintlock camped on a patch of cropland that had been used before, maybe by the old Atakapan Indians, called the Man-eaters since they were rumored to be cannibals, who'd once ruled the swamps. Whoever it was, they'd left a supply of firewood and Flintlock soon had a fire going. Coffee was on the boil and bacon sputtered in the pan when the darkness parted and O'Hara stepped into the circle of firelight.

"I wondered when you'd show up," Flintlock said. "I could have used you today."

"I heard," O'Hara said. He squatted by the fire, grabbed the tin cup that Flintlock had set out for his own use, and poured coffee. He stared over the steaming rim at Flintlock and said, "Alphonse Plume. A tad out of your class, huh? Did you shoot him in the back?"

Flintlock refused to show his anger. "No. I shot him in the front. And the other one."

"Dave Storm. He was no bargain either."

"I got lucky," Flintlock said.

"No, you didn't. The word in the swamp is that Brewster Ritter plans to hang you first chance he gets. Or throw you to his monster."

"Monster?"

"I spoke to Maggie Heron, a Cajun swamp witch and —"

"How the hell do you know her?" Flintlock said, moving around the bacon with his knife.

"I know a lot of people, Sammy. You'd be surprised. I'm half Injun, remember."

"What's that got to do with it?" Flintlock said, irritated.

"Indians know stuff that white folks don't. May I finish?"

"Yeah, go ahead. You spoke to a swamp witch, whatever the hell that is, and . . ."

"And she told me that Ritter plans to drain bayous and swamps this side of the Sabine and start a logging operation. There's big money at stake and Maggie says Ritter has a monster with huge staring eyes under his control and it has already killed seven people and driven others out."

"Seems like a big windy to me," Flintlock said.

"Seven people burned to cinders is real enough," O'Hara said.

"What about the law?" Flintlock said.

"In Louisiana they call Ritter the Baron of the Bayous. He *is* the law in the swamps and his hired guns enforce it." Suddenly O'Hara threw down his cup, rose to his feet and vanished into the darkness.

Flintlock shook his head. O'Hara was as good as Barnabas at disappearing. But a few minutes later, as Flintlock chewed on the last of his bacon, the reason for the breed's flight became clear.

Two men wearing dusters and carrying Greeners stepped out of the night. The

21

muzzles of one of the shotguns shoved against the middle of Flintlock's forehead and its owner said, "Even blink, mister, and I'll scatter your brains."

The other man said, "He ain't too bright, is he, Harry?"

"I'd say a man who commits murder, leaves a clear trail and builds a fire in the middle of a swamp has a lot to learn," Harry said.

"I didn't murder anybody," Flintlock said. "And get that damned scattergun out of my face before I shove it up your ass."

"Sure, buddy," Harry said. He reversed the shotgun and slammed the butt into the side of Flintlock's head. For a moment Flintlock felt pain and then the ground rushed up to meet him and he felt nothing at all.

CHAPTER THREE

"Cypress, Mr. Luke," banker Mathias Cobb said. "Dare I say that that very soon it will be the root of wealth, both yours and mine?"

"Indeed you may, sir," Simon Luke said. "I intend to inform Mr. Ritter that I will buy all the cypress lumber he can sell me. It's in great demand for our great nation's burgeoning shipbuilding and construction industries and prices have never been higher."

Cobb touched a forefinger to the side of his nose. "A word to the wise, Mr. Luke. I have considerable capital invested in this venture and I've begun to doubt Mr. Ritter's methods."

A freight wagon, piled high with beer barrels, rumbled noisily past Cobb's office window and he was silent until it moved on and then said, "He's talking about draining the swamp to force out the inhabitants. An impossibility, I say. And he's putting a lot of faith in his damned flying balloon. There's only one method of dealing with the lower classes, talk to them in a language they understand. Use the whip, the sap and the billy club and, yes, the gun if necessary and send them on their merry way to whatever hell they choose." He looked at the tall, angular man who had his back against the wall by the door. "What's your opinion on that, Mr. Lilly?"

Sebastian Lilly, a skilled pistol fighter out of the Arizona Territory, said, "Ritter would need to drain all of east Texas and the entire state of Louisiana. You're right, banker Cobb, use the gun and kill all them swamp rats, man, woman and child."

Luke, almost a mirror image of Cobb, a heavyset man with a thick gold watch chain across his huge round belly and a diamond ring on the little finger of his left hand, was alarmed.

"My dear, sir," he said to Cobb, "that is harsh treatment indeed. Suppose you're found out?"

"We won't be, Mr. Luke," the banker said. "No one cares about the trash living in the swamps, and if they did, we have ways of silencing them. Is that not right, Mr. Lilly?"

The gunman's smile was both rare and

cold. "You mean I have ways of silencing them."

"Indeed, Mr. Lilly. As always, you are the voice of reason," Cobb said. "I will have a word with Mr. Ritter and tell him what we have decided. Ah, here is the pie at last. You may leave us now, Mr. Lilly."

The tall gunman grinned, shrugged himself off the wall and, his spurs ringing, stepped around one of Cobb's tellers and walked out the door. The teller carried a huge domed pie in both hands and laid it down on the space Cobb had cleared on his desk.

"Ahhh . . . smell the aroma, Mr. Luke," Cobb said, sniffing, his huge jowls aglow. "There's nothing like steak and kidney pie when the first nip of fall is in the air, I always say."

His eyes big, Luke gleefully tucked his napkin into his celluloid collar and said, salivating, "You are a most gracious host, Mr. Cobb, and a credit to the Cattleman's Bank and Trust, may I say."

"There's a spoon beside you there, Mr. Luke," Cobb said. "Great trenchermen like us need no other eating tool. Now, shall we storm the battlements of this splendid culinary creation and assay its contents?"

"Indeed we must," Luke said, spoon

poised, his concerns about the swamp and the massacre of its people for the moment forgotten.

Sebastian Lilly lifted his whiskey and paused, the glass between the bar and his mouth. "He doesn't like the swamp-draining plan and I don't like it either."

Bonifaunt Toohy indicated that the bartender should fill his glass again and when that was accomplished he said, "He has a better plan?"

"Yeah, go into the swamp and kill them all," Lilly said.

"It may come to that," Toohy said. "I don't think the drainage plan will work either. Did he say anything about money?"

"No, not directly. He'll keep on bankrolling Ritter and you can tell him that." He motioned with his glass to the bartender. "Hit me again."

"You'll keep us informed, huh?" Toohy said. "Any hint that the financing will stop and Mathias Cobb is a dead man."

"He's a dead man anyway," Lilly said. "Ritter won't pay him back the money he owes. It will cut into his profits."

"Cobb is a respected businessman in this town," Toohy said. "When the time comes I'll handle that killing myself."

"I'll do it," Lilly said. "I hate his fat guts. He's ordered me around for long enough." He grinned. "Heard you killed a man over to Beaumont way a couple of weeks ago."

"Yeah, a railroad section hand. He didn't like me sparking his woman and went for his gun. He'd been notified." Toohy reached into his pants pocket and laid five double eagles on the bar. "Ritter wants to be kept informed about Cobb. The man worries him."

Lilly scooped up the money and said, "Tell Mr. Ritter that I'll report everything the fat man does and says."

Toohy nodded. "I got to go. Maybe Ritter has somebody who needs killing."

CHAPTER FOUR

Sam Flintlock woke to a throbbing head-ache and morning light.

He tried to sit up and found that he couldn't move his arms or legs. Then he discovered the reason why . . . he was spread-eagled on the ground, his wrists and ankles bound with ropes to wooden stakes.

Flintlock raised his head. "Hey!" he yelled.

A tall man with a carrion-eater's eyes suddenly loomed above him. He held Flintlock's Hawken in his hands. "What the hell is this?" he said.

"What does it look like?" Flintlock said, a question that earned him a hard kick in the ribs.

"Keep a civil tongue in your head," the man said.

Flintlock recognized him as Harry, the man with the Greener from the night before. He wanted to kill him real bad.

Harry turned the Hawken over in his

hands. "Lovely old piece," he said. "I reckon I'll hold on to it."

"It's mine," Flintlock said. "You can't have it."

"But I do have it," Harry said. "See, right here in my hands."

Flintlock tried to get up but the stakes held him fast. He stared at Harry. "I'll kill you for this."

The man turned and said. "Hey, Lem, the man with the big bird on his throat says he's gonna kill me."

Lem, a brutish man with a bull neck and massive shoulders, stepped into Flintlock's view. "Hell, Harry, why don't we just shoot him and be done?" he said.

"Because Brewster Ritter will want details. And one of the details he'll want is that this tramp didn't die quick or easy."

Now it was Lem's turn to deliver a kick into Flintlock's ribs that made him gasp in pain. "Al Plume was a friend of mine," Lem said.

"I'm sure he'll be sadly missed," Flintlock said. He gritted his teeth against the pain he knew was coming and he wasn't disappointed as the square toe of Lem's boot thudded into him.

When he could talk again, Flintlock said, "What are you going to do with me?"

29

"Us? Nothing," Harry said. "But I'll give you a clue to what's gonna happen to you. Show him, Lem."

The man called Lem stepped away and returned a moment later. He held a dead raccoon by one leg and raised it so Flintlock could see it.

"Can you guess?" Lem said.

"Go to hell," Flintlock said.

"Can't guess, huh?" Lem said. He dropped the bloody raccoon onto Flintlock's chest then kneeled behind him and roughly grabbed him by the hair. He jerked up Flintlock's head and forced him to look to his left. "What do you see, huh? Tell me what you see?" Lem said.

Flintlock made no answer and the man grabbed his hair tighter as though trying to wrench it out by the roots. With his free hand he slapped Flintlock back and forth across the face, stinging blows that cracked like pistol shots. Blood trickled from the corner of Flintlock's mouth and his right eye began to swell.

"Damn you, I'll beat it out of you," Lem said through gritted teeth. "What do you see?"

"Lem, don't kill him," Harry said. "He's got to be alive for a while."

"What do you see?" Lem said again.

"A swamp, damn you, a swamp," Flintlock said through split lips.

"Clever boy," Lem said. "And what dwells in the swamp, huh?"

"How the hell should I know?" Flintlock said.

"Well, I'll tell you. He's an elderly ranny who goes by the name Basilisk because the swamp dwellers say just one look from his eyes can turn a man into stone with fear."

The man called Harry took up the story. "The swamp folks say Basilisk is a hundred years old and that he's eaten so many people he has a taste for human flesh." Harry grinned, made claws of his hands and said, "Grrrr . . ."

By nature Sam Flintlock was not an excitable man, but he didn't like the direction this conversation was taking. "What the hell are you boys talking about?" he said.

"Bless your soul, an alligator of course," Lem said. "Basilisk is twenty feet long and can swallow a horse whole." He smiled. "You'll very soon meet him."

"Let's talk about this," Flintlock said.

Lem shook his head. "No need for talk. Like I told you before, Al Plume was a friend of mine."

Lem picked up the dead raccoon and walked to the edge of the swamp. The water

31

was still, without a ripple, and the air smelled of rotten vegetation and of fish shoaling in the Gulf. Moss clung to the snags around the cypress trees and just off the bank a row of turtles sunned on a fallen trunk. Lem cut the raccoon's throat and let blood drip into the water. He then carried the animal, stepping slowly, letting blood drip, back to Flintlock. He threw the bloody raccoon onto his chest. "I've never seen how an alligator eats a man," Lem said. "Maybe you'll get lucky and it will be quick."

"Damn you, why don't you just shoot me and get it over?" Flintlock said.

Lem shook his head. "That would be too easy." He looked at Harry and said, "Let's go and leave our guest to his . . . his . . . what?"

"Fate?" Harry said. "Or maybe his doom would be better."

"Yeah, that's it. We'll leave him to his doom," Lem said.

"I'm surprised lowlifes like you don't stay to watch," Flintlock said.

"Don't have the time," Lem said. "We got better things to do."

Harry grinned. "Well, you take care, tattooed man. We'll see you in Hell."

CHAPTER FIVE

The swamp water was warm from the sun, brown with mud, and from a distance away Sam Flintlock heard a grunting feral hog root among the hyacinths that grew close to the bank. The cypress trees cast no shadows because the sun, white as molten steel, stood at its highest point in the sky. Carrion birds glided overhead, patient as monks illuminating manuscripts with feather pens, and watched and waited.

Flintlock ran a dry tongue over his parched lips, his thirst a raging thing. Mosquitoes as big as sparrows bit his exposed wrists and neck, and flew heavily away, groggy from their blood feast.

His wrists rubbed raw from straining at the ropes, Flintlock dreamed about water, of throwing himself into the swamp and drinking and drinking until the roots of the cypress were revealed. Visions of beer, the color of Baltic amber, ice cold and foaming in tall glass steins, tormented him and gave him no peace.

The sun dropped lower and a gator bellowed once among the cypress and in the following quiet Flintlock thought he heard it slide into the swamp, water hissing along its armored sides.

Flintlock jerked up his aching head, his frightened eyes searching. Was it the big one? The one they called Basilisk? The one with the ravenous appetite for human flesh? His head sank slowly back to the dirt. Suddenly he was very tired, used up by fear and thirst, and he wanted it to end.

By late afternoon Sam Flintlock drifted in and out of consciousness. He saw his mother again, bright red hair, but her features blurred because he could no longer remember her face. She was lost in the swamp. Then her hair was no longer red but gray, and she beckoned to him, her face pleading, begging him to save her, her arms moving like willow branches in a wind. Flintlock moved toward her, but slowly, as though he walked through thick molasses. He called out to her, "Ma, what's my name?" But then a mist came down like a gray cloud and she vanished from sight.

Flintlock woke with a start. He lifted his head and craned his neck, staring toward the swamp. A mist curled between the cypress trunks and over the willow islands and speckled trout jumped at flies and splashed back into the water.

Ripples washed ashore and hissed onto the sandy bank. Flintlock's eyes widened. The ripples were not made by a fish but from something bigger. A lot bigger. His neck aching, Flintlock kept his eyes glued to the surface of the water, now and then catching glimpses through the drifting mist.

Flintlock saw it! A scaly back. Unblinking reptilian eyes level with the water. The slow, lazy undulation of a massive tail. A massive alligator, a cold, emotionless killer, slid through the murky water toward him.

His dry throat croaking his fear, Flintlock frantically tugged at the ropes that bound him. But the stakes were driven in deep and didn't budge. The alligator was closer now. Its huge head lifted and rows of teeth glinted in the fading light like sabers. Flintlock dropped his head and prayed that his horrible death would be quick and painless.

BLAAMM!

The roar of a pistol shot racketed through the swamp and set roosting birds scattering in panic into the sky. Flintlock lifted his head and watched the muddy water boil as

35

an alligator thrashed, showing its white belly. The reptile made a quick turn and slunk away into the swamp, trailing a stream of blood.

A figure stood over Flintlock and blocked the rays of the dying sun.

"Ma?" he said.

And then unconsciousness took him.

CHAPTER SIX

"He's coming to," a man said.

O'Hara's voice.

Sam Flintlock opened his eyes. "O'Hara, you rat," he said, his voice a feeble croak. "First chance I get I'm going to put a bullet in you."

"How do you feel, Flintlock?" O'Hara said.

"Alive or barely. Did you shoot the gator?"

"No, the swamp witch did," O'Hara said. He leaned closer and whispered into Flintlock's ear, "Don't look into her eyes. If you do she'll steal your soul."

"You damned traitor, she saved my life, more than I can say for you," Flintlock said. "Why did you quit on me last night?"

"Later," O'Hara said. "You need to rest."

The man moved aside and Flintlock saw the alligator. It was right above him, its fangs bared! He cried out and tried to rise but strong hands pushed him back onto the cot.

"He's long dead," a woman said. "He can't hurt you now."

"I thought . . . I thought . . ."

"Yes. I know what you thought," the woman said. "I killed that one three years ago and now he hangs from my ceiling as a warning to his kin."

The woman was young and spectacularly beautiful. Her black hair was piled on top of her head in glossy ringlets and waves and coiled tendrils hung over her forehead and cheeks. She had dark eyes, lashes as long as lace fans and a wide, lush mouth, her lips painted a vivid scarlet. She wore a pale pink shirt under a tight black bodice laced at the front with grommets and boned at the front and sides. Her wine-red, bustled taffeta skirt was tied up at the front to better reveal shapely legs in thigh-high red leather boots. A large golden key, decorated with tiny cogwheels taken from pocket watches, hung by a velvet ribbon from her neck.

"You're a swamp witch?" Flintlock said. He didn't look into her eyes.

"Yes. What did you expect? An old crone with no teeth and warts?"

"Something like that," Flintlock said.

"Here, drink this. It will help you sleep

for a while," the woman said. "And I'll put some salve on your lips." Then with a devastating smile she said, "My name is Evangeline and you can look at me. I won't steal your soul. I have one of my own already."

She raised Flintlock's head and helped him drink from a wooden cup. He thought the liquid tasted like sour green apples . . . and then for the third time that day, oblivion swept over him.

Evangeline sat by the great stone fireplace that dominated her cabin. She crossed her long slim legs and said, "I thought at first you might be Rangers."

O'Hara was trying his best to be as stoical as a cigar store Indian. He avoided looking into the witch's eyes and staring at her lovely legs, traps to snare and forever enslave the unwary traveler.

"Flintlock will enter the swamplands to find his mother," he said. "His grandfather says he's an idiot and asked me to look after him. It's not easy. He blunders into things and causes trouble."

"He killed two of Brewster Ritter's best men," Evangeline said. "I imagine that's trouble enough."

"How do you know that?" O'Hara said,

surprised. He'd removed his hat and his long black hair hung over his shoulders. He wore a white shirt and beaded vest.

"I know everything that goes on in the swamp," Evangeline said. "That's why I waited with Mr. Flintlock until you found us. Do you know that Ritter wants to drain the swamp and cut down all the cypress?"

"Can he do that?"

"Of course he can. He has powerful friends in Washington."

"Does he even have the tools to drain the swamp?" O'Hara said.

Flintlock muttered in his sleep and Evangeline looked over at him in concern. "He dreams," she said. "Perhaps he dreams of his mother." She took a sip of red wine from a long-stemmed glass with a silver base and said, "Ritter already has enormous steam pumps, all he needs, and powerful steam-driven saws. The alligators, the fish, turtles, water birds, they will all be gone soon."

"And I'm told he has a monster," O'Hara said.

"Yes, he has that too," Evangeline said.

"What about the folks who live in the swamp?" O'Hara said.

"What about them?"

"They'll lose their homes, their liveli-hoods."

Evangeline smiled. "They're little, unimportant people that no one cares about. Do you think Washington worries about what will happen to them? I can tell you it doesn't. Ritter already has all the senators in his pocket he wants. The people will have to move out or die in the swamp."

"And what about you, Evangeline?" O'Hara said. "Where will you go?"

"Nowhere. If I must, I'll die here in the swamp with the people. They come to me for healing, child birthing and often just for advice. I won't desert them, now or later."

"You are a strange kind of witch."

"Yes, I know. And that's why you can look me in the eye, O'Hara."

"That's the Indian part of me."

"No, it's the ignorant part of you," Evangeline said. "But you'll learn."

"Then tell me why you dress the way you do," O'Hara said.

"Because it pleases me. Why do you dress like an Indian and not an Irishman?"

O'Hara grinned and Evangeline said, "Yes, because it pleases you. See, you're learning already."

"There's no man in your life?" O'Hara said.

"La, la, la, now you pry, Mr. O' Hara."

"Sorry."

41

"Don't be. Yes, there's a man. His name is Cornelius and he's curator of the Museum of the Swamp."

"Where is that?"

"Here in the swamp. But it moves from place to place."

"Will Cornelius stand up to Ritter?" O'Hara said.

"He's a good man, a poet by nature, not a Texas draw fighter," Evangeline said. "But yes, he'll stand up to Brewster Ritter and his gunmen and he'll be killed. That's a story that can have no other ending. You're awake, Mr. Flintlock."

"And you look like hell," O'Hara said.

Flintlock sat up in the cot. He was groggy and his sunburned face hurt, but he felt his strength returning. "I overheard part of your conversation," he said. "My mother is in the swamp, somewhere, maybe living in a bayou. Will she be forced to leave?"

"Flintlock, you heard the lady," O'Hara said. "Your mother will move out or die. Even for a white man that's a simple concept."

Evangeline rose and crossed the rough timber floor, the high boot heels drumming. She put her arms around Flintlock's shoulders and said, "Come and sit down. I'll get you a glass of wine." The woman smelled of red roses and green moss.

As he rose, Flintlock hit his head on the hanging alligator. "Damned crocodiles are going to get me one way or the other," he said.

O'Hara vacated his chair for Flintlock and sat cross-legged on the floor.

"I didn't thank you for saving my life . . . miss . . ." Flintlock said.

"My name is Evangeline. Here, drink this wine. It will help sustain you. I didn't set out to save your life, Mr. —"

"Sam."

The woman smiled. "Then Sam it is. I was hunting Basilisk in the swamp and saw your predicament. It was a most singular situation and a matter of the greatest moment that I save you from the jaws of the reptile."

"You got a bullet into him," Flintlock said.

"Yes, but that wasn't Basilisk," Evangeline said. "It was a much smaller alligator."

"Why do you risk your life trying to kill a giant alligator?" Flintlock said. It hurt his cracked lips to talk.

"Because he killed a friend of mine, an old black man who fished the swamp," Evangeline said. "To borrow your colorful turn of speech, Sam, I got a bullet into him that day. He's hated me ever since."

O'Hara smiled. "Can animals hate?"

"Basilisk can and does. He wants to kill me very badly. How is the wine, Sam?"

"Real good, ma'am," Flintlock said.

"It's made right here in the swamp, from wild grapes."

Suddenly O'Hara was alert. "What's that?" he said.

Flintlock heard it moments later . . . a steady thrumming that seemed to come from above the cabin.

"Step out onto my deck and I'll show you," Evangeline said. "It will be your introduction to Brewster Ritter."

The deck was railed and quite small with just room enough for a heavy rocking chair and side table. But Flintlock didn't notice. His eyes were fixed on the sky.

CHAPTER SEVEN

"This is an excellent way to travel, my dear Ritter," said Simon Luke, owner and chairman of the Lucky Luke Lumber Company of Pennsylvania. "Like a bird. I say, like a bird."

"Thank you, sir," Brewster Ritter said. "As dirigibles go, the *Star Scraper* is small, more a runabout than a long-distance flying machine."

"But it's deuced comfortable," Luke said. "I have room to stretch my legs, a table with a decanter of port and box of cigars at my elbow. What more does a civilized man need?"

Behind Luke a small man wearing a leather helmet and large goggles was at the tiller, a propeller spinning in a shining disc behind him. The man wore a canvas coat fastened by a row of brass buckles and leather gauntlets.

"How is the boiler temperature, Professor

Mealy?" Ritter said. "Is it still fluctuating?"

"No, steady as she goes, Mr. Ritter," Jasper Mealy said. "The engine is performing flawlessly, sir."

Ritter, a small, self-important man with iron gray hair and a short, clipped beard, nodded. "Carry on, Professor Mealy." Then to Luke, "Well, from your lofty perch, what do you think of my plan?"

"I'll buy all the sawn lumber you can send me, Mr. Ritter," Luke said. "Damn my eyes, but there must be thousands of cypress in this swamp."

Ritter smiled. "You've seen only a part of it. There are thousands more to be had."

"You'll make us both rich," Luke said. "Or richer, as the case may be."

"That is my intention," Ritter said. "Now look down there. That's called a bayou."

"Beautiful, isn't it?" Luke said. "I like how the moss clings to the tree roots and there are water blossoms everywhere."

"It will be even more beautiful within a six-month," Ritter said. "Once I drain the bayou I'll build my sawmill there and tent accommodations for the lumbermen. There will also be a company store, a saloon and dancehall and a brothel of course. In short, everything the commoner needs to keep him happy."

Luke raised his glass. "Well, here's to progress. And you will work on the railroad spur?"

"I have friends in Washington who are already working on that," Ritter said. "There's talk that when all the lumber is cut the army might want the land as an artillery range. I'd be paid by the acre of course."

"Then here's to you, Mr. Ritter," Luke said, raising his glass. "You're a shrewd businessman and no mistake. What about the inhabitants of the swamp?"

Ritter made a gesture with his hand. "They'll be swept aside."

"And good riddance," Luke said. A massive gold watch chain crossed his huge belly. "Commoners are a bunch of damned lazy malingerers who want the government to take care of them. I hate them seed, breed and generation."

Ritter yelped as a bullet splintered into the wooden gunnel at his elbow. "Murder!" he yelled.

"Professor Mealy, who is shooting?" Ritter said. He drew a Colt from his shoulder holster.

Mealy looked behind him, then said, "It came from a cabin down on the bayou, a

47

man with a rifle. His wife is pulling him inside."

"Full speed ahead, Professor Mealy. Mr. Toohy, mark that damned hovel."

Bonifaunt Toohy was a scarred man who wore a bowler hat and a tight, red and white striped vest over a white shirt. Like everyone else who might be called on to work on the dirigible's steam engine he wore goggles around the bowler's crown. He carried a short-barreled Colt in a cross-draw holster.

"I got it marked, Mr. Ritter," he said.

"Pay him a visit tonight, Mr. Toohy," Ritter said. Then for Luke's benefit, "A social call, you understand."

"Survivors?" Toohy said, lowering his voice.

"No. No survivors."

Simon Luke was outraged. "Mr. Ritter," he said, "I could have been killed."

"The miscreant will be dealt with, Mr. Luke," Ritter said. "I'll have the law deal with him."

"I certainly hope so," Luke said. "I've no desire to get shot out of a balloon, a glass of port in my hand."

Adam Gantly, his wife, Audrey, and their teenage son, Israel, tried to find solace in the Bible, but after a while Adam said, "I

48

tried to kill somebody today, Audrey. May God forgive me."

Audrey rose and placed her hand on her husband's shoulder. "You were pushed to it, Adam. God will forgive."

"I heard that Brewster Ritter lives in a fine mansion in Galveston," Adam said. "Why does he want my wooden hut?"

"We stand in the way of his plans," Audrey said. "He wants to cut down all the trees."

Adam Gantly was a tall, gaunt man who didn't get enough to eat. He wore suspenders over a red cotton under vest, workmen's boots and baggy pants. "I still shouldn't have tried to kill him," he said. "That was a mortal sin."

"No one will blame you, Adam, least of all God," Audrey said.

A single oil lamp lighted the small, shabby cabin, but suddenly the room filled with dazzling light and the Gantly family looked toward the front window, now a rectangle of the purest white.

"He has come," Audrey whispered. "He has come down from Heaven to comfort us."

But it was Hell, not Heaven, that had come calling.

A voice from outside, made louder by a

49

megaphone, said, "Come outside now. All of you."

Adam told his wife and son to stay where they were and lifted his Winchester from the brackets on the fireplace. He stepped onto his deck and was blinded by two bright reflector lamps, shining like eyes in the darkness.

"What do you want?" he yelled.

"You!" a man's voice said.

Adam brought up his rifle, but was immediately felled by a hail of bullets.

"Adam!" his wife yelled. She ran to her husband and threw herself on his torn body. "Adam, Adam, please talk to me."

"He can't, lady," a voice from the darkness behind the lamps said. "He's dead. And now so are you." A rifle shot rang out and Audrey joined her husband in death.

Israel, fifteen and game, ran onto the deck and took in what had happened at a glance. He picked up the Winchester and had time to throw it to his shoulder before he was hit. Three shots to the middle of the boy's forehead dropped him like a puppet that had just had its strings cut.

"Mr. Hughes," Bonifaunt Toohy said. "Please step into the cabin and see if there's anything else that needs killing."

Elias Hughes looked into the cabin then

called from the deck, "Nobody else. Just those three."

"Good," Toohy said. "Then our work here is done. A jigger of black rum to every man jack of you when we get back."

Seven killers, including steam engineer Mealy, cheered that lighthearted announcement.

CHAPTER EIGHT

"Miz Evangeline!" Zedock Briscoe called out, his ebony face troubled. "You wake up now, Miz Evangeline."

Sometime in the night Evangeline had changed and now as she rose from her rocker her sheer robe of gold silk rustled. "Good morning, Mr. Briscoe," she said.

"Left fish on the po'ch for you, Miz Evangeline," Briscoe said. His tight, black hair was shot through with gray. "But don't you go lookin' at me none. I got young 'uns and you can't turn me into a stone, no."

Evangeline picked up the fish and said, "Beautiful trout, Mr. Briscoe. I'll have some for breakfast."

The black man stood in his pirogue, leaning on the spruce punt pole. He kept his eyes lowered. "Got bad news, Miz Evangeline. I head over to the Gantly place in the mornin', two, three times a week, an' give them poor folks some fish or a piece of hog meat."

Briscoe rubbed his eyes. "Went over there this mornin' and they was all dead. Pa, ma and son, shot through an' through, Miz Evangeline."

Flintlock had stepped onto the deck. His mouth was dry and he felt like hell. "Any sign of who did it?" he said.

"You one o' them warlocks, mister?" Briscoe said. "I want no truck with warlocks. They mate with the female loup-garou, or so folks say."

"No, I'm not a warlock," Flintlock said. "I'm in the swamp looking for my mother."

Briscoe shook his head. "No, no sign. Just three dead white folks."

"I'll go over there, Mr. Briscoe," Evangeline said.

"I wish you would, Miz Evangeline," Briscoe said. "It ain't right for them folks to be murdered and no murderer to be found."

"Thank you again for the fish, Mr. Briscoe," Evangeline said. "You take care now."

"You too, Miz Evangeline. Take care."

"Sam, there's coffee on the stove and cornbread," the woman said. "Eat fast. I want you with me."

"Where's O'Hara?" Flintlock said.

"I don't know. He took his canoe and left

around midnight."

"Damn that breed, he never stays put," Flintlock said. "I don't even have a gun."

"Yes, you do. It's on the shelf beside the cornbread. And there's also a cartridge belt. O'Hara said the cantina proprietor took a heap of convincing to part with Plume's revolver. He said you'd know what he's talking about."

"I know what he's talking about and I know how O'Hara convinces a man. It ain't a pretty thing to watch."

"I'm sure it isn't, Sam. Now I must change."

Compared to the Colt he'd lost, the balance of the new revolver was all wrong. Sam Flintlock decided it needed two more inches of barrel and the front sight filed down. But beggars can't be choosers and he stuck the piece into his waistband and buckled the belt lower on his hips.

Evangeline, as darkly beautiful as a fallen angel, had changed into a split canvas riding skirt, boots and a boned corset of scarlet leather over a black shirt with a high collar. She dropped an engraved Remington derringer into a pocket and said, "Are we ready?"

Flintlock, his hands filled with a coffee

cup and wedge of cornbread, swallowed what he was eating and said, "Yup, I'm ready."

"Then let's go. Sit in the front of the canoe and I'll paddle. By the way, you look much better this morning. You need a shave and a bath, but we'll take care of that later," Evangeline said.

Flintlock stuffed what remained of the cornbread into his mouth, set his cup down on the rail around the deck and climbed into the canoe after Evangeline. Old Barnabas, squatting on top of a cypress, glared down at him, shook his head, and disappeared.

Flintlock didn't know if the old man disapproved of him or Evangeline.

A fleet of pirogues and canoes had gathered around the Gantly cabin. As Evangeline paddled closer Flintlock heard the wailing of women and the hard, quick talk of angry men. Evangeline's status as a swamp witch and dazzling beauty parted the crowd after she and Flintlock stepped onto the deck. A few of the black folks averted their eyes, but most did not. The bodies had been taken inside, but dry, crusted blood still stained the rough timbers of the floor.

"No need to ask who done this," a man in

a worn homespun, butternut shirt said. "It was that devil Brewster Ritter and his gunmen."

Evangeline nodded but said nothing. She stepped into the cabin and came out again a few minutes later, her cheeks pale.

"Can you resurrect them, swamp witch?" a woman asked.

Evangeline shook her head. "Only God has that power."

"Well, where was He when this happened?" the man in the butternut shirt said. He looked around at the crowd. "I say we arm ourselves and go wipe Ritter off the face of the earth."

This drew growls of approval from the menfolk and an alarm bell rang in Flintlock's head. Sheep walking to their own slaughter would suit Ritter's purposes just fine.

He wanted to ask if anyone knew the whereabouts of his mother, but heading off an armed mob must come first.

"You men listen up," Flintlock said. "How many of you have been in a shooting scrape?" He waited and, as he'd expected, got no answer. "How many of you here have killed a man?" Again, no one spoke up. "Ritter has hired gunmen, Texas draw fighters who've been in many a gunfight and have killed men. Sure, you can go up against a score of professional guns, but after the first volleys you'll trip over your own dead trying to get away. You women, let me ask you a question: Are you willing to become widows with orphans to raise?"

The woman exchanged worried glances, but none of them spoke up.

"Who the hell are you, mister?" Butternut shirt said. "You don't belong here in the swamp."

"I'm here to find my mother," Flintlock said. "She's hiding out in the swamps somewhere."

"What's her name?" a woman asked.

Barnabas had never again spoken his daughter's name after she got pregnant by a gambling man and he'd beaten it into Flintlock that it was a forbidden subject. "I don't know," he said.

"Then you've no chance of finding her," Butternut said. "I suggest you get the hell out of the swamp."

"I plan to stay until I find my ma," Flintlock said. "You'll need my gun."

This brought guffaws of disbelief from some of the men and Butternut voiced their misgivings. "You already done told us Ritter has professional gunmen. What the hell can you do that we can't?"

Sam Flintlock was not a bragging man but he had to make a show. As men do often when they're on the prod, four of the more belligerent swamp dwellers had lined up beside Butternut. All wore hats, ideal for the demonstration Flintlock had in mind.

He drew and fired, the steady staccato of his Colt like a fast drumbeat. Five hats flew off five heads and five men clapped startled hands to their parted hair.

Flintlock shoved his Colt back into his waistband and said, "That's what I can do that you can't. And I'm betting a few of Ritter's men can do it better than me."

If the five hatless men were not convinced, their womenfolk were.

"We've come here to pray over the dead," a plump, motherly woman said. She said to Butternut, "Avery, you come inside now and stop this hooliganism."

Chastened by Flintlock's gunplay, the men filed into the cabin, and soon their voices were raised in prayer. That is, all but one. A young man in workman's clothing, a Bible in his hand, said, "I aim to go to Orange City and telegraph the county sheriff. He needs to be here."

"Anyone I know?" Flintlock said.

"Eldon Dowling is his name," the man said. "They say one time he got lead into

John Wesley Hardin, but I don't know if that's true."

"Never heard of him, but he sounds like the kind of lawman you need," Flintlock said.

"Yeah, seems like." The man opened his Bible and stepped into the cabin.

Evangeline frowned. "Sam, was that petulant display really necessary?" she said.

"They need to learn," Flintlock said.

"I think you taught them," Evangeline said. "I only hope you haven't scared those men and taken the fight out of them. Ritter will be laughing up his sleeve. Shall we go inside and pray for the hurting dead?"

"I'm not a praying man, Evangeline," Flintlock said.

"Then at least go through the motions and do as I do," the woman said.

CHAPTER NINE

O'Hara kept his horse at the hogan of an old Jicarilla Apache man who lived near the southern edge of the piney woods country. In answer to O'Hara's question about local newspapers the old man said he knew of only one, situated east of Beaumont in a cow town called Budville.

"I never look at it myself," the man said. "On account of how I can't read."

O'Hara thanked the man, saddled up and rode west, knowing that he might be on a wild goose chase. But anything was better than being holed up in the swamp, even with Evangeline close. As for Flintlock, he'd lost his horse and was stuck where he was, at least until O'Hara could steal him another one.

It was almost noon when O'Hara reached Budville, a dusty, nondescript cow town in the middle of nowhere. But the settlement boasted large cattle pens, three saloons, a restaurant and a railroad spur and seemed to be thriving.

O'Hara rode past the Cattleman's Bank and Trust and several stores, and found the office of the *Budville Democrat* conveniently located between the Alamo and McCarthy saloons.

In answer to his question the gray-haired woman at the front desk, who identified herself as Miss Pearson, said yes, they had done a piece on Brewster Ritter, but it was short and published three months ago. At first O'Hara thought she wasn't going to look up the item, especially since she looked askance at his strange garb — a black beaded vest over a red shirt, battered hat with a feather in the brim — and long hair that fell over his shoulders. But she surprised him when she said, "Come this way. I'll find it for you."

She led O'Hara into a small room that smelled like a library and lifted aside stacked editions of the newspaper and shuffled around others until she found the one she wanted.

"Ah, here it is, right there at the bottom of page three," the woman said. "You can read it at your leisure, though it is very short."

Miss Pearson left the room and O'Hara

sat in a high-backed chair and read:

A NEW FACE IN TOWN

Mr. Brewster Ritter, a visitor from up north, called in at the Democrat office to tell us he was in town and looking for someone to finance a new business venture involving a timber sawmill. To your humble reporter he looked like a man who can get things done. Any new enterprise that employs some of the loafers that currently plague our fair town will be most welcome, Mr. Ritter.

O'Hara sat back in the chair and thought things through. The operation Ritter planned was an expensive undertaking and it seemed logical that he had financial backers. Now O'Hara's suspicion was confirmed by the newspaper story. It was highly probable that Ritter was broke when he arrived in Budville. He told the reporter that he was looking for someone to finance a new business venture and he'd found that person. The question was, who was he?

Then Miss Pearson stepped back into the office and said, "I do remember something I read in one of the eastern newspapers about a man named Brewster Ritter. It was a long time ago, ten years, perhaps longer."

"The same man?"

"Well, it's not such a common name."

"What did you read, Miss Pearson?"

"That a man named Ritter owned a textile factory in Savannah. In 1878 the place burned down and eighty-three women and girls were killed. Apparently the factory was very run-down and the investigating authorities called it a firetrap. Mr. Ritter left Georgia in a hurry and was not heard from again."

"It could be the same Ritter."

"It could be. But I do not like to point a finger at anyone without evidence."

"You're a very wise woman, Miss Pearson," O'Hara said. Then, "Who's the richest man in town?"

The woman smiled. "That would be Mr. Cobb, the banker. But his credentials are unimpeachable. Mathias Cobb is a respected member of the community and a church deacon."

"I'm sure he is, Miss Pearson," O'Hara said, rising to his feet.

"I'd like to give you a word of advice, young man," the woman said. "Cut your hair and dress like a white man and you'll do better in the world."

"I'm only half white man," O'Hara said, smiling. "I'll dress the white half of me as you say."

Miss Pearson was unfazed by O'Hara's sarcasm. "Please see you do. You would look so handsome as half a white man."

Cletus McPhee was a drifting gunman who'd killed a deputy sheriff in Galveston and then lit a shuck north for the good of his health. He heard that a man named Ritter was paying top gun wages and he'd been in Budville a week but hadn't yet made contact. McPhee, who affected the dress and manners of a Southern gentleman, was a man at war with the world with a deep, abiding hatred for humanity in general and Indians in particular. In his time he'd killed eight white men and an unknown number of blacks, Indians and Mexicans and regretted not one of them.

In McPhee's diseased mind, breeds occupied the lowest rung of the ladder, an affront to his sensitivities as a gentleman. When he saw O'Hara enter the restaurant, sit at a table and order bacon and eggs like a white man McPhee marked him for death. And he planned to make a public show of it.

The restaurant was filled with a lunchtime crowd, but O'Hara looked at no one, busy with his grub, bacon and eggs being long a favorite of his. He did take time to note a tall man who flaunted a cared-for imperial, dressed in the garb of a frontier dandy and wore an ivory-handled Colt. But O'Hara dismissed the man as a sporting gent and thought no more about it.

McPhee waited until O'Hara was halfway though his meal before he made his move. He had to wend his way through crowded tables before he reached O'Hara, who sat alone.

"Enjoying that?" McPhee said, looking down at O'Hara.

O'Hara said, "You could say that."

"You aren't going to finish it, not in here you're not," McPhee said. "Take it out and eat with the pigs where you belong."

A hush fell over the restaurant and McPhee was enjoying himself. The breed looked scared and this was going to be easy.

But O'Hara was far from scared. He had the heart of an Indian warrior and the reckless courage of an Irishman and was always ready for a scrap, be it with guns, knives or fists and skull.

He smiled. "What don't you like about me, mister?" he said.

"The fact that you're a stinking breed and shouldn't be here eating with white folks."

"And you aim to draw down on me, huh?"

65

"That's the general idea."

"Then I suppose I must accommodate you," O'Hara said. "Be quick now, my eggs are getting cold."

McPhee liked no part of that speech. The breed sounded too confident, like he'd been here before. And when O'Hara stood and revealed the worn Colt at his hip, he liked that even less. McPhee had shot blanket Indians before but the man facing him was not one of those. He pegged him as a gun and a killer.

"At your convenience," O'Hara said, hellfire in his eyes.

A respectable-looking man sitting at a table said, "Here, that won't do."

McPhee badly wanted an out. In those few moments before he died, he knew he'd bitten off more than he could chew. The thought came to him then, *Damn it, Cletus, never pick on strangers.*

He went for his gun and wasn't even close. At a range of just three feet O'Hara pumped three bullets into McPhee before he hit the ground. The man raised his head and stared at O'Hara. "Fast . . . fast . . ." he said.

"Only middlin'," O'Hara said.

A diner leaned from his chair, looked down at McPhee, shook his head and said,

"He's gone."

"Seems like," O'Hara said. He picked up his plate and fork, shoveled down what was left of his meal, took a gulp of coffee and walked out of the restaurant. He rode out of town aware that people stood in the street and watched him go. But no one tried to stop him. And that was just as well because O'Hara was angry, his rage directed at the man who was causing so much death and misery in the swamp . . .

It was high time Brewster Ritter got a taste of his own medicine.

CHAPTER TEN

"I don't think that shooting all the people in the swamps and bayous is necessary, Mr. Ritter," engineer Leander Byng said. "It is a bit drastic and could attract enforcers."

"You have a better idea?" Brewster Ritter said. He sat at ease in his tent on the Louisiana side of the Sabine. He'd already dismissed the two armed guards who usually stood at the open flap as being unnecessary.

"Perhaps not better, but not as violent," Byng said. He wore a dark brown double-breasted vest, jodhpurs of the same color and tall, lace-up English boots. Like most of Ritter's technicians he had goggles pushed up onto his forehead. "I ask you to allow me to start up my steam pumps, all of them. We can drain the swamp right out from under the miscreants. When their cabins are high and dry, surrounded by mud, dying fish and hungry alligators we'll soon be rid of them."

Ritter ran a hand through his short hair, thinking. He was a small, compact man and as tough as they come and mean as a curly wolf. A ruthless employer, he'd once owned a textile mill near Savannah but the place burned down in the winter of 1878, killing eighty-three women and girls, and he'd left Georgia in a hurry. "How long to get the pumps up and running?" he said.

"Two weeks if we drain right directly into the Sabine," Byng said. "If we empty into the Gulf a week longer, depending on how fast the steam shovels can cut us a channel."

"Then we'll use the Sabine," Ritter said.

"We can expect localized flooding of farmlands," Byng said.

"Like I give a damn," Ritter said. "I want those pumps started, working night and day. Let's get this show on the road."

Byng rose to his feet. "I'll get on it right now."

"Good man," Ritter said. The engineer stooped to go through the tent flap, but Ritter stopped him. "By the way, Byng," he said. "If the pumps aren't up and running in two weeks I'll have you shot."

Byng said nothing, but his face suddenly paled.

■ ■ ■ ■

Zedock Briscoe had traveled far into the swamp and had pulled his canoe into a patch of relatively dry land thickly covered in tupelo trees, black willow, privet and ink-berry. Somewhere among that tangle of growth was a hog that Briscoe badly wanted to shoot. It would keep him, his missus and their five young 'uns in meat for a long time. He'd scouted tracks along the water's edge and he figured the hog was a monster, an easy three hundred pounds of pork on the hoof and maybe more.

Zedock lifted his Winchester from the canoe and walked a hundred feet into the trees, then stopped and listened. A feeding wild hog makes considerable noise, but he heard nothing but the buzz of flying insects and the rustle of small, timid things in the undergrowth.

"Mister Hog, you come out here now and get acquainted," Zedock said. He fingered his rifle. "I got something for you."

He was greeted by only a chirping, squeaking quiet.

His footsteps whispering through sun-dried weeds, he stepped farther into the tupelo growth. The air was humid and thick and smelled of smoke, the sort that trickles from a chimney and carries the odor of frying fish and hushpuppies. What Zedock didn't smell was the musky scent of a hog. His rifle at the ready, he crossed the entire extent of the dry land then stopped at a bayou where a large but run-down cabin on high stilts stood about fifty yards away.

Zedock Briscoe knew the cabin well but avoided it like the plague. The place belonged to a trapper by the name of Obadiah Pendred Anderson, a cantankerous, some said crazy, old coot who harbored a passionate hatred for blacks. He didn't like whites much either, but reserved his special loathing for those of the Negro persuasion. A canvas tarp hung between two posts on his deck, painted in red with the words:

**SHARPS BIG .50 SIGHTED IN AT
100 YARDS
STAY THE HELL AWAY OR GET SHOT**

Anderson had been vocal in his opposition to Brewster Ritter and on a recent trip to Orange for rifle ammunition had threatened to kill the man on sight, a statement heard by many ears.

It was Zedock's destiny to witness how swift and brutal Ritter's retribution could be. As he backed away from the water's edge, from high above the tree canopy Zedock heard a sound he'd heard before, the heavy drone of Ritter's dirigible pounding across the sky.

Zedock stopped in his tracks. He wanted to cry out and warn Anderson that the flying machine was close, but he was very much afraid that he would be rewarded by a bullet from the old man's Sharp and stayed silent.

Moments later Anderson, wearing overalls and a red plaid shirt, stepped onto his deck. He stared at the sky for a moment and then rushed back inside.

Zedock Briscoe would say later that it was Anderson's hatred of blacks that killed him. If he'd dared yell out to him, the man might have been able to jump into the water and swim clear.

The dirigible was over the cabin and something dropped from the gondola. The missile looked like a large cannonball, but it had a fuse that smoked as it tumbled downward. Zedock heard the bomb crash through the cabin's roof. A few moments ticked past and then the cabin exploded with a deafening roar. A sheet of flame erupted into the air and broken spars of wood and flying fragments of metal splashed into the waters of the bayou, churning up the surface.

Zedock had closed his eyes and now he opened them again. The cabin's walls had been blown out and the roof had landed yards away among the cypress. Smoke rose from the flattened cabin and scattered flames fluttered like scarlet moths on pieces of charred wood that spiked at crazy angles from the wreckage.

If there was anything left of Obadiah Anderson it was not evident.

Stunned, Zedock watched the dirigible chatter around the destroyed cabin a few times and then fly south. He didn't move from his spot until he was sure the craft was gone.

CHAPTER ELEVEN

Sam Flintlock had just finished a dinner of boiled trout and some kind of swamp vegetable when a knock came to the door and a moment later O'Hara stepped inside.

"Where the hell have you been?" Flintlock said.

"Scouting," O'Hara said. "Seen stuff. Done stuff."

"What kind of stuff?"

O'Hara, who'd swapped his headband for a top hat stuck all around with white feathers, ignored that and said, "Evangeline, black man outside to see you. He says it's important."

Alarmed, Flintlock grabbed his Colt from the table but O'Hara said, "Says his name is Zedock Briscoe. Do you know him?"

"Yes, I know him," Evangeline said. "Put your gun down, Sam. It was Zedock's fish you just ate."

"He refuses to come inside," O'Hara said.

"I'll talk to him from the deck," Evangeline said. She wore a black casual dress that ended midway down her thighs and knee-high boots. "Zedock doesn't trust witches at close quarters."

Flintlock followed the woman outside, the Colt in his waistband, but O'Hara sat at the table and poured himself coffee.

Zedock stood in his pirogue, a lantern casting a halo of orange light at the bow. Around him the swamp lay in moonlight and mist.

The black man spoke in a rush. "Obadiah Anderson is dead, Miz Evangeline. A bomb fell from the sky and blew him up and it was the flying machine and —"

"Mr. Briscoe, slow down," Evangeline said. "Take a deep breath and then tell me what happened. Obadiah is dead, you say."

"Yes, Miz Evangeline," Zedock said. "Seen it with my own two eyes." A fish leapt out of the water near the man's canoe and he jumped and looked around him.

After a few moments to recover from his fright, he told Evangeline what had happened while he watched from the cover of the tupelo.

"And you're sure Obadiah is dead?" Evangeline said.

"He was inside the cabin when the bomb

came down," Zedock said. "I got to be moving on now, Miz Evangeline. The loup-garou are out, heard them howling at the moon. It ain't good for Christian folks to be abroad when the loup-garou howl, no."

As the black man punted away, O'Hara came out onto the deck, a coffee cup in his hand. "I killed two men today," he said. "Earlier today."

"What men?" Flintlock said.

O'Hara shrugged. "I don't know their names. Look in the corner over there, Sammy."

Flintlock glanced behind him and saw his Hawken propped against the cabin wall. "How the hell —"

"We'll talk about it inside," Evangeline said. "The loup-garou are no friends of mine. I refuse to attend their blood moon balls and they're mad at me for it."

Flintlock thought about pursuing the woman's statement, but decided otherwise. Suffice to say that the southeast Texas swamp country was a mighty strange place, and let it go at that. He picked up his Hawken, held it close like a long-lost child and followed the others inside.

"All right, O'Hara," Flintlock said. "Tell us."

"Tell you what?"

"Damn it, quit being such an Indian. Tell us about the two men you shot today."

"I only shot one," O'Hara said. "I used my knife on the other."

Flintlock feigned patience. "Make things easy for us. First tell us about the one you shot."

A terse man by nature, O'Hara used as few words as possible to recount his time in Budville, his visit to the *Democrat* office and his shooting of Cletus McPhee.

Flintlock and Evangeline listened in silence and when O'Hara was done talking the woman said, "If you're right about Ritter being broke when he got here, who is the moneyman behind him?"

"I don't know," O'Hara said. "The only man with money in Budville is Mathias Cobb, the owner of the bank."

"A bank in a hick town doesn't have the kind of money Brewster Ritter needs to clear the swamp and start logging," Flintlock said. "We're talking tens of thousands, maybe a sight more."

"Budville may be a hick town, but the bank is another story," Evangeline said. "Just about every rancher west of the Sabine has an account there, including Jerome Jackson. His J-Bar-J is the biggest spread in

77

southeast Texas and some say he's a millionaire many times over."

"How do you know this?" Flintlock said.

"Jerome and I walked out a few times," Evangeline said. "He wanted me to live on his ranch but I told him I had to stay in the swamp where my healing powers would do the most good." She smiled. "We parted friends and he always remembers my birthday."

"So Mathias Cobb could be bankrolling Ritter," Flintlock said. "If he is, then he's just as guilty. I think it's time I did some investigating in that town. Damn, I need a horse."

"An Apache I know has horses," O'Hara said. "That's where I left mine. It's a fair piece to his place but you can pick up a mount there. Any one of his horses are better than that nag you were riding."

"She's a good little mare, that mustang of mine," Flintlock said.

"No, she's not," O'Hara said. "She's a sheep."

Evangeline said, "Tell us about the other man you . . . um . . ."

"Killed?" O'Hara said.

"Yes, that," Evangeline said.

"After I left Budville I paid a visit to Brewster Ritter's camp. It's on the Louisiana side of the Sabine," O'Hara said. "He's got himself situated well, on dry land, he and his men living in tents. I counted maybe fifty horses and a dozen freight wagons, huge machines of all kinds lying around the place."

"You mean you just rode in there?" Flintlock said.

"No, I didn't go in like that. There must be two hundred men in camp, most of them workers, but Ritter has guns aplenty. I'm sure I spotted Travis Kershaw, the Pecos County draw fighter, in the crowd. There's another Travis Kershaw, sells his gun out of Denver, but he ain't a patch on this one."

"So many," Evangeline said, her beautiful face troubled.

"That's only the ones I saw," O'Hara said. "There could be more out in the swamp."

"There should only be one hundred and ninety-nine, O'Hara," Flintlock said. "You say you killed one."

"I didn't say I'd killed one of Ritter's men, but in fact I did. I heard other men call him Harry and he had your rifle."

"I remember him," Flintlock said. "I planned to gun him first chance I got."

"Well, I did it for you, Sam, so now you owe me."

Evangeline said, "Mr. O'Hara, please tell

us what happened, but spare me the gory details."

"Well, first of all, Brewster Ritter doesn't keep any kind of guard. I guess he thinks no one can touch him and I decided it was time to teach him otherwise. I saw Harry carry Sam's Hawken into a tent. He was drunk of course, and I went after him. Harry went in the front and I went in from the back. He was lying on his bunk already snoring when I cut his throat. He didn't snore after that."

"O'Hara, how did you get into Ritter's camp?" Flintlock said.

"I found a place at the edge of the swamp where I could leave my horse and then went on foot, maybe two miles. Like I said, there were no guards, just folks walking around. Nobody even noticed me."

"That will change now," Evangeline said. She frowned and brushed a fly off her knee. "There's not a cabin in the entire swamp that's safe from Ritter's flying machine and now he'll use it more."

"Then we'll have to bring it down," Flintlock said.

"How?" O'Hara said. "It will take some doing. I'm told it just shrugs off rifle bullets."

"What about the balloon?" Flintlock said.

"Maybe. If we can put a big enough hole in it."

"We need a cannon," Flintlock said. "Evangeline, you got one of those lying around?"

"No, but I think we should talk with Cornelius," Evangeline said. "He's a museum curator, not really a problem solver, but he often has good ideas."

"Right now I'll talk to anybody," Flintlock said. "The only idea I have kicking around my head is to ride into Ritter's camp and shoot him down like a dog."

"You'd last about ten seconds, Sammy," O'Hara said.

"I know. That's why it's a rotten idea," Flintlock said.

CHAPTER TWELVE

At dawn, Flintlock and O'Hara stepped into Evangeline's pirogue and slid across the calm waters of the swamp, the woman paddling at the bow and O'Hara at the stern. Flintlock sat in the middle, his hand close to his Colt. Mist lay thick on the water and the only sound was the occasional call of a bird and the steady plop, plop of the paddles.

Evangeline turned her head and said, "The Museum of the Swamp was built on a floating island and moves around. We'll try its last location."

Flintlock, balancing coffee and cornbread, said, "What kind of place is it?"

"It's a tall building, seven floors high, and some say the old Spanish men built it as a kind of mansion," Evangeline said. "You must start on the ground floor and examine the exhibits. Then, if you solve the mystery you can proceed to the next floor. But no one can climb higher unless the mystery is solved. Cornelius is very strict about that."

"I'm not very good at solving mysteries," Flintlock said around a mouthful of corn-bread. "What kind of mystery?"

"The mystery of the swamp," Evangeline said. "Brilliant scholars have spent their entire career on the ground floor and never risen any higher."

"How many visitors does the museum get, since it floats around in a swamp?" Flintlock said.

"Oh, it's busy enough," Evangeline said. "There was one scholar in 1870, two in 1876 and another in 1883. Cornelius was very pleased." Then, her voice rising a note, "Hush. I sense that Basilisk is near."

"Over there," O'Hara said, pointing. "On the bank."

It was the biggest alligator, the hugest animal, Flintlock had ever seen. The scaly reptile was on its belly, its huge jaws agape, and it looked like it was big enough to swallow a longhorn steer in one gulp.

"He's not warmed himself yet," Evangeline said. "He won't trouble us."

The alligator scared Flintlock enough, but it was the sight of Barnabas sitting on the creature's back that troubled him most. The old mountain man polished a brass pocket watch with a bright yellow cloth, breathed on it and polished it again. Satisfied, he removed his top hat, hung the watch around his neck and then smiled and patted the monster's back. He picked up the hat, adjusted the goggles on the crown and replaced it on his head. Not once did he glance in Flintlock's direction, a sure sign that his grandson did not meet with the old man's approval.

"There's a patch of mist on Basilisk's back," Evangeline said. She laughed. "For a moment I thought it was a human."

"It was just the mist," Flintlock said. "That's all it was."

"Yes, the mist can play tricks on a person," O'Hara said. "Ain't that right, Sammy?"

"Look!" Evangeline said. "The museum has moved but a few yards."

Sam Flintlock stared over her shoulder at a rickety timber structure that looked like a pair of wooden boxes of diminishing size stacked one on top of the other. The many windows to the front, including a myriad of dormers, were in the Gothic style, as was the entrance to the building, guarded by an iron-studded door. The untidy nests of water birds sprouted like weeds all over the edifice and marred the blue paint with vertical streaks of white.

"Quite a place," Flintlock said. He'd never seen its like before and thought it looked like a house built by a madman.

"Cornelius is very proud of it," Evangeline said, her hair shining in the morning sun. "Before Ritter arrived, he thought about hosting a ball here for the swamp dwellers. But now the Museum of the Swamp could become a prime target for Ritter's bombs, that is no longer a possibility."

The canoe bumped against the tiny dock and Evangeline, with considerable grace, stepped out and held it in place until Flintlock and O'Hara joined her. She tied up the canoe and then led the way along a gravel path to the museum door. A large key handle protruded from a wooden panel at the side of the door and Evangeline turned it as she would wind a clock. After she let the handle go it turned backward by itself and a bell jangled inside. She smiled at Flintlock. "It's a clockwork bell. Clever, don't you think?"

"Usually I just knock," Flintlock said. He looked up at the towering, ramshackle structure above his head. "Is this place safe?" he said.

"Of course it is," Evangeline said. "Well,

at least until now." The door creaked open. "After you, Sam," she said.

CHAPTER THIRTEEN

Sam Flintlock stepped through the door into a large room lit by four large windows, two on each side. Half a dozen glass-topped display cases were placed strategically on the pine floor and the walls were covered in shelves that held stacked, leather-bound books, alligator skulls, turtle shells and skeletal birds, coiled snakes and a variety of stuffed swamp animals. The place smelled musty and slightly damp along with a vague odor of fish.

Evangeline stepped next to Flintlock. "Interesting, isn't it?" she said. "Look in the display case beside you, armor and weapons of the Spanish conquistadores who first explored the swamp more than three hundred years ago. And over there is an ancient Egyptian mummy that was found just a couple of months ago floating in a bayou. No one knows how it got here." She smiled. "The swamp has many mysteries."

"Yeah, I can see that," Flintlock said. He felt uneasy but the weight of the Colt in his waistband reassured him. "Where is Cornelius?"

"He'll be down shortly," Evangeline said. "He likes people to browse for a while before he greets them. O'Hara, over on the shelf to your right is pottery and baskets used by the old Atakapan Indians. Cornelius says they lived in the swamp going back ten thousand years before they all disappeared."

"What happened to them?" O'Hara said.

"No one knows. It's yet another mystery of the swamp."

Light footsteps sounded on a rickety staircase that led up to the next floor. Then a small, slender man appeared. He crossed the floor, bowed and kissed Evangeline's hand. "It's been too long, my dear," he said. He had a birdlike voice. "We live in parlous times."

"This is my friend Mr. Sam Flintlock and his associate Mr. O'Hara," Evangeline said.

"Welcome, gentlemen," Cornelius said. "Have you come to solve the mystery of the swamp?"

"No, we've come to figure some way of making Brewster Ritter eat crow," Flintlock said. "And to see him hang, of course."

"Ah yes, I understand," Cornelius said.

"These are violent times indeed." He seemed distracted, stealing quick glances at the thunderbird tattoo on Flintlock's throat.

The man's appearance did nothing to reassure Flintlock. In contrast to his own stocky, strong masculine presence, Cornelius seemed almost effeminate. He was less than medium height with the face that on a woman would be called pretty, and thin, pale hair fell in strands to his shoulders. He wore a strange, knee-length frock coat in a light tan, a frilled white shirt, and breeches that ended at the calf and were held up by a belt with a huge gold buckle. He wore embroidered Chinese slippers on his feet, the toes upturned, fitted with little silver bells that chimed as he walked.

Cornelius remained silent and Flintlock said, "Evangeline says you may have some advice for us." But to himself he said, *What does a woman like Evangeline see in this little pimp?*

Cornelius didn't answer that question. He said, "Forgive me for staring at you, Mr. Flintlock, but the tattoo on your throat intrigues me."

"Indian put it there when I was a boy," Flintlock said. "It was my grandfather's idea, old Barnabas the mountain man. He said folks would remember me."

"I'm sure they do," Cornelius said. "I know I will."

"Me too," O'Hara said, grinning.

"The Atakapan Indians had a legend that a thunderbird will rise out of the swamp and lead the people to a time of peace and prosperity," Cornelius said. "Perhaps you are the thunderbird, Mr. Flintlock. And you might be the one to solve the mystery of the swamp."

Flintlock wished he was far from here, had a horse under him and was shooting at people he didn't like or maybe robbing a bank or something. Anywhere but here, in the middle of a damned bog, talking to a loco museum curator.

Perhaps Evangeline caught Flintlock's mood because she said, "Cornelius, we will talk of the thunderbird another day. Can you offer us any advice that will help us defeat Brewster Ritter?"

"Yes, I can, my beloved," the little man said. "When you wish to drain the pond, cut off its water at the source. Stop Ritter's money flow and he will wither on the vine."

"That's just what I was thinking," O'Hara said. "Find the money man, gun him and it's over."

"I abhor violence, but it is obvious that Ritter cannot proceed with his plans without funding. As for you, Mr. Flintlock, I can help you in a more tangible way. You think the Colt in your waistband is badly balanced and does not sit well in your hand, is that not so?"

Flintlock was stunned. "How the hell —"

"Let's say I just know," Cornelius said. He stepped to a shelf and removed a walnut box. He returned to Flintlock and opened the lid.

"Three years before he died this Colt revolver was presented to me by President Grant," Cornelius said. "I was a member of his security detail and stepped in the way of an assassin's bullet that was meant to kill him. Despite being wounded here" — Cornelius's hand strayed to the left side of his chest — "I killed the assailant and thus saved the president's life. The assassin was a woman, the widow of a Confederate soldier killed in the war. I have never used a gun since."

"During the war Cornelius served under General Hugh Judson Kilpatrick as a major in the Second United States Cavalry," Evangeline said. "He stayed in the army for some time after the war ended."

"Try the revolver, Mr. Flintlock," Cornelius said. "I wager it's a better balanced weapon than the one you have."

91

"I can't take your Colt," Flintlock said. "I mean, you getting it from President Grant an' all."

"I want you to have it, Mr. Flintlock. Trust me, your need for a fine weapon is greater than mine." Cornelius took the Colt from the case, and spun it with great skill and dexterity, so fast that the spinning revolver blurred into a blue disc. The butt of the Colt slapped into Cornelius's palm. He reversed the revolver and extended it to Flintlock, butt first.

Flintlock reached for the gun but Cornelius executed an expert road agent's spin and he found himself looking into the muzzle. "Way too trusting, Mr. Flintlock," the little man said. "That can get you killed in the swamp."

Irritated, Flintlock grabbed the Colt from Cornelius's hand, spun it faster than he had and a split second later the muzzle jammed into the space between Cornelius's eyebrows. "Old Barnabas taught me the road agent's spin when I was a younker," he said. "I let you fool me was all."

"Yes, because you underestimated me. Another mistake you must never make in the swamp. Do you like the Colt's balance?"

Despite his touchiness Flintlock admitted that the Colt's balance was damn near perfect. "A beautiful revolver," he said.

"Then it's yours and use it wisely and well," Cornelius said.

"I can't —"

"Yes, you can. I have no more need for it."

Flintlock carefully placed the Colt in its case and reverently tucked it under his arm, as though Sam Colt's finest creation was a holy object.

"If you two gunslingers are quite finished showing off, I'd like to ask you a question, Cornelius," O'Hara said.

"That is why the museum is here, to answer questions, Mr. O'Hara."

"What is the mystery of the swamp?" O'Hara said.

"Good question," Cornelius said. "The mystery of the swamp is that there is no mystery. That is why we must find it."

"Oh," O'Hara said.

And Flintlock, his mood warmed by the gun case under his arm, said, "Sounds logical to me."

Chapter Fourteen

Brewster Ritter's anger verged on madness.

He stood beside his horse and said to Bonifaunt Toohy, "Search the swamp. Find him. I want the man who murdered Harry Stake dead, dead, dead."

"I'll find him, boss," Toohy said.

"If you can't, kill a swamp rat every hour until they give him up, understand? Show mercy to no one."

"I'll see that it's done, boss," Toohy said.

"And from now on I want guards posted around the clock," Ritter said. "By God, if there's a repeat of this outrage heads will roll."

"Where are you headed, boss?" Toohy said. "Maybe you should take one of the boys along."

"No, I'm headed for Budville, and Mathias Cobb has guns enough. He said to only contact him if there's a crisis. Well, this is a crisis. The damned swampers are fighting back and that may call for a change of plans."

Ritter swung into the saddle. "See that my orders are carried out, Mr. Toohy," he said before he set spurs to his horse and galloped away.

"I've told you to never come here, Ritter," Mathias Cobb said. He sat forward in his chair and his great belly hung between his knees like a sack of grain. "My association with your enterprise must be a secret. If the ranchers got wind of it . . . well, it could be a disaster."

"This is important," Ritter said. "One of my men was murdered in my camp, his throat cut. That can only mean one thing, that the swamp rats plan to fight back and bring the war to me."

"Handle it, Ritter," Cobb said. "I pay you enough to hire gunmen. Start shooting people and the swamp dwellers will soon lose their will to fight." The fat man opened a tiny pillbox. He selected a white tablet, popped it into his mouth and swallowed it with a glass of water Sebastian Lilly poured for him. "My heart is acting up," Cobb said. "You upset me coming here, Ritter."

Ritter mentioned the orders he'd given Bonifaunt Toohy and said, "The killing will start today."

"That is a practical solution to the problem," Cobb said. "You will also forget any plan you might have for draining the swamp. Even confining that effort to the Texas side of the Sabine would cost a fortune. Even the United States government would not consider such an undertaking."

"My chief engineer assures me that his steam pumps can handle it," Ritter said.

"Balderdash," Cobb said. "The man is a fool. A pistol cartridge costs ten cents. If you must kill an 'undred swamp dwellers it will cost you, or should I say me, just ten dollars. Bullets, not steam pumps, are the solution to your problem. It's good business, Ritter."

Ritter opened his mouth to speak, but Cobb cut him off. "Can the cypress be harvested easily if the swamp is not drained?"

"Yes, of course, But —"

"That's all I wanted to know," Cobb said. He scratched a blue jowl. "Now go about your business and don't come back here unless I send for you. Mr. Lilly, show Mr. Ritter to the door."

Ritter knew further talk of draining the swamp was useless. He got to his feet and stepped to the door, but Cobb's voice stopped him. "Pile up the skulls like the Mongols did in the days of yore, Ritter. You'll soon force out the vermin. I guarantee it. Mr. Lilly, tell Miss Rhonda La Page that she can come in now."

Lilly grinned. "Sure thing, Mr. Cobb," he said.

Brewster Ritter's anger was a volcano ready to erupt. Mathias Cobb had made him feel small and now he wanted to kill, smash, destroy — he was a finger looking for a trigger. The late summer day was radiant, the birds sang and the smell of pines, borne on a north wind, scented the air. But Ritter cared nothing about those things. The swamp people stood in his way and he wanted them dead, all of them, to the last man, woman or child.

He rode east toward the Sabine, then looped southeast, planning to cross at the rocky shallows near a burned-out Butterfield stage stop. His route took him close to the southern edge of the swamp and set up the killing Ritter so badly wanted.

It had been a good fishing day for Zedock Briscoe and as the trout moved so did he. By the time he reached the southern edge of the swamp he reckoned he'd three dozen fish in his pirogue, plenty for his family, plenty to give away. The day was just beginning its shade into evening when he pulled up his lines and began to think fondly of fried fish and cornbread and maybe hotcakes if his wife was in the mood to make them.

Brewster Ritter heard a splash in the swamp to his left and drew rein. His eyes scanned into the distance and he saw a black man punting his canoe out of the shallows and into deeper water.

Ritter didn't know the man nor did he care. He was a swamp dweller and that was all the information he needed . . . an invitation to a killing. He slid the .44-40 Winchester out of the boot under his left knee and racked a round into the chamber. The black man's head turned in his direction as though the sound had startled him. Ritter put the rifle to his shoulder, sighted and fired. Zedock fell backward out of the canoe and Ritter waited to see if he needed a second shot. Facedown in the water, the man's motionless body drifted away from the pirogue and snagged on a cypress knee. Even in the fading light Ritter saw a crimson stain in the water around the corpse.

Ritter smiled and sighed his satisfaction,

like a man does after sex. But the killing of the swamp rat was better than sex, at that moment better than anything. He slid the rifle back in the boot and rode on . . . his anger gone as though it had never been.

CHAPTER FIFTEEN

"You got something on your mind, honey?" Dixie Haley said.

Bonifaunt Toohy sat at the end of his cot in his undershirt and pants. He poured black rum into a jigger and knocked it back. "Why would a whore care about anything?" he said.

The afternoon sun had trapped itself within the canvas and the tent was hot. Dixie had undone her lace corset and rolled her black stockings down to her ankles. She still wore her high-heeled ankle boots.

"I care about you, honey," Dixie said. "The other girls say you slap them around but you never do that to me."

"Not yet anyway," Toohy said. Coarse black hair grew over his shoulders and down his back. "So far you've given me no cause."

Dixie felt a little tremble inside and she said, "Maybe I should go and leave you to your bottle."

"Man takes only what he needs out of a bottle and then he puts the cork in it. You stay."

"I'll stay as long as you need me, Bonifaunt."

"Call me Bon, just that. I hate my goddamn name." Then, "You slept in Travis Kershaw's tent last night. How do you explain that?"

Dixie hesitated before she answered. "Honey, that was business. It's what I do for money."

"Don't I give you enough?"

"Sometimes a girl wants more."

Toohy kneaded the knuckles of his right hand. For Dixie it was a bad sign. The other girls said he did that before he slapped them. She also heard he did it before he killed a man.

Dixie's tremble was back. "For clothes and stuff. Girly stuff," she said.

"What did you tell him about me?"

"Nothing, honey, honest. Like I said, it was strictly business."

"You tell him how I feel about Ritter? You tell him I ain't never killed a woman or hurt a child. Did you tell him that?"

"I didn't even know those things, Bonny. I swear. Maybe I should leave. Mr. Ritter will be back soon."

"He won't be here for a spell yet. It's a ways to Budville. You're a whore, Dixie, with a heart like a rock. Could you put a bullet into a child?"

The woman was horrified. "No. I could never do a thing like that."

"A little boy and a little girl, scatter their brains with a Colt? Could you do that?"

"No. That's a horrible question to ask. You're scaring me." Dixie sat up and grabbed the laces of her corset. "I think I should go."

"I couldn't either. I couldn't kill a child," Toohy said.

"Then why do you even mention such a thing?" Dixie said.

"Because that's what Ritter wants us to do, kill women and children in the swamp. He says we've got to kill all of them."

Dixie folded her arms across her naked breasts. "Maybe we should leave, all five of us girls. Get far away from here."

"You'll stay here. This is where the money is." Toohy's thin lips twisted into a sneer. "And where would you go? What would you do? Become a two-dollar-a-bang whore at a hog ranch, maybe?"

"And what will you do?" Dixie said, some of her courage returning.

"I don't know," Toohy said.

"I'll leave with you, Bonny. We can go anywhere together. Texas is a big place."

Toohy poured himself another drink. "There's ten dollars in my vest pocket, Dixie," he said. "Take it and then get the hell out of here."

The woman laced up and took the money from Toohy's vest, then said, "Should I ask Travis?"

"Ask him what?"

"If he can kill women and children."

"No need to ask him. Kershaw is a low-down, murdering snake. He'll cut any man, woman or child in half with a shotgun for fifty dollars."

Dixie rolled up her stocking, put her scarlet garters in place and at the tent flap said, "I won't come back here until you're in a better mood."

"And when will that be?" Toohy said.

"Probably never," the woman said.

CHAPTER SIXTEEN

At dawn, a man called Ashe Kent, having no room in his small canoe, towed Zedock Briscoe's body to Evangeline's cabin and Sam Flintlock watched him come.

Flintlock and O'Hara manhandled Zedock onto the deck and Evangeline, wearing only a changing robe, kneeled by the body.

"Can you do anything for him, Miss Evangeline?" Kent said, a tall, lanky man who trapped all over the swamp.

Tears misting her eyes, Evangeline said, "I can't raise the dead, Ashe."

"He was shot," Kent said. "He didn't drown."

Evangeline nodded. "Yes. Yes, I can see that."

"Where did you find him?" Flintlock said.

"At the edge of the swamp south a ways. I reckon he was shot by someone on the bank." Kent reached into his pocket and produced an empty cartridge case. "Found this. It's a forty-four-forty and still shiny."

Flintlock took the case and said, "You see anybody, Ashe?"

The man shook his head. "Nobody. Saw some horse tracks on the banks headed east. I reckon the killer crossed the Sabine into Louisiana already."

"One of Brewster Ritter's men most likely," Flintlock said.

"That would be my thinking," Kent said. "Zedock now, he didn't have any enemies and the only things that feared him were the fish."

Evangeline was very pale. "Ashe, will you tell Mrs. Briscoe what happened?"

"I sure will, Miss Evangeline, but it's a hell of a thing to do."

"I know, Ashe, but it has to be done," Evangeline said. "I'll make Zedock's body decent. Mrs. Briscoe can come here or I'll bring Zedock to her. Tell her that."

Kent nodded, grim-faced as a hanging judge, and left to do what had to be done.

"I'll wash Zedock's body right here on the dock and wrap him in a sheet," Evangeline said. "I can't let Mrs. Briscoe see him like this." She wiped a tear from her cheek and said, "You gentlemen may not want to be here for a while."

"No, we don't," Flintlock said. "We'll go scout the bank where Zedock was murdered. Can we take your pirogue?"

Evangeline didn't raise her head. "Of course you can."

O'Hara removed his strange top hat, kneeled beside the body and placed his hand on Zedock's cold forehead. He bowed his head and closed his eyes and stayed like that for long moments. When he finally rose he said, "The Great Spirit has welcomed him."

"It could not be otherwise," Evangeline said.

O'Hara nodded. "That is true, swamp witch. It could not be otherwise."

Sam Flintlock stood in the bright morning sun, the new day coming in clean, and chopped his bladed hand to the east. "That's the way he headed, all right. What do you say, Injun?"

"You read sign as well as I do, Sammy," O'Hara said.

"Then we'll follow the tracks," Flintlock said. "See where they lead."

"They'll lead right to Brewster Ritter's camp," O'Hara said.

"Uh-huh," Flintlock said. President Grant's Colt was tucked into his waistband.

The tracks ended at a ruined stage station on the west bank of the Sabine. "He crossed here," O'Hara said. "Rode down through the willows there and across the shallows."

"Then the murderer was definitely one of Ritter's men," Flintlock said.

"That's a fair guess," O'Hara said. His eyes held on Flintlock for a long time, then he said, "Well, what do we do?"

"What we don't do is walk into Ritter's camp with wet feet and ask him nicely to hand over the murderer of Zedock Briscoe," Flintlock said. "Man could get himself killed that way. There's a sunny patch by the ruin. I say we sit for a spell. My feet are killing me in these boots."

They propped their backs against the stage stop's only standing wall, then O'Hara stretched out and tipped his hat over his eyes.

Five minutes went by and as the morning melted into a drowsy afternoon, wicked old Barnabas, his pants rolled up to his knees, stood in the shallows, a fishing pole in his hands. He looked up at Flintlock and said, "I got news for you, Sam."

"Spill it, you old reprobate," Flintlock said.

Barnabas yawned. "I made a mistake, boy. Your ma ain't in this swamp. She's in the Arizona Territory waiting tables at a saloon they call The Swamp." The old man grinned. "See, that's how come the mix-up. You-know-who played a trick on me. He does that all the time."

"Damn you, Barnabas —"

"I'm already that, Sam."

"You know the trouble I'm in following the wild goose chase you sent me on? I ought to put a bullet in you."

"Wouldn't do you any good, boy, on account of how I'm dead already."

Flintlock jumped to his feet. "What's my ma's name, you evil old coot? And where is she in Arizona?"

"You know I never give out my daughter's name. I refuse to say it."

"Say it now, you old scoundrel. Say my ma's name."

"Elsie. It's Elsie. That's the name I give her."

"Where is she in Arizona?"

"Maybe I'll tell you later."

"Go to hell, Barnabas," Flintlock said.

The old mountain man threw away his fishing pole. And vanished. The river water bubbled and steamed where he'd stood.

O'Hara stepped beside Flintlock. "Riders coming," he said.

"Did you hear that? Did you hear what the old sinner told me?"

O'Hara's face was empty. "Riders coming," he said.

The two riders were still a ways off as Flintlock and O'Hara stepped away from the abandoned stage stop and stood at the edge of the swamp. The men could be a couple of Ritter's hired guns, but they might as well be a pair of out-of-work punchers riding the grub line or even circuit preachers come to that.

It was only when they got closer that Flintlock recognized Lem, the Ritter gunman who'd left him to the tender mercies of the alligator. He didn't know the other man but he was a hard-faced feller who was cut from the same cloth as his companion.

When the two were just a few yards away, Flintlock stepped out of cover and said, "Howdy, Lem. You remember me?"

The man drew rein, startled. "You!" he said.

"Cut the throats of any raccoons recently, Lem?" Flintlock said.

"How did —"

"I escape the alligator? It's a long story, Lem, but you don't have long enough to live to hear it."

Flintlock was conscious of O'Hara on his left. The breed's hand was close to his Colt and he was good with it, a steady gun hand in a pinch.

"Give us the road," Lem said. "I don't deal with low persons."

"I do and there's none lower than you, Lem," Flintlock said.

"You killed Al Plume and I owed you payback," Lem said. "Now clear the way there."

Flintlock smiled. "Lem, are you going to talk all day or draw? I have a feeling you're scared, Lem. You're trembling like a hound dog passin' a peach pit."

The man called Lem roared his anger and went for his gun.

Flintlock shot him out of the saddle with time to spare.

The other man threw up his hands. "Hell, don't shoot. I'm out of it."

"Do you work for Brewster Ritter?" Flintlock said. Grant's Colt trailed smoke in his hand.

"Yeah I do, but —"

"Then you ain't out of it." Flintlock fired. Hit hard, the man swayed in the saddle and

Flintlock shot him again. This time the gun-man pitched to his right and landed with a thud, dead when he hit the ground.

"Ain't one to hold a grudge, are you, Sammy?" O'Hara said.

"A while back, I took to liking raccoons," Flintlock said.

"Ah, then that explains it," O'Hara said.

"I hate to pass on two good horses, but we have to send Ritter a message," Flintlock said. "I want to scare the hell out of him." He watched O'Hara's face as he said, "Does the Injun half of you know how to scalp a man?"

"Yes, it does," O'Hara said, his own features revealing nothing.

"Then scalp them two," Flintlock said.

"You would have made a good Comanche, Sammy," O'Hara said, pulling his knife.

"Damn right," Flintlock said.

Their gory heads dripping blood, the two dead men were tied across their horses with Lem's rope, a relic of his cowboy past. Flintlock and O'Hara led the mounts to the crossing and onto the east side of the Sabine. Flintlock slapped the horses into motion and they trotted away, their stirrups bouncing.

"I'd like to see Ritter's face when he gets

a load of them two," Flintlock said. "He'll know he's in a fight."

O'Hara said, "Your mother isn't here, Sam."

"So you heard him?"

"I always hear him. See him from time to time. Now you don't have to stay here. You can walk away from it."

"Is that what you want to do, O'Hara, walk away from it?"

"No. I'll stick."

"Me too," Flintlock

"Then we're fools," O'Hara said.

Flintlock smiled. "You'll get no argument from me on that score."

CHAPTER SEVENTEEN

Evangeline stood on her deck in the waning light and watched the lights draw closer. The canoes, lit fore and aft with lanterns, carried two dozen black folk, men, women and children, all of them singing the plaintive Negro spiritual, "I'm Going Up."

> Oh, saints and sinners will you go
> And see the heavenly land?
> I'm going up to heaven for to see my robe,
> See the heavenly land.

Mrs. Briscoe, a plump, motherly woman with a round face, caught sight of the long white bundle on the deck and wailed, beating her wrists against the sides of her head.

> Going to see my robe and try it on,
> See the heavenly robe.
> 'Tis brighter than the glittering sun,
> See the heavenly land.

113

Canoes bumped against the deck and a couple of young men, Zedock's sons, got out and reverently lifted the body. A canoe, fitted out with a lining of white muslin and strewn with swamp blossoms, was pushed closer and the body was laid out inside. Without a glance in Evangeline's direction, the canoes turned and one by one drifted away. The singing grew fainter and then Evangeline was left alone in the silent, gathering dark.

She turned to go back into the cabin but noticed an object shining at the corner of the deck. She picked it up, a small silver cross on a chain. Smiling through her tears, Evangeline fastened the cross around her slender neck and stepped into the cabin.

Flintlock and O'Hara forgot where they'd left the canoe and it took an hour of searching and cussing in darkness before they found it.

Flintlock was scathing. "I thought Indians always knew where they left stuff," he said to O'Hara. "The Injun part of you ought to apologize to the white part."

"And you were raised by mountain men," O'Hara said. "I bet a mountain man would know where he left his damned canoe."

"You made me nervous yelling at me to

find it and that's why I couldn't find it," Flintlock said.

"All I said was, 'Can you remember a tree or any other landmark?' That was hardly yelling, Sammy."

"Yeah, well, it sounded like yelling," Flintlock said. "Hey, you don't suppose somebody moved it? Maybe an alligator."

"Nobody moved it," O'Hara said, looking over his shoulder as he paddled. "And it wasn't an alligator."

"How can you say that? How come you're so all-fired certain?"

"Because you tied up the canoe and an alligator can't undo knots."

"Yeah, well, maybe so, but the whole thing was mighty strange all the same," Flintlock said. He slowed his paddling. "Listen. What's that?"

"A mighty big alligator bellowing close by," O'Hara said. "Maybe he's mad because he heard you say he tried to steal the canoe."

"It sounds loud enough to be Basilisk," Flintlock said, his hand straying to his gun and his eyes searching the murky, shadowed swamp.

"Hell, paddle faster," O'Hara said.

"Hell, that's just what I'm doing," Flintlock said.

"Over there!" O'Hara said, stabbing into

darkness with his forefinger.

Flintlock looked . . . and saw . . . eyes.

"It's the swamp monster," O'Hara said. "And it's coming our way."

A huge shape loomed less than a hundred yards away across open water, a pair of glowing eyes lighting its way. Flintlock heard the *chunk, chunk, chunk* of its passing and he felt the hair on the back of his neck rise.

O'Hara turned his head. "We'll get into the water and let it have the canoe," he said.

"The hell we will," Flintlock said. "This pirogue is Evangeline's property. Lose it and she'll turn us into toads for sure."

"Then come up with an idea, white man," O'Hara said. "I'm all out of mine."

A rifle shot slammed through the swamp. A bullet hit a foot in front of the canoe and kicked up a startled exclamation point of water.

"It's trying to kill us," O'Hara said.

"Swamp monsters don't shoot rifles," Flintlock said. He'd laid aside his paddle and had his Colt in his hand. "Get us closer," he said.

"Closer! Are you crazy? It's shooting at us," O'Hara said. As though to emphasize his point a bullet split the air between them and another made a dull *thunk!* as it hit the side of the canoe.

"Do as I say, O'Hara," Flintlock said.

"Damn you, Sammy, if you get me killed I'll haunt you for the rest of your life," O'Hara said.

"Closer," Flintlock said. "What kind of Indian are you?"

"Right now the scared kind."

"It's going to be just fine. I'm going to shoot the monster's eyes out."

"Oh my God!" O'Hara said, but whether it was a prayer or cry of approval Flintlock couldn't tell.

As it was, he got lucky.

Rather than head straight toward the monster O'Hara angled the pirogue to his right away from the probing yellow beams from the monster's eyes and vanished into the gloom.

A man's voice drifted across the water. "Where the hell is the canoe?"

Then another, "Did it get away?"

"No, you sons of bitches, it's right here!" Flintlock yelled.

Sighted fire is impossible in darkness, but Flintlock was schooled in the ways of the draw fighter and the point and shoot. At a distance of twenty yards he scored two hits with five shots . . . and put out both the monster's eyes.

Now angry yells echoed across the water and as Flintlock reloaded, filling all six chambers of the Colt, he heard a difference in the sound as the blinded monster started to back away.

Flintlock yelled to O'Hara, "Paddle!"

"Which way?"

"Damn it, any way so long so as it's not toward the monster."

O'Hara swung the pirogue to his left and paddled quickly. Flintlock could make out the darker bulk of the monster against the backdrop of the swamp. Aware that he was looking at a steam-powered boat of some kind, Flintlock fired as he went, hammering shot after shot into the churning craft, and was rewarded with a loud cry as somebody took a hit. Finally, his Colt shot dry and feeling nautical, Flintlock said, "Proceed with all possible speed, Mr. O'Hara."

O'Hara snorted in outrage and said, "You're a madman, Sammy. You should be locked away in an institution someplace. You just ain't right."

"Put the crawl on them, though, didn't I?"

O'Hara grinned. "You sure did, crazy man."

CHAPTER EIGHTEEN

"My ma's not in the swamp," Sam Flintlock said.

"How do you know that?" Evangeline said.

"He knows," O'Hara said.

Evangeline's eyes moved from O'Hara to Flintlock. "You two are keeping a secret from me," she said.

"She's not here," Flintlock said. "Let it go at that. We talked about calling it quits, me and O'Hara, going after her to the Arizona Territory."

"What did you decide?" the woman said, her beautiful face betraying no emotion.

"We decided to stick," O'Hara said.

Flintlock said, "I reckon we're all that stands between the swamp people and Brewster Ritter. Unless there are pistol fighters among them."

"Only Cornelius, but he's done with that," Evangeline said. "You were lucky tonight, Sam."

"Uh-huh. But your pirogue's got a bullet hole in it."

"I can repair it," Evangeline said. "Ritter has lost three men, Sam. What does he do next?"

"I wish I knew," Flintlock said. "The swamp monster is a boat of some kind."

"Yes. I know that," Evangeline said. "I hope you've put it out of commission for a long time."

She wore a long, ankle-length black coat with a hood that lay over the back of her shoulders. Her boots were also black, buttoned up one side.

"You're dressed for going out," Flintlock said.

"Yes, and I'm already late," Evangeline said. "I thought you would have the pirogue back earlier." She held up a silencing hand. "No need to apologize, Sam. It couldn't be helped."

"Evangeline, it's after midnight," Flintlock said.

"I know, but Isaac Murren's wife's baby is due and I must be there for the delivery."

"Do you want me to come with you?" Flintlock said.

Evangeline smiled. "Sam, I don't think you'd be much good at birthing a baby. I think I can manage."

"I'll wait up for you," Flintlock said.

"I could be gone for hours."

"I know, but I'll still wait up," Flintlock said.

"You're sure sweet on that woman, Sammy," O'Hara said.

"Yeah, I know."

"You going to do something about it?"

"Nope."

"How come that?"

A lost, lonely look came into Flintlock's eyes. "Evangeline wouldn't want to share my life, O'Hara. I'm a rough-living man and I keep company with even rougher companions. I step lightly from one side of the law to the other and I sell my gun to the highest bidder, but most of the time I find myself riding the grub line. If times come down real hard on me, I'm inclined to rob a bank or hold up a stage and I never lie awake o' nights regretting either."

O'Hara said, "I've observed you as I would a wolf who comes too near my camp, Sammy. There's good in you, if a person digs deep enough. You don't abuse women, whores or horses and you're kind to children and old folks. You got sand and you're a first-rate fighting man who lets no one put the crawl on you." O'Hara smiled. "Of course, you're none too bright, Sammy, and you're no woman's idea of what handsome is."

"O'Hara, you were doing all right until that last bit, which incidentally was enough to get you shot," Flintlock said, irritated.

"Well," O'Hara said, "if it makes you feel any better, Evangeline has a mighty strange taste in men. I mean she's keen on Cornelius, so there's hope for you yet, slight though it may be."

Flintlock said, "O'Hara, I'm going to pour myself a drink and then sit out on the deck in Evangeline's rocking chair. If you come out before an hour is past I'll shoot you."

"You're a mighty hard, unfeeling man, Sammy," O'Hara said.

"Ain't I though," Flintlock said.

Evangeline returned at four in the morning, paddling though a mist that lay among the roots of the cypress. Falling strands of Spanish moss garlanded their branches and looked like a widow's tears.

Flintlock helped Evangeline from her pirogue. The woman looked strained, as though the birthing had been difficult. He tried to be cheerful. "Well, so we have a new little swamp person?" he said.

Evangeline turned her head and looked at

the mist made opalescent by the lowering moon. "No, we don't," she said.

Flintlock let the shocked expression on his face ask the question.

"A beautiful baby girl," Evangeline said. "She was stillborn. It seems that the swamp, once so full of life, is now full of death."

In that moment Evangeline looked frail, vulnerable and Flintlock, never a demonstrative man, reached out and took her in his arms. Evangeline was as rigid as a board and did not respond. "I'll be all right, Sam," she said, moving away from him. "I think I'll go inside now.

O'Hara, who had defied Flintlock's dire warning, had stepped onto the deck. He said, "Can I get you anything, Evangeline?"

The woman shook her head. "No, nothing, thank you. Nothing at all."

Flintlock sat in the rocker and stared at the sky. He was still there when the first rays of dawn set the morning sky on fire.

CHAPTER NINETEEN

Brewster Ritter cut the ropes that bound Lem Claxton's feet and wrists and dragged him to the ground. He rolled the dead man onto his back and then ripped his shirt open, the buttons popping one after another.

Ritter stared at the corpse's bloody chest and nodded. "Bonifaunt, bring the other one over here," he said. Toohy did as he was told and Ritter treated the body as he had Claxton's.

"Look at this," Ritter said, nudging Claxton with his toe. "What does it tell you?"

"That he was shot twice," Toohy said.

"Look at the damned bullet holes. You could cover them both with a playing card. And this one" — a kick in the ribs this time — "shot in the center of the chest. He must have been as dead as a rotten stump when he hit the ground."

"Hired gun?" Toohy said.

"It has to be," Ritter said. "The damned swamper trash have got together and hired themselves a draw fighter."

Toohy considered that for a few moments and said, "I heard that Doc Holliday is in Fort Worth. Lafe Croucher is up El Paso way and Vic Moylan was in Crystal City last I heard. Moylan is always looking for work, supports a crippled brother."

"Hell, it could be anybody," Ritter said. "Texas is full of guns for hire. Whoever he is, he's here in the swamp and he's good. You heard what happened last night, huh?"

"Yeah, the monster machine shot up and Travis Kershaw burned across the side of his head."

"An inch to the left and he'd be a dead man," Ritter said. "The hired gun knows how to shoot and he was in a damned canoe."

"I'll find him," Toohy said.

"You'd better," Ritter said. "Or I'll be looking for a new boy." Toohy let that go, and Ritter said, "Tell that damned useless engineer I want to see him. Cobb is right, the hell with draining the swamp, let's start cutting trees."

"We don't have the sawmill built yet, boss," Toohy said.

"That's why I want to talk to the engineer.

125

We can pile the trunks high until he builds the sawmill and gets the steam saws in operation."

"I'll find the engineer," Toohy said.

"And Bonifaunt, I want you to ride over to Budville and tell Mathias Cobb what's happening," Ritter said. "Tell him to alert the railroad that I'll be delivering sawn lumber within a month." He read the doubt in Toohy's face and said, "I don't care if the sawmill doesn't have four walls and a roof, I want the saws running and those hundred and fifty idle loggers working. Hell, that's fifty crews. We can have every cypress in the swamp cut down within a year. Tell Cobb that too."

Toohy nodded. "You got it, boss."

"Well, don't just stand there, beat it," Ritter said.

Bonifaunt Toohy rode past the bank and up the middle of Budville's main street before he looped his horse to the saloon hitching rail and stepped inside. As he knew it would, his presence became known and within a couple of minutes Sebastian Lilly joined him at the bar.

"You got news, Bon?" Lilly said.

"Yeah. It's for Cobb, directly from Ritter."

126

"He knows you're here but he won't talk to you."

"I reckon. That's why I'll tell it to you."

"Then tell it," Lilly said. He raised two fingers to the bartender and the man laid shot glasses in front of him and Toohy and poured whiskey to the brims. "Cheers," Lilly said. He and Toohy downed their drinks and Toohy signaled for two more.

"The swampers have hired themselves a gun," he said. "He's already killed Lem Claxton and Jim O'Connor and gave Travis Kershaw a headache, came damn near to scattering his brains."

Lilly stared hard at Toohy. "You can handle him."

"Sure I can. If I can find him."

"A gun in a swamp shouldn't be too hard to find."

"Let's hope so. Another thing, Ritter is planning to start cutting down trees. He's got a hundred and fifty loggers who've been doing nothing but eating his grub, drinking his whiskey and screwing his whores. Now he's finally putting them to work."

"Is the sawmill finished?"

"Hell, it ain't even started. The steam saws will operate even if they're out in the open, which is likely. Ritter wants Cobb to let the railroad know that he'll be loading sawn

127

lumber within a month."

"Big talk," Lilly said.

"I think he'll deliver."

"What about the swampers?"

"Ritter pays me and another six guns to take care of that problem."

"You up for killing innocent folks?"

"I don't know. After the Gantly family was shot I started to see things different."

"Better make up your mind soon, Bon."

"Yeah, I know."

"You're getting some mighty close attention," Lilly said.

"I've been watching him in the mirror. You know him?"

"Name's Randy Collis. He claims he's a fast gun, says he killed a man in the New Mexico Territory and another over to Corpus Christi way. Whether that's true or not, he wants to build a rep as a badman."

"Why doesn't he brace you, Seb?"

"Because he knows I can shade him any day of the week. He's not so sure about you."

"I don't want any trouble," Toohy said.

"Seems like you got it. He's coming over this way."

"You seeing enough, mister?" Collis said.

He was a hard-faced youngster, his hat pushed back on his head. He had arrogant

128

blue eyes, an impertinent smile and from years of experience Toohy could tell he'd killed his man.

Toohy ignored the youngster, unimpressed by the two guns he wore. He turned his back on Collis and ordered a couple of more whiskeys.

"You were watching me in the mirror," the kid said to the back of Toohy's head. "You some kind of a Mary?"

Usually when a would-be badman was on the prod in a saloon he had an audience. Toohy glanced into the mirror and sure enough, an equally arrogant youngster sat at a table grinning, and hanging on him was a hard-eyed saloon floozy who looked like she was enjoying the show.

Toohy turned. "Boy, go find yourself another pincushion," he said.

Collis put on an act of being offended. "What did you say, Mary?"

"He said to go away," Lilly said.

From the table, the other youngster said, "The Mary is scared of you, Randy. He ain't gonna draw down on you."

"Yeah, you're right, Jake," Collis said. "He's pissin' his pants." He pushed Toohy aside then reached around him and lifted his whiskey. "Only real men drink whiskey in this saloon," Collis said. He drained the

129

glass and threw it hard against a wall, where it shattered. "On your way out pick that up, Mary," he said. "If you don't I'll come looking for you."

Collis turned his back and swaggered back to the table, the guns on his hips hanging out from his side, the brass shells in the cartridge belts gleaming. "Hell, let's go get something to eat," he said to his companions. "Putting the crawl on a man always gives me an appetite."

"I could eat some eggs," the floozy said.

"Sure," Collis said. "But I got to go take a piss first."

The jingle bobs on his spurs ringing, he walked out the back door to the outhouse.

The bartender gave Toohy a long look, but he ignored it. "You got a billy club stashed away somewhere?" he said.

The man reached under the bar and produced a two-foot chunk of turned wood as thick as a man's wrist. "Teak," the bartender said.

Toohy nodded and stepped toward the rear door. "Have fun," Lilly called out after him.

Randy Collis grinned as he heard Bonifaunt Toohy's footsteps approaching the outhouse. He buttoned up, turned his head and said, "I knew it had to be you, Mary. And now I'm gonna kill you."

Toohy said nothing as Collis, smiling his anticipation, stepped out of the outhouse and said, "You're wearing a gun like a man. Let's see if you —"

Bringing the club from behind him Toohy swung and the iron-hard teak slammed against the side of Collis's head. The youngster shrieked and staggered back, his left ear a bloody mess. Toohy, all his pent-up rage searing like acid to the surface, went after him. Groggy but still on his feet, Collis went for his guns. But Toohy was faster. He smashed the club into the man's head for second time and Collis's already mangled ear erupted, jetting blood. The kid dropped to his knees and managed to draw with his right hand, but he was slowed by his injuries. Toohy kicked the Colt out of the youngster's hand and then coldly, systematically, he beat Collis to a pulp. His face a scarlet mask of blood and shattered bone, Collis fell on his back and then rolled over, groaning.

"I hate my given name, boy, but I hate the name you give me even worse," Toohy said. He grabbed Collis by the back of his shirt and dragged him into the saloon where Lilly had pinned the other youngster and the girl in place with his gun.

Toohy dragged the now unconscious Collis and dropped him at his friends' feet. "Take what's left of that outside," he said.

"Damn you, where are his guns?" the youngster said. He had a crop of pimples on both cheeks.

"In the cesspit," Toohy said. "When and if he comes to, he can go get them."

The kid was about to say more, but when he looked into Toohy's eyes he knew that would be a big mistake.

After Collis had been half dragged, half carried outside, Toohy laid the club on the bar. "That needs cleaned," he said to the bartender. "It's got Randy Collis all over it."

"Did you need to beat him that bad, mister?" the bartender said.

"No, I didn't," Toohy said.

"Bon, I'd rather have you as a friend than an enemy," Lilly said.

CHAPTER TWENTY

Sam Flintlock spent the next two days and nights in the swamp on an island of dry land where the vanished Indians, perhaps hundreds of years before, had erected a totem as tall as a man, carved with fish and water birds, its top crowned with a yellowed human skull.

Flintlock neither ate nor drank. He sat with his back against the totem, his head bowed in thought, unmoving as a carved rock. The alligators avoided the place as though remembering that they'd once been hunted there and the long-legged marsh birds searched for frogs among the hyacinths and kept their distance.

By the morning of the third day Flintlock felt weak. He was thirsty and had a pounding headache. The sun slanting through the tall columns of the cypress made the swamp look like the nave of a Gothic cathedral and the morning mist drifted like incense from a censer.

Old Barnabas sat opposite Flintlock and opened the huge book he carried; a foot thick bound with leather and studded iron. The old mountain man wore his usual buckskins, but the top hat with the goggles on the crown remained.

"Ah, here it is, on page nine hundred and sixteen," Barnabas said. "I figured he would be entered in the Book of the Damned."

"Go away, Barnabas," Flintlock said. "I don't want to talk to you."

"Don't you want to know who he was?"

"Who?" Flintlock said.

"The feller at the top of the totem pole."

"No. I don't want to know."

"His name was Don Pedro de Castillo, a noble Spanish knight noted for his great cruelty toward the native Indians. I'm reading now, 'Don Pedro, puffed up with pride and in black armor, marched into the swamp in search of gold with a hundred harquebusiers and two hundred pike men. He and his soldiers perished in the swamp and Don Pedro was killed by a flint arrowhead that entered his throat just above his gorget. He was summarily dragged away and placed in that level of Hell reserved for the cruel and prideful.' "

Barnabas closed the book. "That's who

you've spent the past two nights with, Sam. Why?"

"I needed time to think," Flintlock said.

"Think? You? Think about what?"

"About something I have to do."

"Don't tell me if you don't want to."

"Good, because I don't want to."

Barnabas rose to his feet, the huge tome under his arm. "All right, I'm going now." He hesitated then said, "You planning to get yourself into trouble, boy?"

"I'm going to dig myself a deep hole, Barnabas," Flintlock said.

"Yup, now there's no doubt about it," the old man said. "I raised me up an idiot."

O'Hara, no longer surprised by the weirdness of white men in general and Sam Flintlock in particular, ran his canoe onto the bank of the island. "Waiting for me, I see," he said. "Have you reached a decision?"

"Yeah, I have," Flintlock said. "I'll need your horse."

"Talk to the Apache," O'Hara said. "Do you want I should go with you?"

"No. I'll do this alone."

"Is it a killing?"

"Not a killing. At least not yet. How is Evangeline?"

"Worried about you. We're both worried about you."

"I'm acting real strange, huh?" Flintlock said.

"Seems like."

"It will get stranger."

"You look like hell."

"I feel like hell."

"Then eat and drink first," O'Hara said. He looked at the skull on top of the totem and said, "Friend of yours?"

"Spanish gent. He walked into the wrong swamp."

"We know all about that, huh, Sammy?"

"Damn right," Flintlock said. "Where's the grub?"

"Right here." O'Hara opened a paper sack and passed it to Flintlock. "Fried fish and cornbread. Evangeline packed it herself. Oh, and a canteen of water."

"Let me have the water," Flintlock said. "Is that all Evangeline ever eats, fish and cornbread?"

"I don't know, Sam. I've never seen her eat anything."

"Now I come to think on it neither have I. Maybe witches don't eat."

Flintlock swallowed a pint of water, ate the fish and cornbread and then said, "I'm ready. Take me out of the swamp and I'll go visit the Apache. He ain't wild, is he?"

"Tame. Or as tame as an Apache ever gets. I still think I should go with you, Sammy. Remember I told you that you're an easy man to kill? Well, I haven't changed my mind about that."

"I have to go this alone," Flintlock said. "Now get me out of this damned swamp."

CHAPTER TWENTY-ONE

It was a long walk to the Apache's place. For a man wearing riding boots made on a narrow Texas last it was a torment and when Flintlock reached the Indian's hogan he was hot, tired, thirsty and irritable as hell.

Like O'Hara, the old Jicarilla was sensitive to the moods of white men and he made no argument about giving up the horse. He even fed Flintlock cornbread and coffee, for which he was grateful, even though he was getting mighty tired of corn.

O'Hara sat a McClellan saddle that was designed to favor the horse, not the rider, and by the time Flintlock reached Budville he was glad to dismount and let blood rush back to his aching rear. He stepped into the saloon and ordered a whiskey, steeling himself for what was to come. It was still early in the day and when Flintlock glanced around him he saw only a few patrons, none of whom looked the type to be on the prod, eager to cut another man down to size.

"Quiet," Flintlock said to the bartender.

"Early yet," the man said. He looked over the tattoo on Flintlock's throat, the buckskin shirt turned almost black by sweat and hard use, the expensive, fancy Colt in his waistband and summed him up as some kind of a hard case. "You should have been here yesterday, stranger. One of Brewster Ritter's guns — you heard of Brewster Ritter?" At Flintlock's nod he said, "Well, he had it out with a kid by the name of Randy Collis."

"Shooting scrape?" Flintlock said.

"Nah. That's what the kid wanted, but the Ritter man went after him with this" — he held up the billy club — "and damn near killed him. Now the Collis kid is over to Doc Lighter's office and ain't likely to survive. If he does live, he'll sure regret it. Ain't much of his brains left."

"What name does the Ritter gun go by? Sounds like a good man to avoid," Flintlock said.

"I don't rightly know," the bartender said. "John or Bon, something like that. Wears a bowler hat with a big pair of spectacle things on the brim, kinda unusual around these parts. Another whiskey?"

"No. I got to be moving on, open an account at the bank."

The bartender grinned. "If Mathias Cobb shakes hands with you, count your fingers afterward. He's a money shark is ol' Mathias. Got an eye for the ladies, too."

Flintlock drained his glass, touched his hat to the bartender and said, "Obliged." He stepped out of the cool darkness of the saloon into the bright sunlight of noon.

Flintlock gathered up the reins of the paint then stood for a few moments looking around him. As he'd hoped, the noon hour heat had driven people inside and the street was empty. One hardy old lady, a shopping basket over her arm, stepped into the general store and a little calico cat lazed in the sun on her back, her tiny white paws in the air.

It was time.

Flintlock led his horse to the Cattleman's Bank and Trust and left it at the hitching rail. He stood for a spell to let his hammering heart slow and then stepped inside. There was only one teller, a young man wearing a blue eyeshade. "Can I help you, sir?" he said. There was a noticeable hesitation between *you* and *sir*. Flintlock's appearance did little to instill confidence in bank tellers.

"Yeah, I'd like to open an account, but

since my deposit is quite large I'd like to talk to Mr. Cobb," Flintlock said.

"You have dealt with the Cattleman's Bank and Trust before?"

"Yeah, a couple of years back."

The teller brightened. "I'll ask Mr. Cobb if he can see you now. Your name, sir?" There was no hesitation this time.

"My name is Gunwood H. Hempel. Mr. Cobb will remember me."

The clerk returned with a beaming Cobb in tow. The banker was resplendent in gray broadcloth, a pink cravat bunched at his throat, held in place by a pearl the size of a robin's egg. He held out a pudgy hand. "Of course I remember you, dear sir," Cobb said. "How could I ever forget such a large depositor? You've returned to the right place for honesty and integrity, Mr. Hempel. As my lady wife always says, Mathias Cobb by name, Mathias Cobb by nature. Now, what can I do for you?"

Flintlock pulled his gun and stuck it into Cobb's face. "You can tell your teller to grab all the money he can and shove it in a sack."

"This is an outrage," Cobb said, his jaws purpling.

"Do as I say, fat man, or I'll blow your brains out," Flintlock said. "The choice is yours."

"You won't get away with this," Cobb said. "I have friends in this town."

Flintlock thumbed back the hammer of his Colt. "I won't tell you again. I've got friends in the swamp." He swung the gun on the now thoroughly frightened teller. "You! Fill a sack. Now!"

The teller didn't need to be told twice. He opened drawers and began to stuff bills and coin into a money sack.

"Put plenty in there," Flintlock said. "This money is going to the families of the swamp dwellers that your boss helped murder."

"I didn't murder anyone," Cobb said. His face had drained and he looked as pale as a fish's belly. "How dare you say —"

"You pay the man who does the killing," Flintlock said. "Fat man, you're just as guilty of murder as Brewster Ritter."

"How did you know —" Cobb stopped himself. He was sweating like a pig.

"Everybody knows, Cobb. Did you think you keep a thing like this a secret? You want a cut of the money Ritter will get for the cypress trees and you'll stop at nothing to get it, including murder."

Flintlock glanced at the bulging money sack. "Right, that's enough." He grabbed the bag from the teller's hands. "Cobb," he said, "if another person is murdered in the swamp, I'm not going after Ritter, I'm coming straight for you."

"You'll regret this, Hempel," Cobb said. "I'll have you hunted down and shot like the thieving dog you are."

Flintlock held up the sack. "The swamp people thank you for this, Cobb," he said. "You've been most generous."

He stepped to the door, walked without hurry outside and swung into the saddle. There was no one in the street but a tall man walking on the boardwalk eating a sandwich. The man looked at Flintlock and stopped chewing for a moment. Flintlock waved and kneed his horse into a fast canter. He cleared the limits of town as Cobb waddled out of the bank and yelled, "Lilly, stop him!"

Sebastian Lilly tossed his sandwich away, drew and fired.

Two rounds sang past within inches of Flintlock's head. He grimaced. Damn, that was good shooting from a revolver. But as the galloping paint put more git between him and the town, Lilly's remaining shots went wild.

Flintlock was now in the clear and he held close to the southern edge of the piney woods, keeping the paint to a steady lope. It would take a posse time to saddle horses and mount up and by then he would be long gone.

But now the question he asked himself was: Would his plan work?

CHAPTER TWENTY-TWO

The day was far along when Sam Flintlock rode up to the Apache's hogan. O'Hara was already there, broiling a swamp rabbit on a stick above a hatful of fire, as was the Indian way.

O'Hara glanced at the money sack but said nothing. Then, "The Apache has coffee, get yourself some then come share the rabbit. It will make a change from fish and cornbread."

"I should have known you'd be here, O'Hara," Flintlock said. He tossed the bag at the breed's feet. "Guard that."

"With my life," O'Hara said.

"With your gun is enough."

Flintlock asked the Apache for permission to enter his home, and when this was granted he stopped and walked inside. When he came out again he held a sooty tin cup and a chunk of cornbread.

"I just can't get away from the stuff," he

said as he sat opposite O'Hara.

"What's in the sack?" O'Hara said.

"Money, as though you didn't know."

"How did you get it?"

"Robbed a bank."

"Cobb's bank?"

"Damn right."

"I would have loaned you some money," O'Hara said.

"I don't want your money. I wanted Cobb's money."

"You kill anybody getting it?"

"No, a feller took a couple of pots at me, but he missed."

O'Hara twisted off a piece of the rabbit and tossed the meat to Flintlock. "Enjoy," he said.

Flintlock chewed for a while then said, "You make good rabbit, Injun." O'Hara's only reply was a grunt and Flintlock said, "Well, ain't you going to ask me?"

"Ask you what?"

"Why I robbed the bank."

"I figured you'd come up on it eventually."

"To draw Mathias Cobb out of his rat hole," Flintlock said. "We suspected that Cobb was the moneyman behind Ritter, but couldn't prove it, right?"

"Go on, Sammy."

"Well, I told him I was taking the money for the swamp people and he looked real surprised. He got even more surprised when I told him that everyone knows he bankrolls Ritter and that makes him just as guilty of murder as he is."

O'Hara had emptied the contents of the money bag onto the ground and now as he counted them he tossed bills back into the sack. "What do you hope Cobb will do?" he said.

"For starters I hope he'll panic, maybe even tell Ritter to close down the whole operation. That would take the pressure off Evangeline and the other swamp people."

"Suppose he doesn't panic?"

"He'll do something stupid," Flintlock said, but there was a hint of doubt in his eyes.

"Ten thousand dollars give or take, Sammy. You got a bad ten-dollar bill in there, looks like somebody drew it by hand."

"Damn that teller. I bet he knew it was a forged bill. I can't abide dishonesty in people."

"Well, you can gun him later, make you feel better. Ten thousand is a lot of money, Sam. Cobb might come after it. Does he know your name?"

"I told him my name was Gunwood

Hempel," Flintlock said.

"How did you come up with a handle like that? Gunwood . . . what kind of given name is that for a white man?"

Flintlock said, "It just popped into my head. Suppose Cobb doesn't panic? Now you got me worried."

"What are you going to do with the money?"

"Give it back eventually. It's not Cobb's money, it belongs to the ordinary folks who deposited it in his bank."

"Eat some more rabbit," O'Hara said.

The two men sat in silence for a while, eating, then O'Hara said, "We can't guess what Cobb will do, Sammy. It's up to him to make the next move."

"I hope it's to tell Ritter to close up shop and leave the swamp alone," Flintlock said.

"Yeah, that would be the ideal outcome," O'Hara said. "But I don't think it's going to happen, Sammy. You robbed his bank but Cobb isn't afraid of you. He's too rich, too powerful and too well connected to let a nobody like you scare him. There's a pile of money to be made from the cypress and he knows it. Sorry, Sam, but that's how things stack up in this world."

"Then me robbing the bank was all for nothing?" Flintlock said, his face glum.

"I don't know, Sam," O'Hara said. "I honestly don't know."

Flintlock sat in the back of O'Hara's canoe as they made their way in moonlight to Evangeline's cabin, the money sack lying between them. As they passed night birds rose out of the cypress and willows and on the banks sleeping alligators looked like sculptures of green jade.

Evangeline was on the deck outside the cabin and with her was another woman, old, bent and white-haired.

Flintlock jumped onto the deck while O'Hara secured the canoe.

"Sam, there's fish and cornbread if you want some," Evangeline said. She glanced at the money sack in his hand but said nothing.

"No thanks, I already ate," Flintlock said. "But I could sure use a drink."

"You know where the whiskey is," Evangeline said. She wore a buckled corset and a straight black skirt, a narrow silver chain around her hips. "Oh, allow me to introduce my distinguished guest. This is Lady Carlisle. She came here from England fifty years ago and has lived in the swamp ever since. Lady Carlisle, this is Mr. Sam Flintlock and over there is his friend Mr. O'Hara."

"Delighted to meet you both," Lady Carlisle said. "One grows lonely in the swamp, especially since Lord Carlisle passed away."

The old woman wore lace gloves, a dress of fine yellow silk and a wide-brimmed hat adorned with ostrich feathers. A large emerald ring glowed on the wedding finger of her left hand.

"Has Evangeline told you about the Blue Fox, Mr. Flintlock?" she said. "I ask this only because you seem like a gentleman well used to feats of derring-do."

"No, Lady Carlisle, I haven't told him," Evangeline said. "As you may know, Mr. Flintlock has been busy with other things." Her eyes dropped to the sack again. She seemed worried.

"Ah, I believe you are talking about that awful Mr. Ritter who wants to cut down every cypress, willow and gum tree in the swamp. I wrote to Queen Victoria and demanded she dispatch a regiment of the Grenadier Guards to the southeast Texas swamp forthwith if not instanter."

O'Hara, interested, said, "Did she answer?"

"Yes. Her reply took six weeks to get here by devious routes and she said no."

"That was it, just no?" O'Hara said.

150

"Yes, Mr. O'Hara. One word in the middle of a sheet of very expensive paper with the royal coat of arms at the top. That one word was *NO*." Lady Carlisle drew herself up to her full lanky height, which was considerable. "Damned impudence if you ask me," she said.

Flintlock had taken advantage of the old woman's talk with O'Hara to get himself a drink. He returned with a glass of Old Crow in his hand just as Lady Carlisle said, "Now, what was I talking about?"

Evangeline smiled and said, "The Blue Fox and Mr. Flintlock's feats of derring-do. Please sit down, Lady Carlisle. Do you prefer to sit inside?"

"No. The rocking chair will do nicely. I do love to see the moonlight shine among the cypress." The old lady sat and said, "Evangeline, I'll have what Mr. Flintlock is drinking. Unless you have a nip of gin available?"

"Yes, I believe I have, made right here in the swamp," Evangeline said.

"Excellent, my dear," Lady Carlisle said. Then, "Little nips of whiskey, little drops of gin, make an English lady forget where she's bin." The old woman's laugh sounded like the whinny of a horse, a Thoroughbred to be sure, but still a horse.

When Evangeline returned with the gin,

151

Lady Carlisle took a sip, nodded her approval, then said, "Now, where were we? Ah yes, I was talking about the Battle of New Orleans in 1815, and the less said about it the better. But what of the treasure? Tens of thousands of pounds in gold coin intended to pay British troops and their Indian allies disappeared after the battle. And who took it? You may ask."

"Vera 'The Blue Fox' Scobey," Evangeline said. "She was the first of the swamp witches."

"Swamp witch my eye," Lady Carlisle said. "The Blue Fox was a pirate rogue, a close friend of that other sea robber Jean Lafitte. I say close friend because I'm in polite company. I leave it to you to decide what kind of friend she was. She dressed like a whore in blue corset, blue tights and blue leather boots to her knees and if the truth is to be told what she wore underneath, and there was little enough of that, was blue."

O'Hara, always interested in stories of treasure, said, "And the lady stole the British gold, huh, Lady Carlisle?"

"Yes, she did, young man, and she carried it here to the swamp with three of her buccaneers and buried it. The Blue Fox was an excellent swordswoman and she killed her men and left them to guard the treasure. Lord Carlisle, who searched for the treasure for forty-seven years until the day he died of snakebite, said he saw the ghosts of three pirates in the swamp. But I never saw them. It was Vera's intention to come back with her lover Lafitte and recover the gold. But as far as is known they never did."

"What happened to them?" O'Hara said.

"In 1823 Lafitte found a watery grave off São Miguel Island. The Blue Fox simply vanished from history, but my husband always claimed that she was hung as a pirate from the yardarm of a Spanish warship off the west coast of Africa."

"So the treasure is still in the swamp?" Flintlock said, only vaguely interested. He'd heard a lot of treasure stories, including the golden bell that had nearly cost him his life.

"I know it is," Lady Carlisle said. "It's just a matter of finding it."

"But your husband tried for years and never found it," O'Hara said.

"Yes, he did, but the day he died he told me he was close. The water moccasin killed him just a few hours later. Who knows? The treasure may be cursed."

Lady Carlisle finished her gin and said, "I must be going now, Evangeline. Thank you for allowing me to visit."

"Are you sure you won't stay for dinner, Lady Carlisle?" Evangeline said.

"Ah, what are you having, my dear?"

"Fried trout and cornbread."

"No, I think I'd better get home," Lady Carlisle said. "Ahmed has promised me curried chicken and I don't wish to disappoint him. Oh dear, what did I do with that boy?"

"You told him to wait with your pirogue," Evangeline said.

"Oh dear me, I did." The old woman walked to the edge of the deck and called out, "Coo-ee, Ahmed! I'm ready to go home now."

A canoe, poled along by a young boy, emerged from the darkness. He wore a frayed red and gold livery jacket, unbuttoned, and a turban. "I am here, memsahib," he said. His eyes were big. "Basilisk is hunting tonight."

"Of course he is, you silly boy," Lady Carlisle said. "Basilisk hunts every night, but he wouldn't dare attack an Englishwoman. Now bring my watercraft alongside."

"Let me help you," O'Hara said.

"Oh, thank you, Mr. O'Hara." Once she was safely in the canoe, she said, "Mr. Flintlock, if you wish to hunt for the British gold come and see me. Perhaps I can be of some assistance."

"I sure will," Flintlock said.

He and the others watched the old woman disappear into the darkness, then Evangeline picked up the money sack and said, "I think you gentlemen have some explaining to do."

"I think I need another drink first," Flintlock said.

CHAPTER TWENTY-THREE

"Get that thing in the air, Mr. Ritter," Sebastian Lilly said. "Mr. Cobb wants the bank robber caught and dead. Preferably a death that's a long time coming."

"Look at the sky, Lilly," Ritter said. "This is gonna be a big storm."

The thunderstorm had made landfall to the south after churning across the waters of the Gulf. Already a wind rattled and rippled the loose planks stacked for the sawmill and the tents flapped and strained against their guy ropes. A smattering of rain made Vs across the water and the swamp was white with lightning.

"I don't give a damn," Lilly said. "My orders are to get that flying machine up and find the robber. Mr. Cobb says he's probably in the swamp somewhere giving the bank's money away."

"It's only dawn. We can wait until the storm clears," Ritter said.

"Do I go back to Mr. Cobb and tell him you refused to obey his orders?" Lilly said.

"Hell, man, I could lose the airship and the crew," Ritter said.

"Mr. Cobb will get you a new airship and a new crew," Lilly said. "Now get it done, Mr. Ritter."

Ritter locked eyes with Lilly, the only sound the rain ticking on the roof of his tent. Finally he said, "It's easy to give orders when you're sitting in a dry office in Budville." He turned away and opened the tent flap. A guard wearing a slicker stood outside. "You, get me Professor Mealy, Byng the engineer and Travis Kershaw," he said. "And you'd better bring Bonifaunt Toohy as well."

The guard was surprised. "Now?"

"Yeah, damn it, now," Ritter yelled.

The guard hurried away and a couple of minutes later the four men crowded into Ritter's tent. "Professor Mealy, you're taking the airship up. Travis, you and Byng will go with him."

Mealy looked stricken. "Mr. Ritter . . . the storm."

As though he hadn't heard, Ritter said, "Scout the whole damned swamp and beyond. You're looking for a man wearing a buckskin shirt with a sack of Mathias

Cobb's money. He was riding a paint horse. If you see the horse, you've found him."

Leander Byng said, "Boss, he'll be holed up somewhere. We'll never find him in this storm. And we could lose the *Star Scraper*."

"And our lives," Kershaw said.

"A hundred dollars bonus a man," Ritter said. "I know you won't find him. You know you won't find him. But Cobb wants it, so go through the motions. Quarter the area with the dirigible and then come back down."

"Two hundred dollars," Kershaw said.

"Cheap at that price," Toohy said.

"All right, two hundred," Ritter said. "I'll see that there's hot coffee and black rum waiting for you men when you return."

Thunder shook the tent and the sound of the rain grew louder.

"Mr. Ritter, this is very dangerous," Professor Jasper Mealy said. He looked like a man trying to crawl into his top hat.

"I know it's dangerous," Ritter said. "That's why I'm paying you two hundred dollars to get the job done."

"And if we refuse?" Byng said.

"Then I'll kill all three of you," Ritter said.

"The man isn't joking about that," Toohy said. "Byng, I'd think long and hard before I said anything else."

CHAPTER TWENTY-FOUR

The *Star Scraper* frantically tugged at its securing lines like a bird struggling to get free of a trap. The balloon bounced up and down on the gondola, eager for flight, and made boarding a dangerous proposition, rife with the possibility of broken arms or legs.

After several tries the three men managed to clamber on board, Kershaw with his rifle. By the time the steam engine was fired up, the thunderstorm hit with considerable force. Rain hissed like an angry dragon and lightning clashed, sizzling white in the swamp.

Byng yelled to the men to loose the lines and after a moment's hesitation the dirigible took to the sky, gained altitude and immediately careened over the swamp, driven by the blasting south wind.

"Mealy, can you hold her?" Byng shouted as the balloon hurtled just above the tops of the cypress. The professor held hard to the tiller but he briefly raised a hand, cupped his ear and shook his head.

Byng left the steam engine and staggered his way to the stern. "Can you hold her?"

Mealy nodded. Like Byng he wore his goggles. He pointed north and then swept his arm to the west before grabbing the tiller again. Thunder roared and lightning flashed and the airship rocked wildly. Byng held on to the rim of the gondola until the moment passed and the *Star Scraper* settled again, like a foundering ship in the trough of a wave. Far from scouting the terrain below him, Travis Kershaw, his face green, was being violently sick and had thrown up all over the gondola and himself.

Byng scrambled back and checked the steam engine. So far so good. The propeller spun with a steady rhythm and the boiler pressure was normal. But how much longer could the ship take this pounding? When he glanced to the stern Professor Mealy looked every bit as worried as he did.

Then disaster struck.

The birds were tiny, no bigger than wrens, but they came in a hurtling white cloud driven by the venomous wind. Thousands of them tore across the shattered sky like buckshot from a hundred shotgun blasts.

Hunched in the stern, Mealy took the

160

brunt of the bird strike. His top hat, pulled low onto his ears, was hit multiple times and flew off his head and sailed away in the wind. The back of his head was a crimson mess. Running blood mingled with white feathers and wood splinters from the wrecked propeller. The professor cried out in pain and alarm and dived for the floor of the gondola. Travis Kershaw had raised his head and turned just as the birds struck and he took multiple hits to his face, each one splitting skin and hitting bone. Kershaw stood, his arms cartwheeling as he tried to fight off the birds. But the gondola was an unstable platform for a standing man. It lurched from a furious wind gust just as the sky exploded into thunder and lightning struck the balloon. Kershaw tipped over the side and screamed all the way down. Like Mealy, Byng hugged the floor and escaped serious injury. But the balloon was shredded and the airship violently dropped its nose, flaming from the red-hot coals that erupted from the steam engine's furnace. Trailing a ribbon of black smoke, the dirigible crashed into the swamp, just yards from where Travis Kershaw's body hung in a U shape, his belly rammed through by a sharp, smoking stake, all that was left of a lightning-struck willow.

■ ■ ■ ■

Sam Flintlock, a man who enjoyed thunderstorms so long as he wasn't riding in one, was sitting on Evangeline's deck polishing the maple stock of his Hawken when he saw the dirigible get into difficulties. He called Evangeline and O'Hara to come see the sight and they stepped onto the deck just in time to see the smoking airship disappear behind the cypress, followed by the sound of a crash.

With commendable understatement Flintlock said, "Well, there's a thing you don't see every day."

Evangeline, still frosty over Flintlock's bank robbery and the retribution it could bring down on the swamp, said, "We must help them."

Flintlock let a clap of thunder pass, then said, "No need, Evangeline. They're probably all dead, and besides they're Ritter's men."

"Sam, I'm not talking to you," the woman said. "But if I was, I'd tell you to go see if there are any survivors. We can't leave injured men to the alligators."

"There's a thunderstorm, Evangeline," Flintlock said.

162

"Oh, very well then, I suppose I'll have to go by myself," the woman said.

Flintlock read that female warning sign and said, "O'Hara, let us charge to the rescue."

"I said I'll go," Evangeline said.

"No, you won't," Flintlock said. "Here, take ahold of my Hawken and don't drop it."

Evangeline, who'd planned to visit Cornelius that morning, was dressed like a librarian in a long gray skirt and severe shirt of the same color with a white rounded collar and black tie. A straw boater with a black and red band sat atop her piled-up hair and Flintlock thought she was the most beautiful woman he'd ever seen in his life.

"She's the most beautiful woman I ever seen in my life," Sam Flintlock said as O'Hara poled the pirogue through the swamp, pausing every now and then to scan the tree islands for wreckage.

"She's all of that," O'Hara said. "Evangeline could make a glass eye blink, an' no mistake."

"Ah well, back to business," Flintlock said. "You see anything?"

"Nothing. That flying thing probably broke into — wait! What's that noise?"

"I don't hear anything."

"Sounded like a man yelling."

"Where?"

"Straight ahead of us, Sammy."

"Well, punt this thing, O'Hara. Put your back into it."

"You ever think of taking a turn?"

"No. I'm the white man here, remember?"

"You never let me forget it," O'Hara said.

The knees of a huge bald cypress that might have been a thousand years old stuck out into the channel between two tree islands. O'Hara punted his way around the obstacle and into a large area of clear water. About a hundred yards ahead of them was a small island, covered in willow. Rain lashed the bayou and ticked from the branches of the trees. The thunder had growled its way northward and the air smelled of smoke, rotting vegetation and the sharp ozone tang of the lightning.

"Man over there, Sam," O'Hara said. "See him among the willows?"

Flintlock squinted through the trees and at first he thought it was old Barnabas come to haunt him again. But as the canoe drew closer . . .

"For God's sake look at that," Flintlock said. "Seems like one of them fell out of the airship and landed smack on a willow."

"Is he still alive?" O'Hara said.

"I can't tell. We'll have to get closer."

O'Hara grounded the canoe and he and Flintlock investigated the fallen man. A man impaled through the belly on the pointed spike of a broken tree is as dead as he's ever going to be. "Damn," Flintlock said. "I hope he didn't live too long."

"Terrible death for a man," O'Hara said. "Help me get him off of there. Dying like that is an obscenity."

Flintlock and O'Hara were both strong, stocky men but it was a five-minute struggle to remove the body from the tree. When they were done the body lay at their feet and the stake was covered in blood.

Then, from the other side of the tree island, a man cried out in mortal terror.

Flintlock and O'Hara exchanged a startled glance then drew their guns and headed toward the sound. There it was again, louder this time, the shriek of a man facing certain death.

The ground under their feet muddy, Flintlock and O'Hara did their best to quicken their pace. They were in time to see Professor Jasper Mealy die in the jaws of a gigantic alligator. The animal dived and then went into its death roll, tearing its prey apart. The churning water turned red then the alligator swam away, what was left of Mealy's body in its jaws. A severed arm, still wearing an elbow-length leather gauntlet, bobbed to the surface and then a top hat appeared, goggles on the crown, and drifted away on the muddy current.

Flintlock looked sick. "I couldn't get a shot at him," he said.

"I'm sure that was Basilisk," O'Hara said. "I think your bullet would have bounced off him."

"I wanted to shoot the man, not the alligator."

Feet squelched in mud to Flintlock's right. He swung around, his Colt coming up, and saw a tall man wearing riding breeches and tall lace-up boots. "Who are you?" he said. "State your intentions."

The man stopped dead still in his tracks. His hands rose above his head as he said, "My name is Leander Byng. I was on the *Star Scraper.*"

"On the what?" Flintlock said.

"The dirigible," Byng said. "We got hit by a flock of birds and then lightning and came down."

"Put your hands down," Flintlock said. "But be notified — I may shoot you later."

"When the alligator attacked Professor Mealy I ran away," Byng said. "Oh my God in heaven, is that his arm?"

"Yeah, it is," Flintlock said. "The alligator got the rest of him."

"There was nothing I could do," Byng said. He seemed to be on the edge of hysteria. "I never carry a gun."

"What do you do for Brewster Ritter?"

"I'm an engineer. I'm setting up the sawmill to process the cypress."

"You were setting up the sawmill," Flintlock said. "You ain't doing that any longer."

"Are you going to kill me?" Byng said.

"That depends on how mean I feel," Flintlock said. "It won't take much, a mosquito bite might do it."

Byng looked around him as though checking for mosquitos in the immediate area. Then he said, "Have you found Travis Kershaw?"

"Young feller, wore a gun?" O'Hara said.

"Yes. He always carried a gun."

"He fell onto a broken tree and impaled himself," Flintlock said.

"Then he's dead?"

"As a rotten stump," Flintlock said. He looked at O'Hara. "Do we gun him or take him with us?"

"Sammy, you're in bad enough with Evangeline already. We'd better take him."

Flintlock's eyes were ice-cold on Byng.

"You got lucky in the crash, engineer man, and you got lucky again. Let's go."

"Should we bury Travis first?" Byng said.

"The alligators will bury him," Flintlock said.

CHAPTER TWENTY-FIVE

"They're not coming back," Brewster Ritter said. "They must have crashed in the swamp and got eaten by alligators or the damned swamp trash."

"I'll tell Mr. Cobb you carried out his orders," Sebastian Lilly said. "He'll be so pleased."

"I needed the dirigible. It was supposed to cover my logging crews while they cut the cypress."

"Hell, Ritter, hire more guns and put them into a few flat-bottomed boats," Lilly said. "You don't need a balloon that can't even fly in a storm." He jutted his rock of a chin. "Hell, man, just get the job done."

"I've lost my engineer," Ritter said.

"Then hire another one. The country is full of engineers."

Ritter stared out at the bayou. After the rain, trout and bass rose at flies and spread tiny circles across the flat water. "What about the bank robber?" he said.

"I'll find him," Lilly said. "I'll comb this swamp until I do."

Ritter turned. "You? There are no saloons and dancehalls out there, Lilly, just alligators and rubes with rifles."

"I said I'll find him and I will," Lilly said. "I'll come back tomorrow or the next day and I'll take Bon Toohy with me."

"Toohy doesn't know the swamp either," Ritter said. "He's a draw fighter like you, Lilly. He carries out his business in towns, not swamps."

"Then we'll learn together," Lilly said. "Now start cutting trees."

"What about the sawmill?" Ritter said.

"I'll ask Mr. Cobb about the sawmill. He always has the answer."

"The man is a damned incompetent, a nincompoop," Mathias Cobb said. "Why did he send a ten-thousand-dollar dirigible up in a thunderstorm?"

"I tried to warn him that it was too dangerous, but he insisted, boss," Seb Lilly said. "Ritter lost the balloon and three men, one of then the engineer who was building the sawmill."

"Damned fool," Cobb said. "Is there any sign of the outlaw who robbed my bank?

He's got a big bird tattooed across his throat. A man with a disfigurement like that can't lose himself in a crowd."

Lilly smiled. "I'll find him and I'll get your money back, Mr. Cobb. Give me a chance and I'll get the cypress cut as well."

"It may come to that, Mr. Lilly," Cobb said. "It may come to that. All Ritter has to do is foul up one more time and he's out."

"What about the sawmill?" Lilly said. "Ritter doesn't even have it built yet and now his engineer is dead."

"Just tell Ritter to start cutting the trees," Cobb said. "I'll arrange to have the sawmill built. On your way out, Mr. Lilly, tell Mrs. Sally Turpin to come in." A smile spread across Cobb's jowly face. "A sad case, Mr. Lilly, a sad case indeed. I was about to foreclose on the Turpin family mortgage when dear Sally offered me . . . shall we say sexual favors."

Lilly grinned. "You're an excellent man of business, boss."

"Of course after I tire of her I'll still foreclose," Cobb said. "That is the exquisite irony of the affair. Oh, wait, before you go, a question, Mr. Lilly."

"Ask away, boss," Lilly said.

"How would you feel about getting Brewster Ritter out of the way?"

"You mean gunning him?"

"A crude way of putting it, but yes . . . gunning him."

"I'd feel just fine, Mr. Cobb."

The fat man beamed. "That's exactly the answer I expected from a man of daring and integrity like yourself, Mr. Lilly. But let us just leave it at that for now, though the day may come."

"When that day gets here I'll be ready," Sebastian Lilly said.

CHAPTER TWENTY-SIX

Evangeline stepped onto the cabin deck and watched O'Hara bring the pirogue alongside. A strange young man sat in the canoe between him and Flintlock. "Got a prisoner," Flintlock said. "One of Ritter's killers."

"I'm an engineer," Leander Byng said as he climbed onto the deck, a statement that earned him a swift kick in the butt from Flintlock. "You speak when only you're spoken to," he said.

"There were others," Evangeline said. "I heard Basilisk sing his victory song."

"Yes, the alligators did for one of them, the other was killed when the dirigible crashed." Flintlock decided not to go into details. Then, "O'Hara, bring the rope and I'll tie this ranny to the deck."

"No need," Evangeline said. "He can't go anywhere."

She was still dressed like a librarian, but

the sky was full of clouds drifting from the Gulf with the promise of more rain, and Flintlock figured she'd put off visiting Cornelius to a more pleasant day.

"Maybe not, Evangeline," he said, "but he could murder us while we slept."

Byng risked another kick. "I'm an engineer," he said. "I don't murder people."

"But you work for the people who do and that makes you just as guilty," Flintlock said. "If it was up to me you'd be dead by now, so shut your mouth."

"Sam, you want me to tie him?" O'Hara said. "I can loop the rope through the deck boards and make him snug."

"Yeah, do that," Flintlock said. "Later you may need to use your blade on him to get information about Ritter's plans. So tie him tight."

Evangeline didn't hear that last. She'd gone inside and now she stepped back onto the deck with a basin of water, a towel and something in a tiny brown bottle.

She said, "Your face is cut in several places . . . what is your name?"

"Byng, ma'am. Leander Byng. We got hit by a flock of birds just before we crashed. A couple of them struck my face."

"More than a few, Mr. Byng. Sit there in the rocker and let me do what I can for those cuts."

"Don't baby him, Evangeline," Flintlock said. "He's our enemy."

"Enemy or not, he's wounded, Sam. I'm duty bound as a healer to treat him."

Flintlock muttered under his breath as Evangeline began to dab at Byng's face with the towel. "No, Sam, I'm not an interfering female," she said. "I just can't bear to see another human being suffer."

Flintlock shook his head and whispered to O'Hara, "I swear she can hear the moon rise."

"Yes, I can," Evangeline said. "And the sun set."

"That's all I can tell you," Leander Byng said. "Ritter is to start cutting the cypress within the next few days. The logs will be stacked up until the sawmill is in operation. There's nothing else."

"How many guns does he have?" Flintlock said.

"Maybe a dozen. Bonifaunt Toohy is the best of them, or the worst, depending on your viewpoint."

Rain swept across the bayou and birds lifted briefly on the fair wind and settled again. The bruised sky was thick with purple and mustard cloud but the thunder was silent and there was no lightning.

"What about the loggers?" Evangeline said. "What manner of men are they?"

"They work for wages," Byng said.

"If we shoot a few will the rest pull out?" Flintlock said.

"I don't know. They're not gunmen but they're tough. I think you'd kick over a hornet's nest."

"Will they fight for the brand?" Flintlock said.

Byng took a deep breath. "The loggers work for wages. No, they won't do Brewster Ritter's killing for him, but if you harm one of their own, they will fight, and there's a lot of them."

"When will Ritter get another flying machine?"

"I don't know. Maybe never."

"What about the swamp monster?"

"That was Professor Mealy's project, a steam-powered, armored barge. As far as I know, it's been repaired and ready for launch again. Ritter will probably use it to protect the loggers as they work."

Flintlock said, "What about you, Byng? Will you be missed?"

"No. With the money he's paying, Ritter can easily find another steam engineer. The entire civilized world runs on steam, so there's plenty of them around."

"That's why the world has become such a dirty, grimy place," O'Hara said. "And now we stand to lose the swamps."

Byng smiled slightly. "The British say, 'Where there's muck, there's brass.' In other words it's dirty, grimy factories that make men rich."

"If that's your world, you're welcome to it, engineer," O'Hara said.

"I want no part of it either," Flintlock said. And then, remembering Barnabas's blast furnaces, "Hell must be full of factories."

"Well, what do we do with him?" Evangeline said.

"I say shoot him," Flintlock said. "He's one of Ritter's boys and that's enough for me."

"O'Hara?"

"I'm with Sammy. Gun him and be done."

"He's very young," Evangeline said.

"A lot of the Yankee enemy we shot in the war were very young," Flintlock said. "Age has nothing to do with it."

"He's an engineer," Evangeline said.

"Damn it all, woman, you and him bandy that word around like he was a saint or something," Flintlock said. "If it helps you feel better I'll shoot him with my Hawken."

"What difference does that make?" Evangeline said.

"It will blow a fifty-caliber hole in him. He won't feel a thing."

"No, I don't want that," Evangeline said. "You and O'Hara take him out of the swamp and set him free. He can't harm us now."

"Not unless Ritter gets another flying machine," Flintlock said.

"That's unlikely to happen, Sam. It would be bad luck to kill the engineer. We're defending our swamp. We're not murderers."

"I'd sleep better at night if I gunned him, Evangeline," Flintlock said. "But seeing as how the bank robbery didn't set right with you, I'll oblige you on this one and won't blow Byng's brains out."

"There speaks a true gentleman," O'Hara said. "Sammy, you're a national treasure."

"Evangeline didn't mention you in her amnesty, Injun," Flintlock said.

But he smiled as he said it.

CHAPTER TWENTY-SEVEN

Sebastian Lilly was a horseman. Hunting a man in a swamp was foreign to him, especially in the fading hours of daylight. He had no real hope of success, not in the couple of hours left to him before dark, but he might be able to get a lead on the robber and track him down later.

Lilly wore a slicker against the steady rain and paddled between the cypress trees, Spanish moss garlanded above his head as though he was a Roman general riding a chariot at his triumph. When Lilly was a boy his pa took him duck hunting in the Arizona Territory's Anderson Mesa country. He remembered how a duck would slam into a wall of birdshot and hurtle straight down and splash into the water. Then old Ranger would jump into the water and retrieve the bird. Pa's old cocker spaniel was stone deaf from the roar of the guns but Pa said he was the best waterfowling dog in

Coconino County and beyond. When Ranger died, Pa buried him and erected a wooden marker that said here lies the best hunting dog in Coconino County. But one day the marker blew away in a big wind and Pa never put up another.

That was then and this was now, and Lilly hunted another kind of game.

He'd gotten a pirogue from Ritter but was unused to the craft and his progress through the swamp was slow. The constant rain was a misery and he was about to turn back and wait for fairer weather when he saw the glow of lamps in the distance. It had to be a cabin and Lilly had a decision to make: Should he inquire about the bank robber and risk darkness overtaking him? The idea of a spending the night lost in the swamp did not appeal to him, but Lilly decided to throw the dice. He paddled toward the cabin at a faster pace.

By swamp standards the cabin was large, with a deck out front, half of it covered by an overhang. A weather vane in the shape of a galleon under full sail stood at the top of the roof and pointed the way of the wind. The cabin had two large windows to the front, rectangles of yellowish light in the rain-lashed gloom.

Lilly laid his Winchester across his knees

and yelled, "Hello the house!"

A full minute passed before the door opened and a woman stepped outside. Her hair tumbled in waves over the shoulders of a gleaming black oilskin with a high, stand-up collar. The coat, closed at the front by seven silver buckles, was cut narrow at the waist, clung to her hips and fell to her ankles. Lilly, his mouth suddenly dry, saw the toes of black boots peep out from under the hem of the coat. The woman was lovely in an almost supernatural way, Lilly realized, the kind of dazzling beauty that no mortal female should possess. She seemed half-angel, half-devil and all woman . . . the kind a man would kill to possess.

"What can I do for you?" Evangeline said. "It's unusual for men to be abroad on an evening like this."

It took a while for Lilly to find his voice. When he did he said, "I'm looking for a man, ma'am, an outlaw who robbed the bank in Budville. He's a kind of stocky feller, looks like a real hard case and he wears a buckskin shirt and has a big bird" — he drew a forefinger across his throat — "tattooed across there. Have you seen him?"

"Oh dear me, if I'd seen such a desperate character I'm sure I'd remember," Evangeline said. "Are you the law?"

"I work for the bank, ma'am." Lilly's eyes feasted on Evangeline, her face, her body, her promise.

"I'm sorry I can't help you," she said.

"You shouldn't be out here alone, ma'am," Lilly said. "Maybe I should come inside out of the rain and we can get better acquainted."

Evangeline smiled. "I'm never alone."

Lilly was about to say something, but his mouth snapped shut and he looked frantically around him as he held on to the sides of the canoe. "What bumped me?" he said.

Evangeline saw fear in the man's eyes. "It's only the alligators," she said. "They're my watchdogs."

"Then call them off," Lilly yelled. He had his rifle in his hands.

"When they see you start to leave they'll let you alone," Evangeline said. She pointed. "You see that large one over there?"

Lilly turned and saw a gigantic, reptilian shape undulating through the water toward him. "What the hell is that?" he said.

"His name is Basilisk," Evangeline said. "He's jealous of you, fearing you might harm me. I put a bullet into him years ago and I think it still causes him pain. He very badly wants to kill me."

"Hell, lady, I don't want to kill you," Lilly

said. "I'd something else in mind."

"Basilisk doesn't know that," Evangeline said.

The canoe rocked wildly as one of the larger alligators prodded it with his snout. "Call him off," Lilly yelled.

"Paddle away and you'll be safe," Evangeline said. "At least, I hope you will."

"We'll meet again," Lilly said, using the paddle to push himself off the dock.

"I look forward to it," Evangeline said. "We'll have fried trout and cornbread for dinner."

The alligators parted to give Lilly a passage and he paddled quickly into the gathering gloom of the swamp. He looked back only once and the woman still stood on the dock. The massive alligator she called Basilisk lay still in the water, his head pointed in the direction of the cabin.

Evangeline said, "Not today, Basilisk. Not today."

The alligator lashed its tail, turned and swam into darkness.

CHAPTER TWENTY-EIGHT

In a tent lit by a lantern hanging above the flap, Sebastian Lilly was drinking dangerous amounts of whiskey and even Bonifaunt Toohy became alarmed. Alcohol and guns are a bad combination. Sober, Lilly was a handful. Drunk, he became uncontrollable.

"She set alligators on me," he said. "And me busy talking pretties to her."

Toohy knew he was stepping on eggshells. "Maybe it was a coincidence, Seb. The gators just happened to show up at the wrong time."

"You calling me a liar, Toohy?" Lilly said. "I don't like to be called a liar."

Toohy was good with a gun and he backed up for no man, but in the confines of the tent, shooting at spitting distance, he and Lilly would kill each other and the man was too drunk to realize that.

"I'm not calling you a liar, Seb," he said. "Just putting out an explanation for them alligators."

"There's only one explanation. The big alligator was on the prod and the woman made him that way. If I had to do it over again, I'd put a bullet in her." Tears sprang into Lilly's eyes. "Damn, Bon, she was purty. I can't tell you how purty she was."

Lilly maudlin was better than Lilly mean and Toohy encouraged him. "You plan on seeing her again?"

"Damn right I do. And next time I'll show her what a real man can do for her."

Toohy grinned. "Now you're talking, Seb. Why, I reckon —"

From outside the tent came a guard's voice. "Engineer's coming in."

"Go tell Mr. Ritter," Toohy said. "I'll be right out."

"Sure thing," the guard said.

Toohy shrugged into his slicker, then said to Lilly, "Better stay here and rest, Seb. You've had a trying day."

"I'm coming out," Lilly said, his voice thick. "Maybe the engineer saw that bank robber with the tattoo on his throat."

Leonard Byng was soaked to the skin and his boots were covered in mud. "I've been walking for hours," he said, feeling the need to explain his appearance

"You look like it," Brewster Ritter said. "We'll go into the mess tent and talk. I don't want to stand out here in the rain."

The mess tent was large, lit by hanging oil lamps, and it had two long rows of table and benches. But it was not large enough to accommodate all two hundred of Ritter's men at a time and the loggers ate in shifts.

The hour was late and when Ritter stepped inside with the engineer, Toohy and Lilly, there were only four loggers inside, rugged, bearded men who wore flannel shirts and heavy, lace-up boots. They sat at a table playing poker, but when Ritter came in one of them picked up the deck and the four stepped outside.

Ritter and the others sat, and then he said, "What happened, Byng?"

The young engineer told them about the crash of the *Star Scraper,* the deaths of Professor Mealy and Travis Kershaw and his subsequent rescue.

"The two men wanted to kill me, but the woman at the cabin wouldn't have it," Byng said. "So they took me out of the swamp in a pirogue and left me on the trail. I walked for hours."

"Yeah, you said that already," Lilly said. "Describe this woman."

"She was tall and very beautiful. The most

beautiful woman I ever saw in my life," Byng said. "The two men called her Evangeline."

"And the men?" Ritter said. "What did they look like?"

"One looked like an Indian and the man with the tattoo on his throat called him O'Hara."

"What kind of tattoo was it?" Lilly said. He was still stinking drunk and slurred his words.

"A big bird with its wings outstretched," Byng said. "It looked Indian to me."

"Did you catch this man's name?" Ritter said.

"They called him Sam. I didn't really catch his last name but I think it was Flintlock. Strange kind of name."

"Then the woman lied to me," Lilly said. "She told me she'd hadn't seen anyone like that."

"Maybe there are two beautiful women in the swamp," Byng said.

"I doubt it," Ritter said. "She knows where this Sam ranny is and we need to make her tell us."

"I'll get it out of her," Lilly said. "When I get done with her she'll be glad to tell me where he is."

"Then it's settled," Ritter said, rising to

his feet. "Byng, get to work on the steam saws. Come morning we start cutting trees."

CHAPTER TWENTY-NINE

Sam Flintlock rose from his cot and as usual there was no sign of Evangeline. Just before sleep had taken him he'd seen her come inside and heard her sit in her chair by the stone fireplace. Now, as the first light of dawn grayed the windows, she was gone.

Flintlock put on his hat then stretched, scratched his belly and padded outside in his long johns. No matter the weather O'Hara spread his blankets outside on the deck and he was already awake, staring into the swamp.

He turned when he heard Flintlock open the door. "Coffee's on the bile," he said. "Didn't you smell it?"

"I got to be awake for an hour before I smell anything," Flintlock said. "Where is Evangeline?"

"She left just before sunup. Says she visits Lady Esther once a week to treat her rheumatisms."

Flintlock nodded and his fingers strayed in the direction of his left shoulder. O'Hara said, "The makings are over there by the rocker."

Flintlock grunted, stepped back inside and returned with a cup of coffee in his hand. He sat and built himself a cigarette. O'Hara watched the level of the coffee in Flintlock's cup drop by half before he said, "Do you hear that?"

"Hear what?"

"The buzzing sound."

"Bees," Flintlock said. "Or maybe hornets."

"It's tree saws, Sammy."

That took a while to register in Flintlock's sleep-fogged brain. "Tree saws?"

"Sounds like it's coming from the edge of the swamp," O'Hara said. "I reckon Brewster Ritter is cutting."

Suddenly Flintlock was wide-awake. "Can anything else make that sound?" he said.

"Damn it, Sam, it's tree saws. And no, nothing else makes that sound."

Flintlock drained his cup, stepped inside and when he came out a few minutes later he was fully dressed, his Colt in his waistband. "I'm going to take a look-see, O'Hara," he said. "You wait here until Evangeline gets back." He stepped toward the canoe O'Hara had appropriated, then stopped and said, "Did you think Evangeline seemed a little strange last night?"

"Yeah, now you come to mention it she was real quiet, as though something troubled her."

"Any idea what it could be?"

"No, I don't."

"I'll ask her when I see her again," Flintlock said.

He stepped into the canoe and paddled away from the deck. It seemed to him that the sawing noise was getting louder.

But what Sam Flintlock didn't know was that fate had dealt him a hand from the bottom of the deck. He was on a collision course with Sebastian Lilly, a gunman who could outdraw and outshoot him any day of the week . . . without half trying.

A cypress that had stood for three hundred years fell and splashed into the bayou. A cheer went up from the onlookers on shore, especially the beaming Brewster Ritter, who turned to Bonifaunt Toohy and said, "There she goes, Mr. Toohy, the first of thousands."

"Congratulations, boss," Toohy said, grinning. But he felt an odd little pang. What had been a magnificent tree, cared for by God, was now just a log to be dragged out of the water with chains and sawn into boards. Somehow it just didn't seem right.

Another cypress fell, more cheers, and Ritter did a little jig, clapped his hands and said, "Hot damn, this is going to be a good day."

Sebastian Lilly had no interest in the trees. He had a woman on his mind. But his thoughts about Evangeline were savage, not tender, lustful, not loving, and above all violent in the extreme.

Like an ardent suitor, the gunman paddled with purpose in a direct line for the cabin, wasting no time. Imagine his distress therefore when he saw another canoe heading toward him . . . and the man in the stern wore a buckskin shirt.

As the two pirogues closed the distance Lilly could make out the tattoo on the man's throat. It had to be Sam, the bank robber, the man he'd sworn to kill. Now the damned wretch stood between him and his woman and that was unforgivable.

Lilly raised his Winchester and fired. The man called Sam jerked, the paddle flew out of his hands and he tumbled into the bottom of his canoe.

It had been a good shot, a killing shot, and Lilly grinned. He paddled toward the dead man's canoe, determined to gloat over his fallen enemy. Mr. Cobb would be pleased. ,

Sam Flintlock had raised the paddle for the down stroke when the bullet hit. The lead chunked into the paddle's ash handle and caromed inches past Flintlock's head. He threw the splintered paddle away from him, played dead man and dived for the bottom of the canoe. He heard the steady plop . . . plop . . . plop of a paddle stroking water and he eased over on his right side, groaning horribly like a badly wounded man. Flintlock eased his Colt from the waistband and silently thanked President Grant for commissioning a revolver so finely made that the triple click of the cocking hammer was almost as quiet as the tick of a Waltham watch.

His assailant's canoe came closer. The paddling stopped and then there was silence as the canoe glided for a few feet before it bumped into Flintlock's bow. Lilly's hand held on to the gunwale as he drew the canoes closer . . . and then he peered over the side of his victim's craft.

Flintlock fired. His bullet hit Lilly's forehead a fraction of an inch under his hat, plowed through his brain and blew out the back of his skull. Lilly was dead before his canoe tipped and tumbled him into the water. But Flintlock had no time for the gunman. His own paddle was shattered and the dead man's had fallen out of his canoe and was drifting away.

His Colt still in his hand, and being a poor swimmer, Flintlock floundered after it. Only then did he realize that the water was only about four feet deep at that point and he could walk. He grabbed the paddle and tossed it into his canoe before he scrambled aboard, almost capsizing the narrow pirogue in the process.

The man's body floated facedown in the water and Flintlock turned him over with the paddle. He'd never seen the man before but he was no doubt one of Ritter's guns hunting for swamp people.

"Nearly got yourself killed there, Sam. You was mighty lucky."

Old Barnabas made room for himself on a dead tree trunk by pushing aside a couple of turtles. "What the hell are you doing out here in this swamp paddling a canoe like a damned wild Indian?"

"You know why I'm here, Barnabas," Flintlock said. "I'm trying to save this swamp and the people who live in it."

"What did that feller try to kill you fer?"

"I don't know."

"Probably because I didn't raise you up right and you're an idiot. Where's the Injun?"

"You know where he is, Barnabas."

The old man cackled. "I sure do. He's waiting for the purty lady while you ponce around in a canoe like a great fairy and get your head blowed off."

"If you'll notice, it was the other feller who got his head blowed off. And what does *ponce* mean? I never heard that word before."

"English feller teached it to me. Nice enough chap apart from the fact that he murdered five wives in a row and dissolved their bodies in vats of acid and got hung for it. But he's a fine steam engineer so he's got a big in with you-know-who."

"Barnabas, I just killed a man and I don't feel like talking," Flintlock said. "Go away and leave me alone."

"Whatever you say, Sam. I know when I'm not wanted. When are you headed for the Arizona Territory?"

"When I'm done here."

"You'll like Arizona. It's hot and dry," Barnabas said. "Like where I come from."

Then he was gone and only the turtles

remained.

And the hungry alligators . . .

CHAPTER THIRTY

Despite the dead man floating in the water, Sam Flintlock still had a job to do — find the source of rasping tree saws.

The morning mist still clung to the cypress as he paddled toward what had become known to the swamp dwellers as Ritter's Landing, an innocuous name for a living symbol of greed, callousness and Ritter's lack of respect for any living thing, human or otherwise. The man needed killing and Flintlock kept that fact at the back of his mind, to be taken out and dusted off when the opportunity arose.

For once Flintlock was thankful for the mist, a nuisance that made navigation around the swamp and the land islands well nigh impossible. But as the sun rose the mist thinned, providing him with just enough cover without reducing visibility too much.

As it was Flintlock rounded the spit of a

tree island and almost ran into a three-man logging crew, one of them carrying steel wedges in his belt and a light sledgehammer. But the loggers, muscular fellows standing in thigh-high water, were intent on their task and didn't notice him.

Flintlock back-paddled around the spit to the shelter of the tree island. He needed to get a better view of Ritter's Landing and the sawing operation. He found a place to moor the canoe and then waded through shallow water to reach dry land. Crouching low, he made his way through willow and gum trees to the opposite side of the island . . . and saw a scene of devastation. At least a dozen cypress had been cut, dragged onto land by the armored steam launch that now revealed six iron tractor wheels, two pairs to the rear, a single axle at the front. Teams of loggers busily limbed the trees but they wouldn't be bucked into manageable length until engineer Byng's steam saws were up and running.

So far only a dozen trees had been felled but it was enough for Flintlock to imagine the blighted wasteland that would be left after all the cypress were gone.

He spotted Brewster Ritter overseeing the operation, standing close to the edge of the swamp. The stocky little man was scowling and he continually yelled orders as though unhappy with the loggers' progress. As far as Flintlock was concerned they had already done enough damage that would take nature hundreds of years to put right, if ever.

Ritter was within rifle range but Flintlock had not brought along his Winchester and the one his assailant had used was at the bottom of the swamp. "Another time, Ritter," he whispered. "Another time."

"Have you any idea who he was, Sam?" Evangeline said.

"No. But I guess he didn't like me much," Sam Flintlock said.

"I agree with that," O'Hara said. "Since he took a pot at you."

"He may have been the man who came here asking about you, Sam," Evangeline said. "He was headed in the direction of my cabin."

"He probably was," Flintlock said.

"He had your description, talked about the thunderbird on your throat. He must have recognized you."

"And cut loose," O'Hara said. "And damn near killed you."

"Yeah, I'm aware of that," Flintlock said. Sometimes the breed irritated the hell out of him for his uncanny grasp of the obvious.

"I visited Cornelius this morning, but I didn't know then that the cypress was already being cut," Evangeline said. "I'll ask him to call a meeting of the swamp dwellers. They respect Cornelius and they'll come."

"And decide what?" Flintlock said. "The only thing Ritter understands is violence."

"Then it may come to that," Evangeline said. "We may have to come together and fight."

"And that gives me an idea," Flintlock said. "Mathias Cobb is behind all this and I think I'll give him an invitation to the meeting."

"Sam, you stole the fat man's money and that didn't work," O'Hara said. "But I reckon an invitation to the meeting will."

Flintlock grinned. "Want to do it, O'Hara?"

"Damn right I do. It's been too quiet around here."

"Hell, I nearly got killed today," Flintlock said.

"Yes, nearly. But nearly don't cut it when things are too quiet."

"Evangeline," Flintlock said, "did you make a lick of sense out of that?"

"More or less," the woman said. She wore her boned red leather corset, black tights and black boots and looked divine. She slid her derringer into the garter holster on her thigh and said, "We'll leave right now and talk with Cornelius, tell him about the trees and set a date for the meeting."

Flintlock made a long-suffering face. "I'm getting mighty sick of paddling though this damned swamp."

"I'll do the paddling, Sammy," O'Hara said. "But this time remember to bring your rifle."

CHAPTER THIRTY-ONE

"When we cut deeper into the swamp how many logs will the launch tow back to here at a time?" Brewster Ritter said.

"I can't give you an exact figure, but I believe between six to seven hundred," Leander Byng.

"It won't blow up on us, huh?" Ritter said.

Byng looked confused. "I don't understand the question."

"I mean towing that many logs," Ritter said. "I mean all of a sudden . . . boom!"

"The launch has a high-quality steam engine that I designed myself," Byng said. "She will perform as well, if not better, than any of our great ocean liners or warships."

"How many riflemen can I cram into her while she's towing logs?"

"A dozen at least. All they have to do is find deck space for themselves."

"Then when Lilly gets back I'll tell him to hire more guns. Damn him, he should be back by now. I guess he's spending more time with that little swamp gal than he intended."

"Will that be all, Mr. Ritter?" Byng said. "I must get back to work."

"Get those ripsaws going, Byng," Ritter said. "We need to buck the logs before we load them onto the freight wagons."

"I'll need three more days," the engineer said.

"Don't worry, I'll pile them logs high for you." Ritter said. "It's funny, I just had a thought. Remember what hide hunters did to the buffalo? Well, that's what I'm gonna do to the cypress." He scowled. "I made a good joke, Byng. Why didn't you smile?"

"Because the buffalo are all gone," Byng said.

"That's the whole point. Soon the bald cypress will be all gone as well. Get it?"

Byng nodded. "Yes, yes, a very good joke, Mr. Ritter," he said.

"Where the hell is he?" Brewster Ritter said.

Bonifaunt Toohy removed his bowler hat and wiped sweat from his forehead with the back of his hand. Ritter's tent was hot from the day's sun and the smoking oil lamp smelled. "I guess we'd better go look for him."

"I wonder if he killed that Sam feller. And did he get Cobb's money back?"

"I guess he'll answer that when we see him," Toohy said.

"Damn, if he's still in the sack with that swamp floozy I'll kill him."

Toohy smiled. "Seb will take a lot of killing."

Ritter shook his head in exasperation. "Round up half a dozen men with lanterns and go look for him. Don't go into the swamp. It's too dangerous at night. Just remain on firm ground and call out for him. Understand?"

Toohy lifted the tent flap and glanced outside. "Darkness coming down. I'll get the search party organized."

"Find him, Bon," Ritter said. "He's got questions to answer."

Lanterns bobbed like fireflies at the edge of the swamp and the voices of rough men were raised, shouting Sebastian Lilly's name. The swamp is never silent at night. Insects chattered, frogs croaked, night birds called and alligators bellowed, but there was no answering yell from Lilly.

After an hour of useless shouting the searchers became hoarse and Bonifaunt Toohy's frustration grew. Where was the man? Was he in bed with a woman as Ritter claimed?

One of the search party, a hired gun named Jed Connolly, said to Toohy, "You don't suppose one of the swampers gunned him?"

Toohy shook his head. "That ain't likely. If Lilly is with a woman he isn't going to move until morning. We're wasting our time out here and I'm getting eaten alive by mosquitoes." Toohy raised his voice. "All right boys, let's call it quits. Lilly isn't gonna show up tonight."

One man, a logger, didn't get the message.

He stood in marshy water at the edge of the swamp, his lantern raised high, its yellow light rippling with the current. Then he yelled, "Hey, Toohy, bring more light over here."

"What do you see?" Toohy said.

"Hell, I don't know, but it could be a body."

A man laughed in the gloom. "Be careful there, Charlie. If it's an alligator he'll bite you up the ass."

The man named Charlie said, "That ain't funny."

Toohy and a couple of men walked to where Charlie was still scanning the edge of the swamp. They both raised their lanterns and after a few moments Toohy said, "It is a body. Looks like ol' Seb caught up with that Flintlock feller."

"Should we drag it in?" Charlie said.

Jed Connolly said, "Sure. I'd like to count how many bullet holes Seb made in that ranny."

"Yeah, drag it in," Toohy said. "There's a dead branch lying there. If it's Flintlock we can identify him by the tattoo on his throat."

It took several attempts before Charlie managed to hook the corpse's clothing with the willow branch. Helped by a couple of other men he dragged the body to dry ground. Then everybody stood there and gaped and Toohy voiced their thoughts, "It's Seb, by God," he said. He lowered his lantern and looked closer. "He's been shot."

"One bullet smack in the middle of his brow," Charlie said. "I guess he met up with that there Flintlock ranny you're talking about."

Suddenly Toohy was angry. "Flintlock didn't kill him. Seb was shot at a distance by some swamp rat with a rifle. It's plain to see."

Connolly shook his head. "Seb was gunned by some lowdown yellow belly who was scared to meet him face-to-face."

"It's how it shapes up to me," Toohy said. "Strange that the alligators didn't eat him. I guess ol' Seb was just too tough to chew."

That drew a laugh and Toohy said, "Let's get him back. We can bury him decent come morning."

"Bon, you sure Flintlock didn't kill him?" Charlie said.

"No, damn you, he didn't kill him," Toohy said. "Get the thought out of your head, and that goes for the rest of you. A lowdown swamp rat assassin who shot at a distance killed Seb Lilly. That's the only way it could have happened. There is no other explanation so don't y'all go looking for one. It was nothing to do with Flintlock, who's probably not even in the swamp any longer. You all got that?"

"Anything you say, Bon," Charlie said. "I was just asking, like."

"Then don't say it again, to me or anyone else," Toohy said. "I don't want the man with the tattoo on his throat turning into a boogerman and scaring the hell out of everybody. You hear what I'm saying to you?"

"We get it, Bon," Charlie said. "Like you say, there ain't no way Seb Lilly was killed by Flintlock. Just no way in hell."

Toohy stared into the gibbering night of

207

the swamp and his thoughts narrowed his eyes. "That's right, Charlie," he said. "Just no way in hell."

CHAPTER THIRTY-TWO

Sam Flintlock stepped out of the pirogue and stood with his hand on the butt of his Colt until Evangeline joined him. They both waited until O'Hara tied up the canoe, then all three walked to the door of the Museum of the Swamp and rang the clockwork bell.

Cornelius answered almost immediately, his face registering surprise. "So late? In the dark? But please come inside," he said.

He led the way through the exhibit room into a small, cozy parlor where a lamp glowed, illuminating the crowded furnishings that were fashionable at the time. A stern portrait of Queen Victoria hung on the wall above the fireplace and under it a scrolled wooden sign that read THE EMPIRE FOREVER.

Cornelius saw Flintlock staring at the somber monarch and said, "I received that from the queen's own hand, a reward for my services to the British Empire. Her generosity far exceeds her taste in gifts."

"Oh, I don't know," Flintlock said. "It would make a good pistol target."

"My dear Sam, if her majesty heard you say that she would not be amused," Cornelius said.

"What did you do for the old gal's empire?" O'Hara said.

"I introduced her army officers to the joys of the Gatling gun and showed them how efficiently they could mow down vast numbers of naked savages and be back in their tents in time for tea. Of course a few years later the British army acquired the Maxim gun that could slaughter even more naked savages. I'm told the queen was very pleased with it."

Cornelius smiled and said, "And talking about tea, would anyone care for a cup? I have a pot brewing right now."

Evangeline asked for tea, as did O'Hara, who'd never tried it before. Flintlock kept to bourbon, but he did accept a slice of seed cake.

After the required amount of polite small talk, Evangeline told Cornelius about Brewster Ritter's assault on the cypress and the need for a meeting of all the swamp people. "We need to come up with ideas on how to fight the menace," she said.

"I'm against that for two reasons," Cornelius said. "A gathering of all the swamp people in one place at the same time, and I assume we're talking about here at the museum, might prove to be a tempting target for Ritter and his gunmen. And secondly, as I've said before, the people of this swamp are not fighters. They just want to be left alone to live their lives. I can't ask them to take up arms against expert gunmen. You heard me talk about the Maxim gun and its effect on savages. If we attack Ritter I can assure you that the resulting slaughter of our people will be much the same."

Flintlock said, "Toss us a lifeline here, Cornelius. You've told us what we can't do, now tell us what we can do."

"Sam, I suggest you recruit a small force of volunteers from the swamp dwellers, men you can trust, men who will stand their ground. Use the force to hit and run, slow down Ritter's logging any way you can. In the meantime I plan to leave the swamp and telegraph Washington. I still have friends there and perhaps they can do something to stop this madman."

"How many men?" O'Hara said.

"No more than six," Cornelius said. "I suggest you start with Mrs. Allie Briscoe's sons. Claude and Isaac are fine young men and they are anxious to avenge their father's death."

"Can they use a gun?" Flintlock said.

"I believe they regularly shoot squirrels for the pot," Cornelius said.

Flintlock and O'Hara exchanged glances, each reading in the other man's eyes what was in his own . . . squirrel hunters were not a match for a dozen of Texas's top draw fighters.

Cornelius knew what the two men were thinking. "Sam, you must work with what you can get. Hit and run is the key. Don't stand and fight. Will you take it on?"

"I'll study on it," Flintlock said.

Both he and Cornelius knew that was no answer at all.

"Seems like your museum moved a good ten yards since the last time I was here, Cornelius," Flintlock said as he stepped out the door. "I recollect that the big cypress there was a lot farther away."

"Eleven yards, two feet and seven inches to be exact," Cornelius said. "During the last big storm the island moved a quarter of a mile, but that was unusual."

"When was that?" Flintlock said.

"All of six years ago. We're overdue for

another big one."

O'Hara was positioning himself to assist Evangeline into the pirogue when Flintlock jerked his head and said, "What the hell was that?"

Cornelius raised the lantern he carried. "What happened?"

"Something just flew over my head."

"An owl perhaps," Cornelius said. "They can fly very fast."

But a moment later an arrow thudded into the mooring post where O'Hara stood. Not a man to ponder a situation, he drew as he dropped to the ground and his gun came up fast, pointing into the darkness.

"Evangeline, get back!" Flintlock yelled. He held his Colt ready.

But the woman ignored him. She pulled the derringer from her garter and took a knee beside O'Hara. "Do you see anything?" she said.

O'Hara shook his head. "Only swamp."

For long moments the four people stared into the darkness. There was no sound but the soft lap of water against the canoe and the chirp of insects. Then Cornelius stepped to the post and pulled the arrow free. He studied it for a while then said, "Flint head fletched with hawk feathers and the shaft marked with five yellow rings. It's an Atakapan arrow."

"I thought they were all dead," Flintlock said.

"So did I," Cornelius said.

"Why did they shoot at us and me half Indian?" O'Hara said.

"The Atakapan were experts with the bow," Cornelius said. "O'Hara, if they'd wanted to kill you and Flintlock they could have."

Flintlock said, "Were they trying to warn us off? Telling us to get the hell out of their swamp?"

"Perhaps," Cornelius said. "Or they were trying to tell us something else."

"Couldn't they have just sent us a note?" Flintlock said.

Cornelius smiled. "That's not the Indian way."

Evangeline rose gracefully to her feet. "What were they telling us, Cornelius?"

"Perhaps that we have allies in the fight against Ritter."

"I think," Flintlock said, "that they were trying to scare us. Next time they see us they'll aim better."

Evangeline shoved the derringer back into her garter. "Which of you is right?" she said.

"I guess we'll find out soon enough," Cornelius said.

CHAPTER THIRTY-THREE

"It was the swamp that killed Seb Lilly, Mr. Cobb," Bonifaunt Toohy said. "Don't let anybody tell you different. We buried him this morning at first light and —"

"Like I give a damn about that," Mathias Cobb said. "Lilly was a professional and he was paid to take his chances." The banker struggled from his chair and waddled to the decanters on a wall table. He poured two whiskeys and handed one to Toohy. "It's all getting too close to me, Mr. Toohy. First the bank robbery and now this. I don't like it one bit."

"When we kill Flintlock we'll get your money back," Toohy said. "He can't spend it in a swamp."

"I know, but he can give it away to the swampers."

"We'll get him soon."

"How is Brewster Ritter holding up?"

"The cutting has started. He's talking

215

about hauling out six or seven hundred logs each week."

"And the sawmill?"

"The engineer is setting it up. He says we'll be ready to buck the logs in a few days."

"How many freight wagons does Ritter have? I know I paid for a lot of them."

"We'll get the lumber to the Budville train depot, Mr. Cobb. Don't concern yourself about that."

"The operation has got to run smoothly, like clockwork, you understand?"

"I'll see to it," Toohy said.

Cobb sat in his chair and stared out the window into the busy morning street. Without turning he said after a few moments, "I'm being blackmailed, or should I say someone is making a clumsy attempt to wring money out of me."

"Who might that be?" Toohy said.

"Well, first a little background. Please be seated."

"I'll stand, if that's all right with you," Toohy said.

"Suit yourself." Cobb swung his chair around and leaned both elbows on his desk. "Shall we say that a young married lady of my acquaintance gave me certain sexual favors in return for not foreclosing on her mortgage. Now, let us say that after I tired of that dalliance, I foreclosed on her anyway. Money is more important than a woman, is it not? Imagine then that the young lady, while the balance of her mind was disturbed, hanged herself from a rafter in her barn. Are you with me so far, Mr. Toohy?"

"I'm catching your drift."

"And now we come to the nub, the very essence of the problem. The late young lady's husband owns a one-loop spread down to Anderson Gully way in the swamp country."

Toohy grinned. "More swamps."

"Indeed, but beside the point. The man's name is Larry Stothard and instead of grieving for his dead wife as a Christian should, he decided to gouge me for money or he'll expose my relationship with his wife to the whole town."

As though to steady his nerves, the fat man took a gulp of whiskey and said, "Stothard wants a thousand dollars a month, every month, for as long as I live. You can tell what kind of rogue I'm dealing with."

"Have you paid him anything yet?" Toohy said.

"No. But I told him I would send out a trusted rider with the first payment. Of course that rider would have been Lilly and he would have taken care of my little problem."

"And now you want me to do it? Is that it?"

"The thought had occurred to me," Cobb said.

"My services don't come cheap," Toohy said.

"Five hundred to get the job done."

Toohy smiled. "That's just half your monthly payment."

"It's more than enough. I can hire a thug to do it for fifty dollars, but dear Mrs. Stothard told me her husband was handy with a gun and had killed a man. That makes me think I need a shootist for this job."

"I'll take the five hundred," Toohy said. "Gunning your blackmailer will be a pleasant diversion."

"Don't underestimate Stothard, Mr. Toohy," Cobb said. "I did and it cost me."

"I don't underestimate anybody, Mr. Cobb. A man lives longer that way."

The Stothard spread lay a couple of miles north of Anderson's Gully in grass and post oak country and the sun was low in the sky as Bonifaunt Toohy drew rein and studied the cabin at a distance.

He grinned to himself. If Mrs. Stothard

was as pretty as Cobb said, she sure liked to live rough. The cabin looked as though it was held together with twine and baling wire and the pole corral out front sagged badly, three ponies standing head down, the best of the bunch a palomino mustang that wasn't worth more than fifty dollars. Several longhorns grazed by a narrow creek where a single cottonwood and a few willows grew. The grass around them was thin, overgrazed and muddy. The barn where Mrs. Stothard hanged herself was a ramshackle structure that once had been painted green, but the boards had weathered into a tarnished silver color.

Toohy had seen places as run-down as this one before. It usually meant the man of the house was lazy, sick or a drunk. Which one of those was Larry Stothard?

Toohy adjusted the lie of his holstered Colt, worn high in the way of horsemen, then kneed his horse forward. An earthenware olla hung from the roof of the rickety porch and barn swallows nested in the corners. A vase of flowers withered in the cabin window and the place looked abandoned. Toohy reckoned that Mrs. Stothard had been the only one who held the ranch together.

He drew rein and called out, "Hello the house!"

A minute passed, then another . . .

Toohy was about to dismount and pound on the door when a man's voice from inside yelled, "What the hell do you want?"

"Mathias Cobb sent me," Toohy said. "I have a payment for you."

After a while the door creaked open on its rawhide hinges and a man stepped onto the porch. His black hair was tousled, his eyes bloodshot and he slurred his words. He wore a Colt on his hip.

Toohy felt a pang of disappointment. He'd thought to meet a skilled shootist who'd killed his man. Instead a drunk confronted him. Where was the honor in swapping lead with a drunkard?

"It had better be all there," Stothard said. "I mean, every cent of a thousand dollars." His eyes got mean. "You didn't steal any of it, did you?"

"No, I didn't," Toohy said.

"Let me count it. If you're a damned liar I'll shoot you."

"Look at me," Toohy said. "I ride a fifteen-hundred-dollar horse, have a fifty-dollar Colt on my belt, a one-of-a-thousand Winchester under my knee and I wear a gold watch and chain. Even a drunk like you should recognize the signs."

Stothard blinked like an owl and tried to sort out in his foggy brain what the man in the bowler hat was saying to him.

Then it dawned on him.

"Damn him, Cobb sent a draw fighter! You're here to kill me."

"Crackerjack!" Toohy said, smiling. "You got it."

Stothard cursed and went for his gun. He died before it cleared leather. The young rancher fell, a bright red rose blossoming in the middle of his forehead.

A black man appeared at the corner of the cabin and Toohy swung his gun on him. Startled, the old timer dropped the wildflowers he carried and threw up his hands. "Don't shoot, mister," he said. "It's only old Oristide Theriot, who don't mean no harm to anybody, no."

"What the hell are you doing here?" Toohy said, angry with the man for surprising him.

"Suh, I come to put flowers on Miz Rose Stothard's grave. She's buried over yonder on the rise where the oaks grow."

"Did you work for her?"

"I mended stuff around the cabin she wanted fixed. But she never paid me, no. Fed me good and that was fine by me." Theriot glanced at the dead man. "Mr. Stothard was not a good man. Beat Miz Stothard. Once upon a time she loved this place, but Mr. Stothard, he threw it all away with his empty whiskey bottles." His tired brown eyes lifted to Toohy. "And now you done killed him. Well, I cain't say he didn't deserve it, no."

"Bury him for me," Toohy said. He holstered his gun and took his wallet from his back pocket. He selected a hundred-dollar bill and held it out to the old man. "Take this. Think of it as Mrs. Stothard paying your back wages."

Theriot took the money. "That's a kind thought, mister," he said.

"One thing, don't bury Stothard next to his wife," Toohy said. "He didn't deserve a woman like that and he ain't fit to lie beside her."

The old man smiled. "Mister, I cain't make up my mind. Are you a good man or a bad man?"

"I hope one day somebody will tell me the answer to that," Toohy said.

He swung his horse around and rode away. The old black man stood with his hand raised and watched him until he was out of sight.

CHAPTER THIRTY-FOUR

There were two men in the rowboat along with their lunch in greasy paper sacks, a can of orange paint and a brush. Timothy Gray was the dauber and Fighting Pat Grundy the rower. Both men were in their early forties, both illiterate, and were entered on Ritter's payroll as laborers.

Gray's job was to daub paint on the trunks of the next cypress to be cut, making sure they had a free fall into open water and not onto a tree island where their removal could be difficult.

The task had taken them far into the swamp, marking cypress trees that were not scheduled to be cut for weeks yet. But it was a job that had to be done and it was far better than working for the engineer, carrying all those heavy parts for his steam saws.

"Now did you see that size of that reptile on the bank, Pat?" Gray said in his heavy Irish brogue. "That was a big beast and teeth on him as long as the knife on my belt."

"Indeed I did to be sure," Grundy said. "It was twice the size of our little boat. I think the devil himself had a hand in his creation."

"Well, they will do you no harm if you don't trouble them," Gray said. "At least that's what I was told."

"Sure they won't, and them as ignorant as the pigs of Docherty with not the sense God gave a gnat."

"Over there," Gray said. "There's a bejasus big tree that will fall right into the channel. I'll put a lick of paint on that one and then we'll rest for a while and break out the bottle."

Once the cypress was marked Fighting Pat Grundy shipped the oars and pulled the cork on the whiskey bottle. "You first, Timothy," he said, extending the bottle to his partner. "It is the mannerly thing to do between gentlemen."

"No, it is myself that would never dream of it," Gray said. "You have been doing all the hard graft at the oars so by right the first swig should be yours. And the second if the truth be told."

"The truth. Aye, so it is then." Grundy took a swig, let out a long, satisfied *ahhh* and then passed the bottle to Gray. "You must have the second, being the artist that you are, a-painting of the trees like Mr. Whistler himself."

Gray held up the bottle, its amber contents catching the morning light, and said, "Here's to you, Pat. May you live as long you want and never want as long as you live."

Those were the last words Timothy Gray ever said. The arrow that thudded into his chest stopped his tongue forever. He died with his eyes wide open, a look of surprise on his face and a bottle of whiskey in his hand.

Pat Grundy received his "fighting" accolade as a pugilist and not a shootist. There was no gun in the boat. He grasped the oars and frantically tried to row away from there, his dead partner staring at him the whole time without a sound. He managed to travel a few yards before the arrows pounded into his back. Bristling like a porcupine Grundy bent over the oars and joined his partner in death.

The rowboat drifted and made slow circles in the sluggish current and the whiskey ran out of the bottle and scented the air with the peaty fragrance of good Irish booze.

"I don't need this," Brewster Ritter said. "Why is this stuff happening?"

"Because you're cutting down the trees, boss," Bonifaunt Toohy said.

Ritter looked up at him, his eyes deadly. "That wasn't funny." He reached for the bottle beside his cot and poured himself rum. "There are no Indians in this swamp. They've been dead for hundreds of years, wiped out by smallpox. Why have they come back now?"

"Ghosts?" one of Ritter's less intelligent gun hands said.

Ritter threw an arrow at the man. "Does that look like it was shot by a spook? Now we got Indians in the swamp. Why does this always happen to me?"

Toohy said, "Boss, maybe they just wanted to kill white men and got the opportunity. It doesn't necessarily mean they're planning to make war on us. Hell, they may be blanket Indians who wanted the dauber team's whiskey."

"Yeah, maybe that's right," Ritter said. "Or maybe it was white men who shot those arrows. Or breeds. Hell, the swamp is full of breeds."

"Could be," Toohy said.

Ritter was quiet for a spell, then his latent viciousness oozed to the surface. "I've been so busy logging that I've let the swamp rats run wild," he said. "It's time to slap 'em down again and teach them a lesson they'll never forget."

"You got a plan, boss?" Toohy said.

"Yeah, I got a plan," Ritter said. But it didn't call for Toohy, a man he didn't quite trust because he suspected that he might have a conscience. "Neville, Bayes, you stay here. The rest of you get out."

Jonas Neville and Arch Bayes were contract killers, men who murdered with the gun, knife, club or poison, whatever got the job done. Highly paid assassins, they were as sly as outhouse rats and deadly as rattlesnakes. Between them they'd killed twenty-seven men and five women and their consciences didn't trouble them in the least.

Ritter had called for those two men and as Toohy walked away from his tent he knew Brewster planned on bringing Hell to the swamp.

Brewster Ritter held up two fingers. "Two, and I want them alive. Bring them here. Understand?"

"Any two?" Jonas Neville said. Like his

partner Arch Bayes he looked and dressed like a small-town parson, favoring a faded brown frock coat to his knees, a white shirt with a cravat of the same color and button-up knee-high gaiters.

"Any two. The choice is yours, boys," Ritter said.

"We kill people," Bayes said. He was a cold man that no human emotion could ever touch. The only Commandment he ever broke with regularity was the sixth. "You sure you want them alive? That is not our way."

"In this instance, yes," Ritter said. Talking to those two unnerved him. It was like trying to hold a conversation with a pair of hooded cobras.

Neville had the eyes of a carrion eater. "When?"

"As soon as possible, gentlemen. But tomorrow would be just fine."

"When you are done with the people, we must kill them," Neville said. "If we don't, our job will not be completed and our reputation ruined."

Ritter smiled. "Oh, you can be in at the kill, if you wish. I plan to hang them."

"We wish it," Bayes said. "And we have hanged people before."

Ritter beamed. "Good, then it is settled.

Would you boys care for a drink before you go?"

"Why would we drink with an employer?" Bayes said. "That is not businesslike."

"Oh, I don't know. Because we're all friends here, I guess."

"You are not our friend," Bayes said. "Why would you say such a strange thing? You are our employer."

"We don't have any friends," Neville said. "We kill people. Who knows, one day we may be contracted to kill you."

To his annoyance, Ritter's hand shook as he poured himself another drink. His smile was forced. "Let's hope that never happens, huh?"

"We don't care," Neville said. "We kill people. That is our profession. Perhaps we already put poison in your glass."

Horrified, Ritter jerked the glass from his mouth.

The grin of the alligators in the swamp was warmer than Neville's smile. "I made a good joke," he said. "It made you jump like a jack-in-the-box."

"Yes, yes, of course you did," Ritter said. He was sweating. "That was very funny."

After the killers left, he tossed away the whiskey in his glass and took a long, shuddering gulp from the bottle.

CHAPTER THIRTY-FIVE

The cypress were being cut, the bank robbery had not brought Mathias Cobb out of his hole and now the Indians could tip the balance even further in Ritter's direction . . . and Sam Flintlock gloomily decided he was losing the war.

"We're losing the war, Evangeline," he said. "Seems like we take one step forward and two back."

"Not if the Atakapan help us," Evangeline said.

"Why would they help a bunch of people who moved into their swamp without as much as a do you mind?" Flintlock said.

"Because the Atakapan don't want the cypress cut. If there are no trees there is no swamp, just a mudhole."

"What do you think about Cornelius's hit-and-run force?" Flintlock said.

"Not much. You'd need well-trained men for that, Sam, and you don't have them."

Evangeline watched Flintlock dip a chunk of cornbread into his buttermilk then said, "The butcher's bill would be high, more than the swamp people could sustain."

Flintlock nodded. "That's pretty much how I figure it." He yawned then said, "Where's O'Hara?"

"Fishing," Evangeline said.

"The whole damned world is falling down about our ears and the Injun is fishing.'

Evangeline smiled. "He said he was going fishing, but I suspect he's trying to make contact with the Atakapan."

"Does he know that they're headhunters?"

"I suppose he does. O'Hara is half Indian himself. He might do well."

"He's also half Irish. I bet them savages will hate the mick of him."

Evangeline smiled. "What did the Irish ever do to the Atakapan?"

"I don't know. But I'm sure they did something."

"You don't like the Irish, Sam?"

"I like them just fine, but what I'm saying is that the Indians don't."

"Then the next Atakapan I see, I'll ask him," Evangeline said. "You've got buttermilk on your mustache."

She wore an ankle-length red dress, buckled down the front, and her long, slim legs were encased in high black boots.

Flintlock wiped off his mustache with the back of his hand and said, "Where do you keep all them clothes you wear, Evangeline?"

"I'm a swamp witch," Evangeline said. But said it absently, her eyes looking over Flintlock's shoulder. "Sam, inside," she said. "There are two men coming toward us in a rowboat and they're probably looking for you."

"Well, let them come," Flintlock said.

"No. I can send them away without any shooting. Hurry, get inside."

Evangeline rose to her feet and Flintlock said, "Where is your derringer?"

"Inside. Now go. Another minute and they'll see you."

Flintlock lifted the Colt from his waistband. "Here, take this. Hide it behind you."

Rather than argue, Evangeline took the revolver and said, "I'll get rid of them."

"Hell, I feel like them two rannies are putting the crawl on me," Flintlock said.

"Go inside, Sam, and do it now," Evangeline said.

Reluctantly Flintlock stepped into the cabin. He rested his Winchester against the wall beside the door and then for some reason he could never explain he got his

Hawken, already charged with powder and ball, and held it in his hands. He was primed. Ready as a rooster with its spurs up.

Evangeline's first impression was that two men in the boat were parsons come to preach to her about the evils of witchcraft as one or two had done in the past.

But when the man in the bow jumped onto the deck with the ease and grace of an athlete she changed her mind. These men were trouble.

"What can I do for you?" Evangeline said. The man she spoke to troubled her. He had the dead eyes of a corpse.

"You will come with us," the man said. Most males looked at Evangeline and smiled, but this man's expression didn't change, as though he didn't even recognize her as a woman.

He was joined by his companion, a man equally emotionless. That one said, "Get into the boat and do it now."

"You see, we kill people," Jonas Neville said. "And we will kill you if you don't do as we say."

Evangeline, holding the Colt behind her, backed toward the door of the cabin. "I warn you, get away from here," she said.

"My husband will return very soon."

"Good, then we will also take him," Arch Bayes said.

"Will you come with us or do you really wish us to kill you?" Neville said.

"We can do it quite easily," Bayes said.

"Bang-bang, you're dead," Neville said. He brushed his coat away from his holstered Remington. "Say the word."

Evangeline had her back to the door, thinking that now was the time for Sam to come to the rescue. He did. But he bungled it badly.

Flintlock kicked the door open and hit Evangeline so hard she stumbled forward and fell, the Colt slipping from her grasp. Flintlock's Hawken came up and he triggered the old rifle from the hip. Click! The flint fell on damp powder. It took a split second for him to realize what had happened. Then he let the Hawken drop and reached for the Winchester. Too late. Bayes pointed his revolver, hammer back, at Evangeline's head and said, "Leave the rifle alone or your woman dies."

"She's not anybody's woman," Flintlock said. But his hand dropped to his side.

"Both of you, into the boat," Neville said.

"Where are you taking us?" Evangeline said. She seemed unhurt from her fall.

"Why, to Mr. Ritter," Neville said. "You two will be the guests of honor at a hanging he's planning." He smiled. "Hah, I made a good joke. Now please follow Mr. Bayes into the boat. Step carefully now, we don't want any broken bones."

Once Flintlock and Evangeline were settled in the middle of the boat Neville said, "You, put your hands behind your back. Any move I don't like I'll shoot the woman."

Flintlock did as he was told and Bayes tied his wrists together, the jerking rope cutting painfully deep. "Now both of you sit there quietly and you won't get hurt," Neville said. "Please enjoy our little cruise."

Flintlock looked into Evangeline's eyes and said, "I'm sorry."

"It's not your fault," she said. And then for the first time since he'd met her he heard Evangeline say something negative. "As you said, Sam, we're losing this war."

CHAPTER THIRTY-SIX

Again, cracking like a rifle shot, the back of Brewster Ritter's hand crashed across Sam Flintlock's face. "Where is the money?"

Through split lips, Flintlock said, "Go to hell."

Crack! Another slap rocked Flintlock's head back on his shoulders. He'd badly bitten his tongue and the raw iron taste of blood was in his mouth and his right eye was so swollen from repeated blows he couldn't see out of it.

"Go to hell," Flintlock said, a feeble croak thick with blood and mucus.

"Stand him up," Ritter said.

A pair of his grinning gunmen lifted Flintlock to his feet. Ritter drew back his fist and rammed a wicked right into Flintlock's belly. He gasped in pain and his bloody head fell on his chest, his mouth gaping like a stranded fish.

"Where is the money?" Ritter said.

"Go . . . to . . ." Flintlock lapsed into unconsciousness.

"Let him go," Ritter said. The gunmen took their hands off him and Flintlock collapsed to the floor of the tent. "Connolly, are you sure you searched the cabin well?"

"I sure did, boss. It wasn't there," Jed Connolly said.

Ritter kicked the unconscious form at his feet. "Damn him, he's hidden it somewhere in the swamp. Connolly, you and Wraith take him to an empty tent and stand guard. Tell me when he comes to and we'll start work on the woman. Maybe that will make him talk."

The gunmen dragged Flintlock outside and Ritter said to Bonifaunt Toohy, "He's damned stubborn, that one."

"He's tough," Toohy said. "Tough as they come."

"When he sees the woman getting hurt he'll talk fast enough," Ritter said. "Once I recover the money I'll be in good with Cobb."

"After you get the money what are you going to do with those two?" Toohy said.

"Hang them," Ritter said. "We'll rig a gallows in the middle of the swamp and let them dangle until they rot. That will cow the swamp rats into submission, them that don't make a run for it."

"The woman is beautiful," Toohy said. "Seems a pity to destroy beauty like that."

"Hell, I don't give a damn," Ritter said. "I'd throw a rock through a Rembrandt if there was money in it." He poured two whiskeys, handed one to Toohy, then said, "You know what this means, Bon? It means we've won. Flintlock was the ringleader and with him gone there's nobody else." He clinked glasses. "When this is over and all the trees are cut you'll have enough money to keep yourself in whiskey and whores for the rest of your life. How does that set with you?"

"Just fine, boss," Toohy said. "Just fine. And what about you? What will you do?"

"I don't know. I'll find something. Maybe I'll buy myself a schooner and get into the West African slave trade. They say taking just one cargo of savages to Arabia or the Jamaican rum plantations can make a man rich."

Ritter stared at his cut and swollen knuckles and pouted. He poured whiskey from his glass over them and then wrapped a handkerchief around his hand. "The woman will be easier," he said. "She won't hurt my hand as much. Go see if Flintlock has recovered consciousness. If he has, tell Connolly and Jake Wraith to bring him here. Then get the woman. She's in the engineer's tent."

"Don't hurt her too much, boss," Toohy said. "She's —"

"Yeah, yeah, I know, she's as pretty as a field of bluebonnets. Whether or not she stays that way is up to Flintlock. By God, Toohy, I'll cut her real bad if I have to."

"Yeah, he's awake and cussin' up a storm," Jed Connolly said. He stood guard outside the tent.

"Take him to Ritter and I'll go get the woman," Toohy said. He looked at the sky. "Why are there so many seagulls around, you figure?"

"They're flying inland," Connolly said. "To feed in the swamp maybe?"

"Could be, or they're lighting a shuck ahead of a big storm."

"Too early for that. The fall is when the storms blow up in the Gulf."

"Yeah, I know. But it's strange all the same. There must be hundreds, thousands of them up there." Toohy smiled. "Well, Ritter isn't paying us to watch birds. I'll go get the woman."

The open tent flap slapped in the wind and

Bonifaunt Toohy felt a surge of alarm. He hurried his step and looked inside. Leander Byng sprawled across his cot, his goggles askew on a face that still bore the terrified expression of his last moments. But his head was not on his body. It hung by rawhide strips from the ridgepole. The hilt of a dagger, bound in scarlet leather, stuck out of Byng's chest and fat blue swamp flies filled the tent with their buzzing.

There was no sign of Evangeline.

"Evangeline is a witch, you damned fool," Sam Flintlock said though broken lips. "You can't hold her in a tent."

Brewster Ritter drew his fist back for a punch, but he remembered the damage he'd already done to his hand from Flintlock's rocky chin and craggy cheekbones and thought better of it. "Hit him, Toohy," he said.

Having no such problems, Toohy draw back and slammed a straight right into Flintlock's face, a punishing blow that dropped him to the floor of the tent.

"She cut his head off and hung it in the tent?" Ritter said.

"Yeah, it was pretty bloody."

"Could it have been the Indians?"

"Maybe. If they set enough store by the

woman to rescue her."

"Damn, I've lost my engineer," Ritter said. "Do we have anybody else that can set up the steam saws and get them working?"

"Boss, you got lumberjacks, laborers, and hired guns. That's about it."

"Then Mathias Cobb needs to find me a steam engineer."

Flintlock groaned, tried to rise and Toohy kicked him back into place. "What about him?" he said.

"I need him to tell me where he stashed Cobb's money. I can't spill the beans to Cobb that we had his bank robber in chains and couldn't get the whereabouts of his ten thousand out of him."

Ritter snapped his fingers. "Here's a lark! We'll drag him behind the steam launch and let the alligators question him. A few close shaves and he'll tell us, all right. What do you think, Toohy?"

"I've met men like Flintlock before. They'll face up to gun hands that are all horns and rattles and stare down an angry grizzly. But they'll hike up their skirts and run like your maiden aunt from a spider in the outhouse. So alligators could do the trick."

Ritter grinned. "Then I'll get it organized."

"There's only one problem," Toohy said.

The little man frowned. "What the hell is it?"

"The only man who can operate that scow is the engineer, and he's dead."

"Damn it all!" Ritter yelled. "And damn that engineer! All right, then we improvise. Tie his hands behind his back and haul him behind a rowboat." He kicked Flintlock in the ribs. "You hear that? You're going to take a little swim with the alligators."

"When do you want it done, boss?" Toohy said.

"He's too out of it today. Leave it until tomorrow morning at first light when he knows what's happening to him. Tie him to the cot and put a man on guard. Now drag him out of here. And Toohy, make sure the engineer is buried and don't forget his head. I knew it was a useless chucklehead the first time I set eyes on it."

CHAPTER THIRTY-SEVEN

Sam Flintlock reckoned he couldn't place a dime on any part of his body that didn't hurt. He was so tightly bound hand and foot to a cot that he felt blood sticky on his wrists and when he clenched his fist his fingers felt grotesquely swollen. A white moth fluttered around the oil lamp that burned above the cot and he heard the night sounds of the swamp and the steady back-and-forth tromp, tromp, tromp, of the booted guard.

Flintlock had heard Ritter say he was gator bait, a thought that brought him little peace of mind. The trouble was he didn't know where the money was. Evangeline had taken it and hidden it somewhere and only she knew where.

"Sam, you'll get the money back when you're ready to return it to the bank and not before," she'd said.

Easy for her to say . . . she wasn't about

to become an alligator's lunch.

"Got yourself in another jam, huh, boy?" Barnabas sat at the foot of his coat, still wearing his top hat and goggles. "Getting et by a crocodile ain't no fun."

"Alligator. Go away, Barnabas."

"See that what I got in my hand? It's a steam pressure gauge only it ain't working real well. I'll have to figure out what's ailing it. Your face is a real mess, boy."

"I reckon," Flintlock said.

"Why did you use the old Hawken on them two characters instead of a perfectly good Winchester?"

"I don't know."

"I do. It's because I raised up an idiot. I hear people coming so I got to go, Sam. I just dropped by to cheer you up some."

Barnabas disappeared, leaving behind him the smell of engine oil.

Outside Flintlock heard a brief struggle and then a man made a terrible gurgle in his throat accompanied by the sound of gouging feet. Then silence. The tent flap opened.

Flintlock raised his head and a white skull stared back at him. The skull came closer and peered down at him. But this was no bony apparition but a flesh-and-blood man, his face painted in black and white, long tangled hair falling over his shoulders. Without a word the Indian, for that's what Flintlock deduced he was, cut the ropes from his wrists and ankles and with surprising gentleness helped him to a sitting position. "Can you walk?" the man said.

"Not fast and not far," Flintlock said.

From outside a man's angry shout, then the slam of a rifle.

"Quickly. We must go," the Indian said.

Two bodies lay outside the tent, the guard and a dead Indian. Flintlock saw shapes moving toward them in the darkness. Guns flared and bullets kicked up dirt around him. From somewhere to his left a bow twanged and he heard a man scream as the arrow hit. The Indian grabbed Flintlock's arm and dragged him toward the swamp.

"They're getting away! Stop them!" came Brewster Ritter's voice.

As his eyes grew accustomed to the gloom Flintlock saw three Indians, one of them bent over from the pain of a wound, head in the direction of the water. Bullets slapped into the swamp and he thought he saw a second Indian take a hit.

"Take." The Indian let go of his arm and shoved a Colt at him. Flintlock recognized it as the General Grant. "Shoot," the man said.

Flintlock shoved a swollen finger the size of a sausage into the trigger guard as his battered, half-shut eyes reached into the darkness. He knew he couldn't score hits but there was no shortage of targets. A dozen men had spread out and, made wary by the arrow strike, were advancing slowly on him.

"Flintlock, give yourself up," Ritter yelled. "Surrender and we won't harm you. We'll talk."

"Go to hell, Ritter," Flintlock said.

Fully aware of how it was going to hurt, he thumbed the Colt and fired. Moved to his left, fired again. His swollen hand was taking a beating, but he kept shooting as the Indian dragged him toward the swamp edge.

"Get into the canoe," the man said.

The shapes in the distance had slowed to a walk, but the gunmen kept up a steady firing, shooting at shadows in the darkness.

Flintlock emptied his gun into the gloom and as far as he knew scored no hits. But Ritter's gunmen were coming close. A bullet tugged at Flintlock's sleeve and a moment later he heard a grunt of pain as the Indian who shoved him into the canoe took a bullet.

Two of the Indians seemed to have escaped wounds and they paddled quickly away from shore, bullets plopping around them into the flat water.

Flintlock heard Ritter yell, "Get into the boats!" And he prayed the skull-faced Indians heard that as well and would paddle faster.

Birds fluttered out of the cypress as the canoe slid through the water and several alligators, alarmed by the shooting, scampered onto an island. Felled trees impeded the progress of the paddlers and behind them Ritter's voice carried across the water, urging his men to row faster. But it was pitch dark out there in the bayou and the shooting stopped as Ritter's rowers sought to close the distance between them and the Indian canoe.

"They're gaining on us," Flintlock said. He got no response and tried again. "I mean gaining on us fast." But he might as well have been talking to five cigar-store Indians for all the reaction he got.

If he'd had cartridges for his Colt Flintlock reckoned he could make a fight of it, but he had none. And the Indians didn't seem to put much faith in their bows. "Well, we're done for," he said. And as though to emphasize that point, a couple of Ritter's men cut loose. Their shots went wide but it was only a matter of a couple of minutes before they'd get the range.

Flintlock shook his head as the stoical Indians paddled at an almost leisurely pace, Ritter snapping at their heels. "It's curtains for all of us," he said. And to his surprise the Indian sitting in front of him turned and grinned . . . like a skull.

O'Hara hoped this was going to work. If it didn't he was a dead man . . . they were all dead men.

The passage between the tree islands was narrow, about thirty feet, and it was so dark he couldn't see the opposite island where Evangeline waited, a derringer in her garter and no doubt a lump in her throat. She'd ten Atakapan warriors with her, two more than O'Hara had on his island. But one of his men was armed with Flintlock's Winchester and O'Hara hoped the Atakapan could hit what he aimed at. The shooting was closer now and O'Hara levered a round into his rifle and readied himself.

"You boys remember to shoot them arrows low," he said. "I don't want any landing on the other island and puncturing our own men. Do you savvy that?"

Not one of the Indians looked like he understood a word and O'Hara could only shrug and hope for the best.

The Indian canoe emerged from the darkness, the paddlers moving faster now. O'Hara caught sight of Flintlock sitting in the stern, but in the gloom he couldn't tell if he was hurt or not.

Then the canoe was past and moments behind it Ritter's two boats, crammed with men, appeared in the channel. When she'd made this plan Evangeline said she'd fire one shot to open the ball and O'Hara waited for it . . . and waited . . .

Damn! What was keeping the woman? The two boats were in the middle of the channel . . .

The crack of Evangeline's derringer shattered the night like a rock through glass and a moment later arrows hissed like angry snakes. O'Hara worked his rifle and fired shot after shot into the boats. Beside him the Indian shot slowly and methodically. As arrows fell among them, two men fell from the boats and splashed into the water, then a third.

"Back! Back!" Ritter yelled.

The rowers needed no further encouragement and both boats began to quickly retreat. But Ritter's Texas draw fighters were not easy men to scare. They kept their heads and despite taking casualties from the arrow storm fired steadily into the islands. An Indian standing near O'Hara took a bullet in the chest and went down. A moment later another took a hit, cried out and staggered back out of the fight, his bow dropping from his hand.

Had Ritter had more sand his men might have prevailed, but the man panicked and screamed at the rowers to light a shuck back to the landing. The two rowboats backed away and were swallowed by the night. The Indians kept up a steady arrow deluge but as far as O'Hara could tell scored no more hits.

But the butcher's bill was high.

Two Indians had been killed and another wounded on Evangeline's island. O'Hara had one killed and one wounded, a young warrior who was not expected to live. The bodies of three of Ritter's men floated in the water, all of them dead.

CHAPTER THIRTY-EIGHT

"Ow . . . that hurts," Sam Flintlock said as Evangeline dabbed something that stung on his battered face. "You're killing me here, woman."

"I use this on children's cuts," Evangeline said. "They don't make near the fuss you do, Sam."

"An Indian would never cry out like that," O'Hara said. "They know how to bear pain like men."

"O'Hara, I wonder if you could bear the pain of my boot up your ass," Flintlock said. Then, "Begging your pardon, Evangeline."

"I've heard worse. Now sit still. This will sting."

"Worse than the last stuff? Owww . . ."

"I told you it would sting."

"Nope, you'll never hear an Indian yelp like that," O'Hara said. "Look, Evangeline, right there under his eye. You missed a spot."

"Oh yes, I see it. Just a little dab, Sam."

"Ow," Flintlock said. His irritation still sharp in his voice, he said, "How did you manage to escape, Evangeline?"

"Men like Leander Byng underestimate women and he didn't closely guard me. It was dark and I just walked out."

"Did you cast a spell?" O'Hara said. "Make yourself invisible?"

"I'm not that kind of witch," Evangeline said. "No, I just slipped out of the tent and kept to the shadows. No one saw me. But then I was discovered by the Atakapan and they took me to a canoe. Later they told me they'd cut off Byng's head because he was the engineer who made the machines that cut the cypress."

"That Byng feller is dead?" Flintlock said as Evangeline tightly bandaged his broken ribs.

"As dead as a man without a head can be."

"The Indians plan to help us, Sam," O'Hara said.

"Not quite," Evangeline said. "The Atakapan will fight for their swamp. Regarding us, it's a case of the enemy of my enemy is my friend. There are three headless bodies floating in the water out there. Now Brewster Ritter knows that the Atakapan make good friends and formidable enemies."

"They fought well enough tonight," Flintlock said. "For a spell there I thought I was a goner."

"Now they'll mourn their dead for three days and we won't see them," Evangeline said.

Flintlock took a deep breath, then said, "Damn, it hurts me to breathe."

"Broken ribs take time to heal," Evangeline said. "You'd better stay close to the cabin."

After looking around, Flintlock said, "Where is my Winchester?"

"Oh, I gave it to one of the Indians," O'Hara said. "By way of thanks."

"You make pretty free with other people's property, O'Hara," Flintlock said, irritated all over again.

O'Hara shrugged. "Those boys needed a rifle."

"And I don't?" Flintlock said.

"I never reckoned you were much good with it, Sammy."

"Well, you're wrong. I'm a good rifle shot when I have a rifle."

"You're passin' fair with the Colt's gun, though."

"O'Hara, you try to take President Grant's Colt to give to an Injun and I'll plug you for sure," Flintlock said.

"And leave you unarmed? I wouldn't dream of it. Besides, you still have the Hawken, though after what happened maybe you should leave it alone."

"And that reminds me," Flintlock said. "Evangeline, Ritter told me he'd feed me to the alligators if I didn't tell him where I stashed the money from the bank robbery. I couldn't tell him because I didn't know."

"And now you wonder where I hid it?" Evangeline said.

"Yeah, I guess I do."

"It's under your bed, behind my hatbox."

Flintlock looked stricken. "The money sack was there all the time?"

"Yes, it was. When men search for stuff they never move things out of the way, so I knew it was safe."

"That was sneaky, Evangeline," O'Hara said.

"No, just common sense."

"And knowing the ways of men," Flintlock said.

"Yes. The ways of men are not a mystery to me."

Earlier Evangeline had been staring out the cabin window. Now she said, "The seabirds are flying inland. I saw a flock of ibis and they're always the last to leave the coast before a big storm hits." She looked pensive. "It's still too early in the year for storms in the Gulf."

"Birds aren't that smart," Flintlock said. "I've seen a lot of chickens in my time and every one of them was as dumb as a snubbin' post."

"Birds can sense when a storm is coming, Sam," Evangeline said. "They get well out of its way."

"Evangeline, you've lived in the swamp for a while," O'Hara said. "What do you think?"

"I don't know, not yet. A storm is like a wolf prowling outside your door in the darkness. By the time you sense his presence it's too late."

Flintlock smiled, or tried to. All his battered face could manage was a distorted grimace. "Well, if a storm comes we'll follow the birds and head north onto dry land."

"Maybe the birds are wrong and it won't happen," O'Hara said.

"Yes, that's right," Evangeline said. "Maybe it won't happen."

But her troubled face gave the lie to that statement.

CHAPTER THIRTY-NINE

Like a whipped cur, Brewster Ritter sulked in his tent brooding over five men killed and two wounded, all of them hired guns. It was a loss he could ill afford, especially after the death of his engineer.

The entry of Indians into the fight had been an unexpected development and one that did not bode well. Already the loggers were muttering among themselves about refusing to go back into the swamp without the protection of a regiment of U.S. infantry.

Work was grinding to a standstill and something had to be done, Ritter told himself. But what?

Bonifaunt Toohy's suggestion that he lay the matter at the feet of Mathias Cobb and let him sort it out, he'd turned down at once.

But now on reflection he wasn't so sure.

Cobb stood to make more money than anyone else on this venture, so it was in his interest to come up with a solution. It involved the hiring of an engineer and more guns and so be it. He could well afford the additional cost.

Ritter downed a glass of rum and then told the guard at his tent to find Toohy and bring him. The gunman was surly, as was every man in camp, and even the whores had deserted, seeking safer pastures.

Toohy, who had been cut across the cheek by an arrow, arrived with more bad news. The loggers were now refusing to enter the swamp and a dozen had already pulled stakes, hoofing it to Budville, where they could catch a train headed north into timber country.

"Boss, you're not going to cut any more cypress until you can convince the rest of the men to stay," Toohy said. "Jed Connolly died a couple of minutes ago, still with an arrowhead in him. He was fast on the draw and shoot and a lot of the boys set store by him."

"Then we have to hire a bunch more like Connolly," Ritter said. "I want you to go tell Cobb what's happened here. Tell him we need an engineer, all the hired guns he can find and tell him . . . yeah, tell him we need immediate cash to pay bonuses to the loggers and the guns we have left or we'll lose them all."

"Anything else?" Toohy said.

"Yes and this is urgent. We need whores and whiskey."

"How do you reckon Cobb will take this?"

"He'll have to take it and like it. It's his money that's at stake."

"All right, boss, I'll go talk with him, tell him how things are with us."

"And tell him we have a good idea where the bank money is and we'll get it back soon."

"Well, that ought to put him in a good frame of mind. If he believes it."

"Make him believe it, Toohy," Ritter said.

When Toohy rode into Budville a wedding party was spilling out of the church, a pretty young bride, a handsome groom and a score of noisy well-wishers. He drew rein and watched the fun for a while. The bride smiled at him and he smiled back, tipped his bowler hat and rode on.

After he gave his name to a teller he was ushered almost immediately into Mathias Cobb's office. The fat man did not look well, ashen gray with large purple pouches under his eyes.

After telling Toohy to take a seat, Cobb settled his hands across his great belly and said, "Good news, I hope. I could use some."

"I've got news, Mr. Cobb, all of it bad," Toohy said.

"I thought so," Cobb said. "I read it in your face as soon as you stepped through the door. Go ahead, Mr. Toohy."

Toohy's cold eyes lifted to the young, fox-faced man who stood behind and to the left of the banker's chair. "Get rid of the gun," he said.

Before Cobb could speak the man said, "I'll leave when I feel like it."

"Now, now, Rolfe, don't take that tone," Cobb said. "Mr. Toohy, this is Mr. Val Rolfe, my bodyguard."

"He isn't a patch on Seb," Toohy said. "I can tell that just by looking at him. I never met a man who wore two guns that amounted to a hill of beans."

"Mr. Cobb, do I have to take this?" Rolfe said. Again and again he flexed his gloved right hand, as though getting ready to draw.

"Yes, you do, Mr. Rolfe," Cobb said. "Probably for the first and last time. Now, Mr. Toohy, tell me what's happening with my associate Mr. Ritter."

Toohy cut to the chase, told about the disasters that had befallen Ritter and his men and then gave the list of his demands.

259

Cobb made no immediate reply, but he buried his face in his hands and his massive body shuddered.

Rolfe inserted himself into the silence. "Hell, send me down there and I'll get it sorted out, Mr. Cobb. I may have to kill a few men, but I'll get the tree saws started again."

Toohy's eyes locked on the young gunman's face, but he said nothing.

Cobb dropped his hands. In the space of just a few seconds he looked ten years older. "From the very outset of this undertaking Brewster Ritter has been guilty of gross mismanagement," he said. "He must be replaced by someone who knows how to handle men, money and materials."

"In fairness to Ritter, there was no accounting for Indians taking a hand," Toohy said.

"A good manager must adapt to adverse circumstances, turn them to his own advantage, Mr. Toohy. He had plenty of men to take care of a few savages if they'd been handled right. And he still hasn't recovered my money and yet you say he had the culprit in his grasp and then let him escape. Why, sir, that is blatant incompetence at its very worst."

Rolfe had been building a cigarette and

now his hand blurred as he brought up the lighted match, letting Toohy know how fast he was.

"Send me down there, Mr. Cobb," he said again, smoke trickling from his nose. "I'll get it running right."

Cobb ignored that. He met Toohy's eyes and said, "Did you see the wedding as you came into town?"

"Sure did. I thought the bride was real pretty."

"She's Rose Stothard's sister and she holds me responsible for the woman's suicide and the killing of her husband," Cobb said. "She's trying to get the whole town to take a set against me and people are talking."

"Want me to take care of that little problem?" Rolfe said.

"No, I don't. At least not yet," Cobb said. "Mr. Toohy, I have a competent manager who can take charge of the bank while I'm gone. I think I should leave Budville for a while to let the idle talk die down."

"You mean replace Ritter yourself?" Toohy said.

"Yes. I think I should be there to look after my investment and future profits. And unlike Ritter I am a competent manager."

"He'll take it hard," Toohy said.

261

"I know. That's why Rolfe will be with me. I'm told he is the best there is and he came highly recommended."

Toohy was appalled. "Ritter's Landing is ––"

"Is that what they're calling my operational headquarters?" Cobb said. At Toohy's nod he said, "Well, now it will be known as Cobb's Landing."

"What I was trying to say is that it's a place for a young man," Toohy said. "Mosquitoes, living in tents, alligators, bad food . . . and now hostile Indians. Are you sure you want to be there?"

"I'm tougher than you think, Mr. Toohy," Cobb said. "I believe I will thrive in such a rugged environment. I will leave it to my manager to supply the money, foodstuffs and yes, whores and whiskey as needed."

"What we need is a steam engineer," Toohy said. "And more hired guns."

"And both those prerequisites will be met in due course," Cobb said. "All we have to do is hang on until they arrive. Ruthlessness is the key to this affair, Mr. Toohy, the willingness to use violence to realize our ends. By God, sir, I'm willing to kill every living creature in the swamp to get my trees cut. Hundreds of thousands of dollars are at stake and I'll let nothing stand in my way of getting them. We must pursue this great, decisive aim with all the force and determination we can muster."

Cobb turned his attention to Rolfe. "Take Mr. Toohy to the saloon and buy him a drink while I brief my manager on what has to be done in my absence," he said.

The young gunman didn't like it but he peeled himself off the wall, motioned to Toohy and stepped to the door.

Cobb said, "Remember, Mr. Toohy, we live in a pitiless world and we must be pitiless to cope with it."

For fifteen minutes Bonifaunt Toohy and Val Rolfe drank in silence at the saloon bar, then the young gunman opened a conversation. "Tell me about Seb Lilly."

"What do you want to know?" Toohy said.

"Was he fast on the draw?"

"He was good with a gun."

"How good?" Rolfe's Colt suddenly appeared in his hand. "As good as that?"

"Hard to tell. It would be a close run thing."

"How about you, Toohy? How good are you?"

"Oh, fair to middlin', I guess."

"As fast as me?"

"I doubt it."

"Then remember that when we get to where we're going. I like to be top dog, cock of the walk, understand?"

"I surely do," Toohy said.

"One thing I will tell you, don't cross me. Don't ever cross me," Rolfe said.

"I won't," Toohy said. "You scare me too much."

The irony in Toohy's voice went right over Rolfe's head and he smiled and looked mighty pleased with himself. "Hell, Toohy, I like you," he said. "I'm right partial to a man who knows his place."

"Me too," Toohy said. "It's good for a fellow to know the order of things."

"That fancy hat of yours, Toohy, I'll want that one day when I dress up to go sparking a gal," Rolfe said.

"Sure," Toohy said. "Come see me any time you feel like taking it."

For a second time Toohy's irony was lost on Rolfe. The young man slapped Toohy on the back and said, "Hey, you're all right. Have another drink."

"I don't mind if I do," Toohy said. His eyes were as cold as iced-over bullets.

An hour later Mathias Cobb stopped his surrey outside the saloon, a good-looking black mare in the traces. Toohy and Rolfe stepped outside and Cobb said, "Mr. Toohy, you ride alongside. Rolfe, tie your horse at the rear and come up on the seat beside me. Bring your rifle." Cobb held up some kind of machine part. It was made of brass and had a white dial about the size of a pocket watch. "And Mr. Toohy, did you leave this behind on my desk by any chance?"

Toohy shook his head. "No. What is it?"

"Some kind of steam pressure gauge, I think," Cobb said.

"I never saw it before now," Toohy said.

"Ah well, then a depositor must have left it behind. They leave all kinds of things, gloves, umbrellas, even baskets of groceries. I'm sure the owner will return for it."

When Toohy was mounted and Rolfe took his place in the surrey, Cobb said, "Well, Mr. Toohy, are you ready to embark on our great undertaking?"

"You can depend on me," Toohy said.

"He knows his place, Mr. Cobb," Rolfe said.

"Excellent. Let us be off then and turn a pestilent morass into money for all of us."

CHAPTER FORTY

There was a change in the light and a sinister amber glow to the sky that made Sam Flintlock uneasy. There was no wind, not a breath, and the swamp was oddly silent. Even the alligators were hushed as they drifted among the green stretches of water hyacinth and there were few birds. Flintlock was not a man of vivid imagination who hears a rustle in every bush, but he felt the presence of . . . something . . . an entity wild and untamed and of immense power.

"You can't paddle a canoe with broken ribs," Evangeline said. "And besides, you don't know the way. I'll come with you."

"Do you think I'm acting like a scared child afraid of boogermen?" Flintlock said.

"Oh, yeah, for sure," O'Hara said.

"No, I don't," Evangeline said. "O'Hara, Sam is right, there's something headed our way and I suspect it's a storm but Lady Esther will know for sure. Why are you so interested, Sam? I can assure you, I've lived through storms before."

"I want to know when it will hit," Flintlock said. "I mean, tomorrow? The next day? I need to know for sure."

O'Hara said, "What's cooking in that mind of yours, Sammy?"

"I can tell you better after I talk with Lady Esther."

"Sam, you're a man of mystery," O'Hara said.

"Help yourself to more coffee, Sam," Evangeline said. "Then I'll get changed and we'll go."

Flintlock poured coffee, grabbed a chunk of cornbread and followed O'Hara onto the deck. The morning sun was warm on his battered face and it felt good.

"All right, Sammy, what's on your mind?" O'Hara said. "You can tell me now that it won't scare the womenfolk."

Flintlock smiled. "You ever seen Evangeline scared?"

"No, I haven't. So out with it. Scare me."

"I want to use the storm as an ally," Flintlock said. "Hit Ritter while it's raging, the very time he'd least expect it."

"Hit him with what?" O'Hara said.

"You, me, the Atakapan if they're out of

mourning. It all depends on when the storm will hit."

"And you figure the old English lady will know?"

"She should. Lady Esther has lived in the swamp for fifty years. She must have lived through a heap of storms. Maybe she's seen enough to tell me when it will get here."

"Sammy, if we can fight in a storm, so can Ritter's boys," O'Hara said. "Have you thought about that?"

"Sure I have. But we'll have surprise on our side. Catch 'em with their pants down."

"You know, it's just crazy enough to work."

"It's all in the timing, Injun. All in the timing."

Evangeline, wearing a black bustle skirt, buckled corset and boots, stepped onto the deck. Her hair was pulled back in an elaborately pinned bun and she wore an English riding top hat.

"Evangeline, you look . . . beautiful," Flintlock said.

"Well, thank you, kind sir. When one is visiting a lady one tries to look one's best," Evangeline said. She looked over Flintlock's battered hat, stained shirt, baggy pants and scuffed boots and said, "Sam, I suppose you'll just have to do."

Lady Esther Carlisle's cabin lay on the bank of a shallow bayou between two massive cypress. She'd modeled the front of the cabin to look like the façade of an Elizabethan country house, her childhood home in miniature.

Only after a ritualized tea ceremony that included fish-paste sandwiches and sponge cake did Flintlock feel he could bring up the subject of the approaching storm. To his surprise Lady Esther answered the question he had not yet asked.

"Ah yes," she said. "It won't be a hurricane, derived from the Carib word *Hurican* that was the name for their God of Evil, don't you know? Now where was I? Oh yes, it won't be a hurricane but we can expect a powerful tropical storm. Judging by the sky, I'd say it will hit us the day after tomorrow in the early afternoon. More tea, Mr. Flintlock? It's Earl Grey, Lord Carlisle's favorite."

"Are you sure about the time, Lady Esther?" Evangeline said.

"Time for what, my dear?"

"The storm."

"Oh yes. It will be here the day after tomorrow in the afternoon. What was it

Lord Carlisle always said? 'Batten down the hatches, we're in for a blow.' Yes, that was it. He was so funny, was Lord Carlisle."

"Will you be all right during the storm, Lady Esther?" Evangeline said. "You're welcome to come to my cabin."

"No, I'll be just fine, my dear. And I have Ahmed here to protect me." The old woman touched her wrinkled forehead with her fingertips. "Oh dear, I'm afraid it's time for my nap. It was so nice of both of you to visit. We must do it again soon. Ahmed will see you out."

"I wish you'd let me do the paddling, Evangeline," Flintlock said. "Sitting back here trailing my fingertips in the water, well, it ain't manly."

"Shh . . . Sam, I'm thinking," Evangeline said.

"Thinking about what?"

"Now you finally told me what you're planning, we must get in touch with the Atakapan."

"Where are they?"

"They move around the swamp like ghosts. I've never sought them out before. And they are still mourning and will be even harder to find."

"Without the Indians I have no plan,"

Flintlock said. "O'Hara and me are good men in a scrap, but we ain't that good."

"I know that but . . . oh dear, Sam, we're in big trouble."

"Is it the Indians?"

"No, ahead of us, two men in the rowboat. Their names are Neville and Bayes. Do you recognize them?"

Flintlock looked and then he said, "Yeah, I recognize them. And you're right. We're in a heap of trouble."

The job was not finished, the contract not completed. Jonas Neville and Arch Bayes could not let that stand. The fact that the man called Flintlock was still alive was an affront to their reputation.

It was Neville's plan to go to Evangeline's cabin and wait for Flintlock there. But a longhaired man in a beaded shirt squatted on the deck armed with a rifle and swapping lead with him would hardly be good business. They wanted Flintlock's scalp, his only and no one else's.

"We stay close to the cabin and strike when Flintlock appears," Neville said.

"But what if he's gone?" Bayes said. "What then?"

"Then our wait will have been in vain and we must search for him in other places.

When we find him and kill him only then is our business with Brewster Ritter concluded."

Bayes glanced at the sky then said, "The swamp seems strange today. The light has changed and there are no birds."

"It must be the approach of fall. Let us concentrate on the job at hand, Mr. Bayes. Keep a wary eye open. I feel in the marrow of my bones that the ball is about to open."

Sam Flintlock looked over the side of the canoe. As far as he could tell the murky water in this part of the bayou, thick with hyacinth, was not deep, only several feet. But he couldn't be sure. Well, there was only one way to find out. He pulled his Colt, rose to his feet and jumped out. To his relief the level came to the middle of his thighs.

His eyes on the approaching rowboat, he waded to the prow of the canoe and pushed it back into deeper water, an effort that punished his broken ribs. "Evangeline," he said, "get the hell out of here."

"Sam, what are —"

"Git out of here, woman. Now go!"

Flintlock forced his way through the hyacinth then dipped under the surface until the water reached the top of his shoulders. He held the Colt high and waded farther into the cover of the hyacinth, praying that the muddy bed would not suddenly drop under his feet.

Of course, Neville and Bayes had seen Flintlock get into the water and they ignored the canoe and went after him. Like a mustached alligator, Flintlock kept his eyes just above the hyacinth, coming up now and again to breathe.

Only Bayes was rowing, slowly, using the oar like a paddle. He and Neville had lost sight of their prey, never a good thing in a swamp.

"You see him, Mr. Neville?" Bayes said.

"No, Mr. Bayes. He's somewhere among the vegetation. Stop rowing now. He can't stay in there forever."

Flintlock heard that exchange and considered his options. They were few. The water was surprisingly cold and he knew he'd have to move again or stiffen up. And at any time alligators could decide to poke their ugly noses into his business. He'd be up to his armpits in alligators and no way of finding the drain to the swamp.

"Flintlock, do you hear me?" Neville's voice. Flintlock kept silent. He had no wish to give his position away. "Stand up, Flintlock. Meet your end like a man instead of some cowering, cowardly creature."

Flintlock estimated the distance between him and the assassins. It was at least thirty feet, too far for him to get his work in with any hope of scoring hits.

He stayed where he was. There was pollen on the surface of the water and he badly wanted to sneeze. He figured he'd be the first man in the West to be killed because of a sneeze. He recalled that John Wesley Hardin had shot a man for snoring. Would he kill somebody for sneezing? Probably. And so would Jonas Neville.

A shot! A bullet probed the hyacinths about three feet from where Flintlock squatted in the water. Then another. He couldn't tell where that round went. And then a third . . . but that was not the boom of a Colt but the sharper sound of a shorter-barreled gun. Maybe a derringer!

Flintlock raised his head above the level of the hyacinth. Jonas Neville stood in the boat, looking off to his right. Bayes still sat but he too had turned, trying to determine the location of the shooter.

Flintlock took his chance. He waded forward and so far the bottom under his feet remained level. He closed the range . . . twenty feet . . . fifteen . . .

It was now or never.

Flintlock rose, water streaming off him in

sheets. He fired at Neville but hurried the shot. The man winced as Flintlock's bullet burned across the meat of his left shoulder. Neville raised his Remington and fired. But his shot went wild because as he triggered the revolver he took a hit. The derringer again. Damned good shooting. Bleeding from a wound on his right side, Neville sat down abruptly on the rowboat's seat, at least for the moment out of the fight.

But now Flintlock had Arch Bayes to contend with and the man was a steady hand with a gun. Flintlock dived underwater just as Bayes fired. The bullet stung him on the hip a split second before Flintlock's head and shoulders hit the mud at the bottom of the bayou. Blinded by a rising cloud of dirt, he swam forward. He had no idea how fast or far. But, his lungs bursting, he finally clawed for the surface. Here the water was deeper, up to the level of the thunderbird tattoo on his neck.

Standing on tiptoe, his hat gone, Flintlock shook water from his eyes. Where the hell was he? The answer was that he was about five feet behind the rowboat, but Neville had him spotted. The man two-handed his Remington to his eyes and he and Flintlock fired at the same time. Neville was close, very close. His bullet raised a V of water just an inch in front of Flintlock's face. But despite the handle of his Colt being slippery from pond scum, Flintlock scored a hit. The big .45 took Neville in the middle of his chest and the man went out of the boat backward and splashed into the water.

Now Flintlock cringed, expecting an aimed shot from Bayes. But when he turned the assassin was bent over on his seat, blood dripping onto his legs from a wound in his head.

Then Flintlock heard Evangeline's voice. "Sam, are you all right? Are you wounded?"

"I'm over here," he yelled. "I think I got shot up the ass."

"Bad place to get shot," Evangeline said. She paddled the canoe closer and Flintlock hoisted himself aboard. "We'd better find my hat," he said. And then, realizing how silly that sounded, he said, "Evangeline, you saved my life. I'm beholden to you."

The woman smiled. "The whole time I fired my derringer I wished it was a rifle."

"Two shots. Two hits. You did well," Flintlock said.

"Four shots, Sam. I always carry a couple of cartridges in a pocket. And I shot only Neville."

"What about Bayes?"

"He killed himself. When he saw that

Neville was dead, he put his revolver to his temple and pulled the trigger. I think that his grief over his friend's death was just too much to bear."

"Who the hell does that?" Flintlock said, genuinely confused.

"A man in love, Sam."

"With another man?"

"That would be the case, yes."

Flintlock was silent for a while, then said, "I always heard that fellers who were that way shot themselves. I guess it was true."

"You're all wet, Sam," Evangeline said. "So would you mind helping me get Neville's body out of the water?"

"Ah, let the alligators have him," Flintlock said.

"Sam, a storm is coming. Trust me, we don't want bodies floating around the bayou when the big winds hit."

"You mean bury him and the other one?"

"Yes, that's what I mean."

"I already told you where I got shot and I've got two busted ribs that are hurting me real bad," Flintlock said. "I can't bury anybody."

"O'Hara and I can do the burying," Evangeline said. "Now all we have to do is to get the body into the boat."

Flintlock sighed and jumped into the water.

"When we get back to the cabin I'll treat your wound," Evangeline said.

"No, you won't," Flintlock said. "I'll get O'Hara to do it."

Evangeline's smile was dazzling. "Why, Sam, I didn't know you were so shy."

"Well, I am," Flintlock said.

Then he disappeared as he stepped into a deep hole and the water closed over his head.

Chapter Forty-One

"You mean you're taking over?" Brewster Ritter said.

"No, not at all," Mathias Cobb said. "I'm here to assist you in any way I can. We must get this operation running smoothly again."

"I need a steam engineer," Ritter said.

"And you'll get one, two if you want," Cobb said. The smell of the fat man's sweat in the close confines of his tent was cloying and Ritter, a fastidious little man, pretended he had a cold and kept a handkerchief to his nose. "We must pull together, Mr. Ritter, and make our venture a profitable one for both of us."

"You said you spoke to the logger foreman earlier," Ritter said.

"Yes, I did, and he and the others have accepted my offer of a fifty-dollar bonus every time a logger steps into the swamp. Cutting resumes again tomorrow and it seems that the fates are smiling on us, Mr.

Ritter. The weather is perfect, just perfect, for logging. No wind, cool temperatures, we can make great strides in the next few weeks."

"I lost my engineer, so we still don't have the steam saws set up to buck the cypress logs," Ritter said.

"Just pile them up, Mr. Ritter. When the engineer gets here the bucking will go very quickly."

"When will I have the engineer? I need those saws working. We can't pile logs forever. We need to move the rough-sawn timber to Budville."

"Soon, my dear fellow. Very soon," Cobb said. "Now, a glass of brandy for you?"

"No. I'll go talk with the loggers and see if their mood is as cooperative as you say it is."

"Money talks better than you do, Mr. Ritter. But if you must speak with the hired help then go right ahead. No one is stopping you."

After Ritter left, Cobb turned to Val Rolfe and said, "The man is a spineless fool."

Rolfe nodded. "He sure wants an engineer to set up his saws."

"I've already made arrangement for an engineer, a man named Claypoole. He'll be here in a week or two." Cobb smiled.

"Unfortunately, by then Mr. Ritter will be no longer with us."

"I'll see to that," Rolfe said, grinning.

"I know you will," Cobb said. "Now, to more pleasant things. Are all the whores gone or are there still one or two left?"

"I don't know, Mr. Cobb, but I'll find out for you."

"Good. I'm in the mood for some feminine company tonight."

"He thinks he's getting the lion's share of the timber money, but he's not," Brewster Ritter said. "Once the trees are cut and on flat cars headed north, Mr. Cobb and I will have a little talk."

Bonifaunt Toohy said, "How do you plan to cut him out of the profits?"

"I don't know quite yet. But I'll come up with something, lay to that."

"Killing him is always an option," Toohy said.

"Yes, but it has implications. Whoever takes over the bank will expect a return on his investment."

"Unless you take it over," Toohy said.

"How would I do that?"

"You get Cobb to sign over a deed of ownership."

"He'd never do that."

"He might be glad to if somebody had a bowie knife to his balls. He loves whores, you know. In fact, young women in general."

Ritter smiled. "And who will hold the knife?"

"Jonas Neville and Arch Bayes spring to mind, if they haven't pulled out by then. If they have, I'll do it myself."

"Force him to sign the bank over to me, and after he does . . ."

"He disappears into the swamp."

"Damn it all, Bon, it just might work," Ritter said.

"It will work," Toohy said. "But I'll expect my share of the money."

"Pull this off and you'll get it," Ritter said. "I'll make sure you won't lose by it. How would you like to manage a bank? At a very large salary, of course."

"That would set just fine by me. I'll swap these duds for broadcloth any time."

"You needn't do the dirty work yourself, Bon," Ritter said. "Round up Neville and the other feller and see if you can convince them to stay until both the cypress and Mathias Cobb are cut."

"I didn't see them around today, but I'll find them."

"Maybe they went into the swamp after Flintlock," Ritter said.

"Could be. If that's the case they'll be back soon. It will be dark in an hour."

"Tell them that they don't really have to geld Cobb, just threaten him with it until he signs over the deed." Ritter smiled. "Of course, if they really want to cut him, then they can go right ahead — but only after he signs on the dotted line."

Like a morning fog lifting from a forest trail, Bonifaunt Toohy now began to see his future path more clearly. The way was so simple it was laughable. All he had to do was wait until all the cypress was cut, then arrange a little accident for Ritter. With him out of the way he could deal with Cobb, perhaps with violence, more likely with blackmail. There were a lot of killings he could pin on the fat man and he'd cave to Toohy's demands, especially since he was already under suspicion for ordering the Stothard shooting. Either way a huge chunk of the profits would be Toohy's, a man born to wear broadcloth as ever was.

It was time for dinner, but Toohy was too excited to eat. What he needed was a bottle and a quiet hour to think and refine his plans. As he walked to his tent he was amazed how quiet was the evening and how soft the wind. Good omens, Toohy told himself, surely indicating bigger and better things to come.

Bonifaunt Toohy was a happy man.

CHAPTER FORTY-TWO: STORM

A week before Bonifaunt Toohy made his plans, water vapor from the warm Atlantic Ocean condensed into clouds and released its heat into the air. The warm air rose and was absorbed by a vast column of clouds, building them higher and higher. Winds blowing off the African coast moved the clouds around a center, like water circling a drain. The whirling disturbance absorbed more clouds and within a couple of days developed into a cluster of violent thunderstorms. As the storms grew higher and wider the air at the top of the columns became cool and unstable and the clouds spun faster, driven by a wind that quickly reached the speed of a highballing steam locomotive.

When the wind speeds reached seventy-four miles an hour they spawned a tropical cyclone, fifty thousand feet high and a hundred and twenty-five miles across. The trade winds pushed the storm westward into the Gulf of Mexico and like a ravenous beast it readied itself to savage southeast Texas . . .

CHAPTER FORTY-THREE

The indignities heaped on Sam Flintlock's posterior by Evangeline's salves and stinging lotions were too much to bear, and when she finally slapped his butt and told him to pull up his pants Flintlock was in a thoroughly bad mood.

Earlier, Evangeline and O'Hara had buried the bodies of the two dead men on a tree island, a task that took them several hours to complete. Her face spattered with mud, her clothes a mess, when Evangeline returned to the cabin she had O'Hara place her copper bathtub in front of the fire and asked him to fill it with hot swamp water, the cleanest he could find. She then banished the two men to the deck and an hour later, dressed in a long cotton robe, she told Flintlock that it was now time to treat his misery. Despite his many and loud objections, the job was done and now he seethed over his own weakness at being so easily dominated by a woman.

O'Hara was notified, just as soon as Flintlock regained his pants and at least some of his dignity. "Say anything, Injun, and I'll plug you for sure."

O'Hara shook his head and said with a straight face. "Me? I won't say a word. I don't want you to be the butt of my jokes, Sammy. It would make me feel like a real ass."

Flintlock scowled and Evangeline suppressed a smile, but the moment passed because their attention was directed at the canoe that parted the dark curtain of the night and came toward them.

The two Atakapan warriors who moored their canoe and then stepped on deck were fine, big fellows wearing deerskin breechcloths and Apache-style leggings to their knees. One carried a bow, the other Flintlock's Winchester. Both their faces were painted for war with vertical stripes of black and white, the red paint of mourning gone.

The older man with the bow came right to the point. "When do we make war again?"

"Coffee?" Evangeline said.

The Indian nodded and Flintlock said, "Tomorrow, during the storm."

"Fighting in big wind no good." He made a fluttering motion with his hand. "Arrows get blown away. Men get blown away."

"It's the only chance we have to save the trees," Flintlock said.

The Indian stared hard at the thunderbird on Flintlock's throat and said, "Will you fight?"

"I will fight tomorrow," Flintlock said. "During the storm."

The Indian shook his head. "You are very foolish."

"I am not afraid of a big wind. I am a warrior, not an old woman."

The implied insult hit home, and the Indian stiffened. "You are not wise."

"Tomorrow is a time to be brave, not wise. We face a mighty enemy and the old women must stay home."

"Easy there, Sammy," O'Hara said. "You're overdoing it and you're not making any friends."

The younger Atakapan said to O'Hara, "You are part Indian and you gave me this fine rifle. Will you be brave tomorrow?"

"I will fight in the whirlwind," O'Hara said. He pointed at Flintlock's throat. "The thunderbird brings the lightning and stirs the storm. Flintlock has powerful medicine and the winds will blow in our favor."

"Coffee," Evangeline said. She passed a cup to both Indians and said, "Will the Atakapan fight in the storm?"

"We will talk about this thing," the older Indian said. He stepped toward a dark corner of the deck and motioned the younger man to follow.

As though to fill in the silence, Evangeline said, "Sam, are you having any pain?"

"From where?" Flintlock said, suspicion in his tone.

"Not from your derrière —"

"My what?"

"She means your ass, Sammy," O'Hara said.

Flintlock angled a hard look at O'Hara and said, "My ribs hurt like hell."

"That is what I was afraid of," Evangeline said. "Are you sure you want to get into a fight tomorrow? Perhaps you should wait until after the storm."

"As it is we'll be outnumbered and outgunned," Flintlock said. "The storm is the only edge we have, attacking while Ritter least expects it." He glanced at the Indians huddled in the corner. "Of course, right now it all depends on how the Atakapan state their intentions."

"They'll fight," Evangeline said.

"How do you know?" Flintlock said.

"I just know."

"I hope you're right. Those two boys are

doing a heap of cussin' and discussin'. They don't consider things like Christian folks."

But no sooner did the words leave Flintlock's mouth than the Indians stepped out of the shadows and the older one said, "We have talked about the coming battle and this is what I have to say. The Atakapan are few and getting fewer. We already have grieving widows and crying orphans and by tomorrow there will be more when the moon rises after the storm. This, we have talked about."

"And your decision?" Flintlock said, dreading the answer.

"Ten warriors, young men who have not yet taken a wife, will answer your call," the Indian said. "They will come here in the morning before the storm. One of them" — he laid his hand on the shoulder of the younger man — "will be my son. You may call him Puma, because he is brave, strong and stealthy in the darkness."

Flintlock stuck out his hand. "Glad to have you with us, Puma."

The Indian took it then said, "Until tomorrow. I will call you Thunderbird Man."

"Sets just fine with me," Flintlock said.

"You cried out in your sleep, Sam."

Evangeline stood beside Flintlock's cot.

She wore a shimmering silk nightdress and in the darkness she burned like a candle flame.

Flintlock sat up, his face troubled. "I don't feel right, Evangeline. I think maybe I'm sick."

"What do you feel, Sam?"

"A kind of sickness in my belly, and I dreamed I couldn't breathe, like I had an anvil on my chest. And then I was running somewhere, running through trees, being chased by . . . I don't know what was chasing me."

"You're not sick, Sam. You're afraid."

"Woman, I don't ever get scared."

"But you are now and you just don't recognize it as fear."

As though trying to clear his thoughts, Flintlock shook his head and said, "Could that be what it is? Is it why I feel sick to my stomach, like I'm going to throw up?"

"Being scared is nothing to be ashamed of, Sam."

"Suppose come the dawn I turn yellow and I'm afraid to leave my cot?"

"You won't be, Sam. You'll be scared tomorrow but you will overcome your fear because that's what brave men do."

Evangeline untied the ribbon at her neck and let the silk gown slide from her body and pool at her feet. As beautiful and graceful as a Greek marble, she took Flintlock's hand and said, "Come, Sam, you will sleep with me. For tonight at least I will take away all your fears."

Outside on the deck O'Hara pulled his blankets to his chin and stared into the silent darkness of the brooding swamp.

CHAPTER FORTY-FOUR

The whores had all gone and Mathias Cobb was a disappointed man.

He tried to take solace in the black rum that Ritter had given him, found it disgusting, and decided to take a short walk around the compound before retiring for the night.

Cobb slipped a .38 self-cocker into the pocket of his broadcloth coat and stepped out of his tent into darkness. There was no wind and the swamp, usually full of night sounds, was strangely quiet. Lamps glowed in the tents of the loggers and now and then a man's voice raised in a laugh. Somewhere a guitar picked out the melody of "Juanita" and a man crooned its simple tale of unrequited love.

Cobb passed a logger who looked at him and then looked again, a well-dressed man with a huge belly and waddling gait out of place among a community of lean loggers and laborers.

"I say, my man," Cobb said. "Stop a moment."

Catching the ring of authority in the fat man's command, the logger stopped and knuckled his forehead. "What can I do for you, mister?" he said.

"What's your name?" Cobb said.

"Grover Shaw."

"And what do you do around here?"

"I'm a bucksawyer. Been a bucksawyer all my life, man and boy." Then, taking Cobb for a tenderfoot, "I cut the cypress logs to size."

"Then, my fine fellow, you'll be glad when the steam saws are set up, will you not?"

"Make my life easier," Shaw said. Then, a puzzled look on his grizzled face, "Who are you, mister?"

"My name is Mathias Cobb. I'm taking over from Mr. Ritter as overseer of this enterprise."

"Well, I'm surprised. But it's nice to meet you, Mr. Cobb."

"Don't worry, I plan to make changes around here," Cobb said. "And I'll make sure that there will be plenty of whores and whiskey for you boys, lay to that."

"Well, I don't drink and I'm a married man," Shaw said. "But some of the others will appreciate that, I'm sure."

Cobb smiled. "Well, carry on with your excellent work, Mr. Shaw."

You sanctimonious, prune-juice-drinking little puke.

His mood little improved by his encounter with Shaw, Cobb decided to seek out Ritter and reassert his authority. He stepped to Ritter's tent and from outside said, "Brewster. Will you walk with me?" Ritter opened the flap. He stuck out his head and cringed when he saw Cobb. "Will you walk with me, Brewster?" the fat man said again.

"Of course. Be delighted," Ritter said. He emerged from the tent wearing shirt, pants and boots. "Wait, I'd better get my gun," he said.

"No need, Brewster," Cobb said. "I have a self-cocker in my pocket."

Ritter stood beside the fat man. "Where do you want to walk, Mathias?" he said.

"Perhaps down by the swamp, but first I must clear up a little misunderstanding. I am your superior and you must call me Mr. Cobb."

"But you called me Brewster. I thought —"

"You thought wrongly," Cobb said. "You are my inferior and therefore I may call you by your given name. But you must always say Mr. Cobb. Is that understood?"

Ritter was a simmering cauldron of suppressed rage, but he managed to say, "It's understood."

"Excellent," Cobb said. "Then we are perfect friends again. Now, shall we promenade and enjoy this wonderful evening?"

"Some of the loggers say a storm is brewing," Ritter said.

"Nonsense," Cobb said. "I haven't lived in Texas for very long, but I assure you I know our great state's weather. It's going to be balmy, Brewster, balmy. My, how quiet the swamp is tonight, and how dark. I can't even see my cypress."

"Don't get too close to the water's edge," Ritter said. "There are always alligators around."

"Is that right?" Cobb said. He reached into his pocket and pulled out his .38. "Perhaps I'll get a chance to take a pot at one."

Ritter said, "Fire a shot this late and you'll alarm the whole camp."

"It's good for the men. Keep them on their toes." Then, his eyes searching the swamp, he said, "Why did you send the whores away?"

"I didn't. They left because they thought it was getting too dangerous around here."

"Another symptom of your gross mismanagement, Brewster. Unlike rats, whores never desert a sinking ship. They stay where the money is to the bitter end. Hola! What is that?"

"Where?" Ritter said, seething.

"Over there among those floating plants."

"It's a log caught up in the hyacinth."

Cobb looked down at the soggy ground under his feet then took a couple of steps closer to the water. "I'll be damned if it is," he said. "That's an alligator."

"Are you sure?" Ritter said.

"Of course I'm sure. Unlike you, Brewster, I'm always sure." He raised his revolver to eye level. "Watch him kick!"

So intent was Cobb on his prey that he never saw Basilisk's head rise from the water. From a standing start, over a distance of thirty feet, an alligator can outrun a horse and when Basilisk, who weighed half a ton, hit Cobb his speed was twenty miles an hour. His bite tore the fat man's left leg off just above the knee and sent him sprawling.

A short silence . . . Cobb in deep shock . . . feeling no pain . . . and then shrill screams that ripped apart the fabric of the night.

Ritter rushed to the fallen man, grabbed the shoulders of his coat and tried to haul him onto drier ground. But Cobb was a fat man and so heavy that Ritter could not budge him.

Basilisk drifted a few yards out, his blind, reptilian eyes above water. Ritter ignored him, still hauling on the shrieking Cobb's broadcloth coat. Blood from the man's severed leg spurted everywhere and Ritter's hands and face were scarlet. Bonifaunt Toohy and several miners arrived and pulled Cobb back from the edge of the swamp. Toohy sidestepped the squealing banker and stepped to the water's edge. He cut loose with his Colt, but Basilisk quickly submerged and all Toohy's bullets did was churn the water.

Cobb was in mortal agony and his frantic shrieks scraped across the night like fingernails on chalkboard. "A doctor!" he yelled. "Get me a doctor."

The ground where Cobb lay glistened with blood and two inches of white bone protruded from the ragged stump of his thigh. The man's eyes were wide from pain and fear and his mouth was a scarlet O in his ashen face as he tried to bear the unbearable.

Bonifaunt Toohy reloaded his Colt slowly as he eyed the screaming fat man. The damned fool had allowed himself to get attacked by an alligator and had ruined all of

Toohy's carefully laid plans. He felt no emotion but anger as he raised the Colt and fired a bullet into the center of the O of Cobb's mouth.

"I wouldn't wish that death on any man," Brewster Ritter said. He passed Toohy a glass of rum. "At least you ended it for him."

"Where does Cobb's death leave you?" Toohy said.

"I haven't thought about it yet."

"You'd better. Now he's dead, who owns the bank?"

"There must be shareholders," Ritter said. "Tomorrow I'll ride into Budville and talk to the bank manager."

"What about the cypress?"

"We continue with the cutting. There's a fortune at stake here. But we need money to keep the loggers happy."

"Surely the shareholders will see reason," Toohy said.

"They should, if there are any. Maybe Cobb thought he'd never die."

"Son of a bitch died like a dog," Toohy said. "And he lived like a dog. My guess is that there are shareholders. And that he cheated and swindled them as he did everybody else. They may be so glad to see Cobb go they'll give you anything you want."

"I hope that's the case."

"You'll find out tomorrow," Toohy said. "The loggers would never have worked for Cobb anyhow. One of the foremen told me he'd blow the whistle if they saw a fat man in the woods. It was a sign that there would be three accidents in a row."

Ritter smiled. "Didn't bode well for Cobb, did it?" Then, "What are the loggers saying about the storm?"

"What storm?"

"Some of them say a big blow is coming."

"I just told you that they're a superstitious bunch, even worse than mariners. Judging by the sky, the weather will remain fair and we can cut a lot of trees. Hey, I wonder where Cobb's leg is?"

"In the gator's belly, I expect," Ritter said.

"Pity. We could have buried it with the rest of him."

As Bonifaunt Toohy walked back to his tent he stopped in midstride. Cobb had brought luggage with him. Hell, he may have a carpetbag stuffed with money. Shocked at the manner of the fat man's death Ritter hadn't thought of that yet, but he would.

A lamp still burned inside Cobb's tent. After a quick look to make sure no one was watching him, Toohy ducked under the flap.

To make himself less visible, he lowered the wick on the lamp and then looked around him. There were not one, but two carpetbags, and neither looked like it had been opened since Cobb's arrival. Toohy uncorked the rum bottle, took a swig and then laid the first bag on the cot. The tent flapped a little in a growing breeze, but he thought little of it. The bag was filled with clothing and a leather shaving set, razor, soap and brush. A silver-backed hairbrush, a jar of pomade, a bottle of lavender water and, wrapped in an oily rag, a Remington derringer. Toohy slipped the gun into his pocket and then tossed the bag away.

The second carpetbag was an even greater disappointment. Cobb had stuffed it with color-tinted photographs of near-naked women, a pair of light wrist shackles, a dog whip and a hundred dollars in single bills, obviously to pay his whores. As he had with the derringer, Toohy stuffed the money into his pocket then thumbed through the pictures. Finally he shoved them into the bag, tossed it into a corner of the tent and stepped outside into rain.

CHAPTER FORTY-FIVE

"It's raining and the wind has picked up," O'Hara said as Flintlock carried his morning coffee onto the deck. "Sleep well?"

Flintlock took time to build and light a cigarette, then, "She was being kind. That was all."

"I didn't ask about that," O'Hara said.

"I had a bad dream and I was scared about today," Flintlock said. "Evangeline let me sleep with her." Flintlock gave a slight smile. "Well, I slept. Evangeline doesn't sleep. Strange sky."

O'Hara nodded. "The clouds are building."

"And the wind," Flintlock said.

"Are you still scared about today?"

"Yeah. You?"

"I'm not looking forward to it. I know that is not the warrior's way, but it's how I feel."

"What can we expect, O'Hara?"

"A shooting scrape in wind and rain.

Thunder and lightning too."

"Good coffee," Flintlock said. "Evangeline made it. I heard her."

"When the fight comes, you'll be ready, Sammy."

"So will you."

O'Hara nodded. "How's the coffee?"

"Like I said, it's good."

"Then I'll get me a cup."

After O'Hara went inside Flintlock built another cigarette and because of the rising wind had trouble lighting it. The rain was light, a promise of things to come, just a faint hiss among the hyacinth. The sky was as gray as a shotgun barrel, the clouds banding in great sweeping arcs. The two canoes moored to the deck bobbed in the restless water.

Still troubled by his fears of the night, Flintlock stuck out his right hand and spread the fingers. His hand was steady with no sign of tremor and he was much relieved.

Evangeline came onto the deck with O'Hara. "Angry sky," she said.

"And getting angrier," Flintlock said.

"When do we go?" Evangeline said.

Flintlock started to say, "You're not —" but bit off the words mid-sentence. He knew telling Evangeline what she could and couldn't do was an impossible task, like trying to sweep sunshine off the front porch. "When the Atakapan get here," he said.

"It will be soon," Evangeline said. "The storm is coming in faster than we thought. I'll get myself ready."

After Evangeline left Flintlock rubbed his stubby chin. "Maybe I should shave," he said. "Make a better-looking corpse if I get shot."

"Sammy, there's nothing anybody could do that would make your corpse look better," O'Hara said. "But if you stop a bullet I'll shave you before we plant you."

Flintlock angled a look at O'Hara. "Do you know something I don't, Injun? Has Evangeline seen something in her crystal ball?"

"She doesn't have a crystal ball, Sammy. And no, she hasn't seen anything and neither have I. Have you been talking with old Barnabas again?"

"No, I haven't seen him in a while. He keeps busy."

"You'll come through this fight like Wild Bill Hickok, trust me." O'Hara said.

"Wild Bill got shot in the back," Flintlock said.

"Yeah, and he made a sight prettier corpse than you ever will."

"O'Hara, when this is over and if I'm still

alive, remind me to put a bullet in you."

"I sure will, Sam."

Flintlock shook his head and said, "I've never been scared before and I've been in some mighty bad shooting scrapes. What the hell is wrong with me?"

"Only one thing wrong with you, Sam. You're in love with Evangeline, so this time you've got something to lose."

Flintlock was silent for long moments, staring at the timber boards between his feet. "You're right," he said.

O'Hara nodded. "I know I'm right."

"What can I do about it?"

"There's nothing you can do, Sammy. Being in love is a natural fact that you can't change."

"Now I know what ails me I feel better," Flintlock said. "For a while there I thought I'd turned yellow."

"You're not the brightest of men, Sam, but I'm sure in the end you would have worked it out for yourself."

The storm grew in intensity as the morning progressed. Wind and rain increased and thunder rumbled. By noon the wind shrieked and debris cartwheeled though the swamp. Agitated water splashed over the cabin deck and the canoes danced and banged into one another. The black sky thundered and lightning scrawled across the clouds like the signature of a demented god.

Through this maelstrom, war paint running in blue, red and yellow streaks down their bronzed faces and onto their naked necks and chests, came the Atakapan, ten warriors in a pair of dugout canoes.

When Puma stepped onto the deck the morning was as dark as evening from the pall of gloom that lay over the torn and tattered swamp. Even the mighty cypress bowed their heads to the ferocity of the tempest and the alligators had fled to deeper water. Only the fish and the frogs remained.

There was little talk, the wind tearing words, half-formed, from every mouth. Evangeline appeared dressed for war, her hair pulled back with a red ribbon. She wore black tights, boots, boned leather corset, a plain white shirt and two holstered Colts in crossed cartridge belts clung close to her hips. Flintlock thought her magnificent, a warrior princess in the rain.

Flintlock motioned to the bucking canoes and after a lot of cussing and a few false starts he and the others managed to board. The Atakapan hid amused grins behind their hands.

CHAPTER FORTY-SIX

On what was destined to be the last day of his life Bonifaunt Toohy woke to a crash of thunder and the steam locomotive hiss of torrential rain. Stunned, he stared at the ridge of his wildly flapping tent but a split second later he saw only a black, lightning-scarred sky as the tent fluttered skyward like an injured bird.

Toohy sprang out of his cot and managed to grab his pants as they sailed off with his shirt in the wake of the tent. As he tugged on his boots he was aware of frantic horses galloping back and forth, loggers yelling to one another as they sought any kind of shelter and from somewhere far off Brewster Ritter shrieking orders to his men that nobody heeded.

Buckling on his gunbelt, Toohy looked around at the devastation wrought by the storm. Ritter's Landing was flattened. Every inch of canvas had blown away, including the big mess tent, and lay scattered across the bayou like stranded whales. Toohy stood stock still as wild-eyed horses galloped past and frightened loggers followed them, seeking drier ground. The loggers ignored Toohy's calls to stop. Panic is the bastard child of fear and, lashed mercilessly by wind and rain, deafened by thunder and harried by lightning, they ran headlong from the swamp, away from the proximity of the Gulf, toward . . . toward what they didn't know. In battle, panicked men don't think, they just run and run until they can't run any longer. And so it was with the loggers as they tried to escape a ruthless and infinitely more powerful enemy.

Ritter's hired guns were steadier. Val Rolfe and four others clustered around their boss as he staggered toward Toohy, buffeted by the howling wind. Ritter yelled something to Toohy that he didn't understand. Rain fell in sheets, thunder boomed and a searing bolt of lightning blasted just a few feet from where Ritter and his men stood. The two great steam saws, each longer and taller than a brewery wagon, were hit. For several seconds they sparked and bled thick black smoke as a billion volts of electricity, nine times hotter than the surface of the sun, blasted their insides and huge gearwheels.

Then as fast as it happened it was over. Ritter and two of his men lay sprawled on the ground and Toohy walked toward them, his body bent against the wind.

Val Rolfe stepped in Toohy's direction, his hand on his gun. Like everyone else he was hatless, the wind a notorious thief of headwear. "Toohy!" he yelled. "Stay the hell where you are!"

The young gunman's words were lost in the roar of thunder and the wail of the wind. But then Rolfe stopped in his tracks and his face took on an expression of surprise. A moment later his surprise gave way to shock. He lifted up on his toes and the wind slammed him facedown into the dirt. Two arrows protruded from his back.

Brewster Ritter was on his hands and knees, the side of his face exposed to the lightning bolt was bright red. He turned his head as Rolfe thumped beside him, then screamed when he saw the arrows sticking out of the gunman's back.

Toohy drew his revolver and looked around for a target. But the wind and rain and constantly moving water oak and swamp privet at the edge of the morass made it a difficult task. An arrow thudded into the ground at Toohy's feet and he snapped off a fast shot at a glimpse of brown skin among the vegetation. He didn't know if he'd scored a hit or not. Ritter and his surviving gunmen were shooting at phantoms and one of the gunmen went down as a rifle roared from somewhere within the swamp.

Showing remarkable skill and a cool head, a gray-haired gunman backed away from the stricken camp, firing alternate shots from two Colts. Pounded by rain and abused by the wind, he managed to keep his feet and sustain a steady fire.

Flintlock, walking through a whirlwind of torn leaves and plant debris, appeared on the road behind the skilled draw fighter.

Toohy roared, "Behind you!" He fired at Flintlock. A miss.

The gunman swung to his left, saw Flintlock and worked his Colts. The hammers clicked on spent rounds. A stricken expression on his face, the man yelled, "Toohy!"

Bonifaunt Toohy and Flintlock fired at the same time.

Unnerved by the gunman's shout, Toohy hurried his shot and made his second miss of the day. Flintlock, not an elite draw fighter but a first-rate bounty hunter, had taught himself to be steady and unhurried in a fight. He fired. His bullet hit the hammer of Toohy's Colt, severed the top joint of the man's right thumb and then what was left of the fragmented .45 struck the right side of his chest like a charge of buckshot. The fragments lacked velocity and the wound was not severe — but the loss of Toohy's thumb was.

The gunman turned away, bent over his cradled right hand, just as the gray-haired man fired at Flintlock. At a distance of ten yards Flintlock returned fire. But the wild, wind-blasted conditions were not favorable for accurate shooting and neither man did any execution. Thumbing his Colt, Flintlock walked forward, closing the distance. He took a hit high on the right shoulder and another bullet nicked his gun arm, but he fired at a distance of fifteen feet and scored a center chest hit, fired again as the Colt recoiled and missed. But his first shot had been effective and the gray-haired man fell without a whimper.

Out of the fight, Bonifaunt Toohy transferred his Colt to his left hand and stumbled along the edge of the swamp. Behind him what had been a thriving camp of two hundred souls was now a deserted wasteland, but agonized shrieks and screams of terror carried in the wind. Toohy guessed that the Indians were killing the scattered loggers and laborers, settling old scores.

Pelted by rain, whipped by tossing branches, Toohy's plan was to loop around the scene of slaughter, reach dry land and head for Budville, where he could find a doctor. He had no doubt that his draw fighter days were over. He could train his left hand, but it would never be as fast and accurate. As for his plans of wealth, something might still be salvaged. He just needed to get away from the death and dying and take time to think. But it was Bonifaunt Toohy's great misfortune that he met Evangeline in the storm.

She stood talking to an Indian, her face concerned. Toohy supposed the man was some kind of chief and she was telling him to end the slaughter of the mostly unarmed loggers. The rain had soaked her shirt and her golden skin glowed under the wet fabric. Toohy stopped, watching her, and wondered if he could take Evangeline with him. The pain in his thumb was so great, the shock of a battle lost to a saddle tramp and a few savages, that Toohy wasn't thinking straight. Now all he could think about was taking the woman.

Firing the Colt in his left hand he could kill the Indian and then drag the woman with him. No one could track them in a roaring, flashing storm that threated to tear the world apart.

Toohy took a step toward Evangeline and Puma, and a twig cracked under his boot. He stopped, staring at the woman, his gun coming up.

Evangeline saw only a man with a gun and instantly realized the danger he represented. She drew both her Colts and in the space of a single hell-firing moment hammered four shots into Toohy.

Hit hard, the man dropped to his knees. And his eyes locked on Evangeline.

"You . . ." he said. "No, not you . . . never you . . ."

He died with a look of wonderment on his face.

CHAPTER FORTY-SEVEN

"Twenty-eight loggers and laboring men are dead," Sam Flintlock said. "There were no wounded. As far as I can tell all eight of Ritter's hired guns are dead. On our side an Indian was killed when a cypress log fell on him and three more have bullet wounds."

"What about Ritter?" O'Hara said.

"I don't know. He may have died in the storm." Flintlock met O'Hara's eyes. "You saved lives today."

"I tried to stop the Atakapan from killing unarmed or injured men and saved a few loggers, but whether or not they eventually survived I don't know. The Indians wanted to kill them for cutting the cypress."

Flintlock said, "Evangeline, you did —"

"I know what I did, Sam. I killed a man. I had no choice."

"It was Toohy who gave you no choice."

"Toohy did what he had to do, and so did I," Evangeline said.

Flintlock stepped to the window and stared into the day's dying light. "The moon is coming up," he said. "There's a lot of wreckage scattered around the swamp, but all the trees are still standing."

"It will be cleared," Evangeline said.

"And the flying machine."

"Yes. That too."

Evangeline sat in a robe by the fire, her long, shapely legs bared. She had a glass of whiskey in her hand that glowed amber in the light. O'Hara, who seemed incapable of sitting, squatted on the floor, but Flintlock kept up his restless pacing. Finally he built a cigarette and stepped outside. The storm had passed but the swamp was still quiet. As he lit his smoke an alligator glided past, just inches away.

Old Barnabas sat on the edge of the deck. He'd taken off his boots and dangled his feet in the water. His top hat and goggles lay beside him and in his hands he held a book. Without turning his head he said, "This book is called *Twenty Thousand Leagues Under the Sea* written by a feller by the name of Jules Verne. But since it's all in French I can't read a word of it."

"Then why do you have it?" Flintlock said.

"I liked the title, though I don't know what the hell leagues are." Barnabas tossed the book into the swamp, where it instantly caught fire and burned. "Time you was moving on, Sam. You got things to do, places to see. Catch up to your ma over here to the Arizony Territory."

"I know."

"The woman will keep you here, won't she, Sam?"

"Maybe. I don't know."

"Hell, boy, you're ugly enough to clabber a mud hole. Why would a right handsome woman like that want you?"

"For the first time in your life, and death, you may be right, Barnabas," Flintlock said. "Why would she want me?"

"Now you're talking sense, boy." Barnabas laced up his boots, put on his hat and goggles and rose to his feet. "It was bad here today, Sam, huh? Too many dead men."

"You know it."

"Then git out of here. You go find your ma, boy, and get your rightful name." Barnabas smiled. "The fat man that got et by the crocodile, I tried to warn him, left a busted steam valve in his office. But he ignored it."

"Not much of a warning, Barnabas," Flintlock said.

"It was warning enough, boy. See you in Arizony."

Barnabas vanished into moonlight. Flintlock flicked his sparking cigarette butt into the swamp and stepped into the cabin.

"Sam, who were you talking to out there?" Evangeline said.

"Myself," Flintlock said. Then, "O'Hara, can you leave us for just a spell?"

"Sure thing," O'Hara said. He rose to his feet but stepped to the table and poured whiskey into a glass. "Here, Sammy, take this," he said. "You may need it."

After O'Hara left, Flintlock took the seat opposite Evangeline. "I have something to say to you," he said. He took a swig of whiskey, then, "I know my face would clabber a mud hole, but —"

"You have a fine, strong face, Sam," Evangeline said. She rose and got herself another drink. When she sat again she said, "I know what you want to say to me, Sam."

"Has that damned Injun been talking out of turn again?" Flintlock said.

Evangeline smiled. "Sam, don't you think a woman knows when a man is in love with her?" Flintlock made no answer to that and she said, "You're a brave, loyal and honest man."

"Fairly honest," Flintlock said. "I have lapses."

"And I wouldn't hurt you for the world," Evangeline said.

"But you don't love me," Flintlock said.

"No, I don't. Even if I did it wouldn't make any difference. I'm already married, Sam."

That last was a knife twisting in Flintlock's heart. "Who?"

"Cornelius. We've been married for a long time."

"But —"

"We don't live together?"

"Yes. That."

"We live separate lives, Cornelius and I. He has his work and I have mine. But we love one another, Sam. We love each other deeply."

Flintlock said, "So I don't fit in anywhere, do I?"

"You can fit in as a friend, Sam. To both of us."

"It's strange, but I've never loved a woman before," Flintlock said. "Now I feel . . . I don't know, I guess I feel empty. It seems that the bottom has fallen out of my life and now there's nothing left."

"I'm so sorry, Sam," Evangeline said. "I wish I could help you feel better."

Flintlock managed a wan smile. "I think maybe time will take care of that. I don't want you to feel bad, Evangeline. It's not your fault, it's mine for being so damned stupid."

"Sam, no one who loves can be completely unhappy. Even love unreturned has its rewards."

Flintlock's smile was more genuine. "Do you think I'll ever find them? Those rewards, I mean."

"I'm sure you will," Evangeline said.

O'Hara tapped on the door and said loudly, "Can I come in?"

"Yeah, come in," Flintlock said.

O'Hara stepped inside and said, "I'm not spoiling anything, am I?"

"Not a thing," Flintlock said.

"I hate to talk this way, but a man's body just drifted past the cabin. Sam, we have to get those dead men buried."

"I know. We can't leave white men to the buzzards," Flintlock said.

"I'll talk to the Atakapan and the swamp people," Evangeline said. "There ought to be enough of us to bury them decent."

"It wasn't Ritter," O'Hara said. "I'd sure like to know what happened to him."

"Me too," Flintlock said.

He glanced at Evangeline, seeking her eyes, but she stared fixedly into the fire. What had passed between them had already set out on the long road to the land of faded memories.

CHAPTER FORTY-EIGHT

Sam Flintlock and O'Hara spent the next two weeks helping to bury the dead and remove debris from the swamp. At least fifty people showed up to assist with the work, half of them middle-aged Louisiana couples living their last adventure. Cornelius was still in Washington and took no part in the cleanup.

And then it was time to leave.

Flintlock wanted to get it over quickly and Evangeline seemed to understand. She kissed O'Hara but the kiss she gave Flintlock lingered a few seconds longer. Then she handed them a packed lunch of cornbread and fried fish and said, "Sam, come back one day after you've found your mother. Please, come back and see us."

Flintlock said he would. But he uttered empty words. It was not a visit he could imagine in his future.

The money sack to be returned to Mathias

322

Cobb's bank was stashed in the canoe, and two hours later, after a visit to the Apache, it hung from Flintlock's saddle horn.

"Seems to me there ain't much sense in giving this up," he said. "I mean with Cobb dead and all."

"I'm sure the bank manager can take care of that," O'Hara said.

"It will never be missed," Flintlock said.

"The money doesn't belong to the bank, Sammy. It belongs to the depositors and for some of them it's probably all they have in the world."

Irritated, Flintlock said, "Damn it, O'Hara, for a half-Injun you sure talk like a white man sometimes. Like a parson."

"After all the dead men, all the destruction from the storm, we should do the right thing, Sam."

"And that's to give back the money."

"Yes, Sammy, that's the right thing."

"Suppose they don't want it?"

"Then we'll keep it."

"Yeah, well, there's no point in asking. I know the bank won't want the money back. There's way too much bookkeeping involved."

"Sam, what would Evangeline say? I know the last thing she said to me was to make sure Sam returns the money and squares himself with the law."

"Hell, O'Hara, I'm never square with the law. Hold up a stagecoach or rob a bank and it treats you like a criminal."

"Truer words were never spoke, Sam, but Evangeline —"

"I know. You don't need to tell me. All right, I'll return the damned money, but it's the biggest mistake I'll ever make in my life. And you're the poorest excuse for a half-Injun outlaw I ever came across."

"If it makes you feel any better we can rob a bank in the Arizona Territory and you can recoup your loss," O'Hara said.

Flintlock shook his head. "Nah, I don't think so. The bank-robbing profession has gone to hell since Jesse got killed. It's no longer a gentleman's calling. Too many roughs getting into it and one time Jesse warned me it would happen. 'Sam,' he said, 'find another line of work. I think a man like you might prosper in the bounty-hunting business. I hear it pays well if you only go after those men on the scout who come from the better classes.' "

For a few moments O'Hara watched jays quarrel in the pines, then said, "So that's how you became a bounty hunter."

"Sure is. And I only go after the best and the baddest. I don't waste my time on chicken thieves."

"Plenty of them bad ones in Arizona," O'Hara said.

"I reckon," Flintlock said.

"But it sure goes against the grain to give back the money to a bank you just robbed. I bet poor Jesse is spinning in his grave."

Budville had sustained some damage from the storm, but the bank was undamaged and, as usual, thanks to the intervention of holy Saint Brigid, the patron saint of drunks, so was the saloon . . . at least according to the Irish bartender.

"I suppose you've heard about the death of Mathias Cobb?" Flintlock said. Lacking a Winchester, he cradled his Hawken in his left arm.

"Yes, poor man, what a terrible death," the bartender said. He wore a red brocade vest and arm garters of the same color. "They say he was eaten by a gigantic alligator."

"Only his leg," O'Hara said. "We buried what was left of him."

The bartender crossed himself. "Jesus, Mary and Joseph and all the saints in heaven, I hope he has both his legs now."

"I'm sure he does," O'Hara said. "Or at least a full set of wings."

Flintlock tried his bourbon and then said, "Who is taking care of the bank now that Cobb is deceased?"

"That would be Mr. Crowhurst, the former manager. He entered into a partnership with Mr. Brewster Ritter, the man who lost his lumber business in the storm, and they'll run the bank together. The town is very pleased with the arrangement, especially since Mr. Ritter says he'll make good on the funds lost in the robbery. And . . ." The bartender stared at Flintlock and his eyes lingered on the big bird on his throat.

"And?" Flintlock said.

The bartender seemed flustered. "Oh, nothing. Just that the honest citizens of this town are glad to have their bank back again." The man smiled. "Do you gentlemen need another drink? I have to pop out for a minute and buy some smoking tobacco."

"No, we're fine," Flintlock said. "We'll wait until you get back."

The bartender untied his apron, dropped it on the bar and hurried outside.

"You know he recognized you from your description and he's gone for help?" O'Hara said.

"I know. But we're giving back the money. We'll be heroes," Flintlock said. He read doubt in O'Hara's face and said, "Won't we?"

O'Hara swallowed hard and said, "Yeah, of course we will."

"Injun," Flintlock said, "if you get me hung I'll haunt you for the rest of your life. I'll be a hundred times, a thousand times, worse than Barnabas."

"Nah, you won't get hung. We'll be heroes, just like you said, Sammy. Trust me."

CHAPTER FORTY-NINE

Sam Flintlock's luck ran out in Budville.

It was unfortunate that the bank manager recognized him as the outlaw who robbed the bank and doubly ill-fated was the fact that three Texas Rangers happened to be in town that day.

When the bartender returned he brought the manager, three big mustaches with cold eyes, a torch and pitchfork crowd demanding Sam Flintlock's head . . . and Brewster Ritter.

"Hell," Flintlock said, "I came into town to give the money back. Tell them, O'Hara."

"He's right. That's why he's here," O'Hara said.

"A likely story," the manager said. "I bet he came back to rob us again."

"Every last penny of the money is in the sack," Flintlock said. "Why would I come back and rob you?"

"Rangers, I know this man," Ritter said.

"He came into my lumber camp and told me he was on the scout. He asked me if he could hide out for a spell and offered me a thousand dollars if I'd lie to any lawmen that came around asking questions. Of course I sent him on his way and reported the matter to the bank owner, the now deceased Mr. Cobb."

The tallest Ranger, the one with the biggest mustache, said, "Put that old cannon on the bar, mister."

"Now look here —" Flintlock said.

"Do it now or I'll kill you," the Ranger said. He pushed the muzzle of his long-barreled Colt between Flintlock's eyes and said, "Am I going to have trouble with you?"

"Not a bit," Flintlock said. He laid the Hawken and the Colt on the bar.

"Crowhurst, count the money and see if it's all there," the Ranger said. Then to Ritter, "Was the Indian part of the bank robbery?"

"He sure was," Ritter said. "He and Flintlock are partners."

"Flintlock? Is that your name?" the Ranger said.

"Yeah. Sam Flintlock."

"Mine is Stanley Box. It ain't much better. What's your handle, Indian?"

"They call me O'Hara. I'm half Irish."

"Which half?" Box said.

"Take your pick," O'Hara said.

"The money seems to be all here," Crowhurst said.

"I told you so," Flintlock said. "Now O'Hara and me will be on our way."

Box shook his head. "You two boys aren't going anywhere except to the hoosegow. I'm charging you with the armed robbery of the Cattleman's Bank and Trust, and in Texas that means you're facing twenty to twenty-five in Huntsville."

"Ritter is a crook and a murderer," O'Hara said. "And he and Crowhurst are in cahoots. Me and Flintlock have buried men who died on Ritter's orders."

"Everybody is a crook and murderer except you two, huh?" Ritter said. "Sergeant Box, I say you string 'em up right now."

"What you say doesn't matter a damn, Ritter, except in the witness stand," Box said. "We're taking these boys to Austin and we'll expect you and Crowhurst to be there when they stand trial."

"We'll be there," Ritter said. He looked at Flintlock, the hatred in his eyes burning like coals. "I want to see these damned outlaws in chains."

Flintlock's smile was genuine. "Ritter, you're a murdering lowlife and one day I'm going to take great pleasure in gunning you."

"Sure," Ritter said. "Think about it when you're doing twenty-five years at hard labor in Huntsville."

"All right, boys," Ranger Box said. "You two bank robbers have a long, long way to travel."

CHAPTER FIFTY

In Texas, then and now, three Rangers were a force to be reckoned with, but there were always badmen who would seek to challenge that assertion.

One of those was Gideon Lash, a heartless outlaw who preyed on the weak, the defenseless and those who plain didn't know any better. Lash had no reputation as a shootist, though the number of people he'd killed was close to a hundred. But he was an efficient, cruel and pitiless murderer who made his living from terror. He had done evil things that no human being ever should.

You ever hold a man's hand in the fire until the flesh burns and blackens and the white bones show and then drop one by one into the coals? You ever wonder how loud he screams?

Lash asked those questions of one of his many teenage "brides" on her wedding night. The girl fled from the hotel and ran into the darkness and kept running, or so they say, until she reached the New Mexico Territory. Gideon Lash laughed about that.

But lest you think fire was his terror of choice, his most cherished possession was his skinning knife, with which he was very adept. "Man or woman, I never trust anybody until they've been skun," he once told a judge in an El Paso courthouse. The outraged jurist sentenced Lash to be hanged, but he escaped, killing two Deputy United States Marshals in the process.

Now he lurked in the darkness and ahead of him the Rangers' fire spread an orange tint on the surrounding pine canopies. Five men, two of then trussed, prisoners and of no account. He identified Sergeant Stanley Box, a dangerous man, and another Ranger named Luke Clover. Then he saw the man he'd come to kill. Denny Hawk, the man whose bullet had carried away a chunk of Lash's left cheekbone and left him with a grotesque cavity scar that repelled even hog-ranch whores. He'd been tracking Hawk for three months and at last the man was there, just a few yards away.

Gideon Lash studied the sleeping camp and made his plan.

■ ■ ■ ■

It had been a long day for the Rangers and they slept around the campfire, but how soundly O'Hara didn't know. Likely the chirp of a sick cricket would be enough to bolt them to their feet, guns blazing.

O'Hara's strong fingers worked on the tight knot of the tie-down rope around Flintlock's wrists. After an hour O'Hara's fingertips bled, but Flintlock's wrists were free.

O'Hara whispered. "Knife. Down the side of my moccasin." Then, "No, the other leg, damn it."

Flintlock lifted the Green River knife, firelight glinting on its five-inch blade, and cut the rope away from his booted ankles. He sat perfectly still and waited. Over by the fire one of the Rangers stirred restlessly in his sleep and Flintlock's heart jumped into this mouth. But after a few moments the man settled down and his mutterings were replaced by soft snores.

It was time for Flintlock to act. He planned to shove the knife blade against Box's throat and then take the man's gun. And after that he'd play the cards that were dealt to him.

But then Gideon Lash emerged from the darkness and spoiled everything.

Lash's plan was to cut Denny Hawk's throat as he slept, just one whisper-thin stroke of the knife and it would be done. He would then melt back into the pines and get his horse. His mount was black, he wore a long black coat to his ankles and a black hat and he'd never be seen in the blackness of night if the surviving Rangers gave chase.

Wearing moccasins, Lash crept soundlessly toward his prey . . . then he saw Flintlock watching him. Lash stopped, put a finger to his lips and then, his knife ready, bent to make the cut.

Flintlock had a split second to think about it. With one Ranger down his escape would be that much easier . . . but he couldn't stand by and see a man slaughtered in his sleep, law officer or not.

One thing old Barnabas had taught Flintlock well was the way of the Green River hunting knife and how to throw it. Lash was a dark, bent figure hovering over the Ranger. He looked like a sinister bird of prey.

Flintlock drew his arm back and threw the knife. He had aimed to stick the man's right shoulder and disable his cutting hand, but the jolt of pain in his still-healing ribs threw his aim off. The blade hit Lash just above the coat collar, a couple of inches below his massive jawbone. Buried to the haft, the blade killed quickly. Lash had time to utter a terrible cry and then his heavy body fell across the sleeping Ranger. Hawk, an excitable man, kicked away the heavy corpse and then jumped to his feet, his bucking Colt blazing at shadows among the trees.

"What the hell!" Stanley Box threw aside his blankets, ran to Hawk and almost stumbled over the dead man. He had a Colt in his hand and his eyes searched the gloom between the pines.

"The only man here is dead at your feet, Box," Flintlock said.

The sergeant told Hawk to put his gun away and then took a knee beside Lash's body. "Denny, come take a look at this," he said.

"My God, it's Gideon Lash," Hawk said.

"He was aiming to cut your throat, Denny," Flintlock said.

"You threw the knife?" Box said.

"Yeah, I did. I got my hands loose and took the knife out of my boot." He exchanged a look with O'Hara. "Then I saw the deceased sneak into camp. He was leaning over Hawk with a knife in his hand when

I stuck him."

Box made a note of the distance involved then said, "You know how to throw a blade, mister."

"One of the few things I'm good at."

"You planned to use the knife to escape?" Box said.

"That was my intention. I have no love for peace officers. I've written my name of the walls of too many calabooses in my day, but I won't stand by and let a sleeping man get this throat cut."

"Do you know who this is?" Box said.

"No. He didn't take time to properly introduce himself."

"His name is Gideon Lash. Mean anything to you?"

"I've heard he'd been hung years ago up El Paso way."

"Was he a friend of yours?" Box said.

"If you mean was he riding to my rescue, the answer is no. You don't stick a man who's trying to save your butt. Even a lawman should know that."

"Well, what I do know is that you saved my butt tonight, Flintlock," Hawk said. "I'll make sure I mention it at your trial."

"I guess all three of us will do that," Box said. "Ain't that right, Luke?"

"Sure thing," Clover said. "You played the

white man tonight, mister, and when the time comes I'll do the same for you."

"What about my friend?" Flintlock said.

"The Injun? Why, sure, sure, if we remember," Box said.

CHAPTER FIFTY-ONE

Brewster Ritter stood by his saddled horse under a pale blue sky and said to Charlie Crowhurst, "I'll ride over to the swamp and see if there's anything worth salvaging. The big ripsaws got struck by lightning but maybe they can repaired."

Crowhurst, always a sour-faced man, looked troubled. "Brewster, the bank" — he looked around him — "is broke. When I liquidate I'll be able to pay twenty cents on the dollar, if that."

"And get yourself lynched," Ritter said. "Just hang on. We'll get the logs rolling again very soon."

"That's impossible," Crowhurst said. "We'll need to hire loggers, replace the freight wagons and draft horses, get the saws up and running . . . all that takes money."

"There's always Simon Luke. He told Mathias Cobb that he'd buy all the cypress logs we can send him. I think he might agree to put up money in return for a lower price."

"Do you think he'll bite?"

"I'll wire him when I get back and we'll take it from there. In the meantime you sit tight and keep your head, Charlie. This thing isn't over yet and it won't be until, from here to New Orleans, every damned cypress in the swamp is cut."

"Talk is cheap, Brewster. Cutting trees isn't," Crowhurst said.

Ritter swung into the saddle and then said, "Unlike Cobb I can get things done." He opened his coat and showed the Colt in a shoulder holster. "And I'll kill anybody who gets in my way. That includes you, Charlie."

"Are you threatening me, Brewster?" Crowhurst said.

Ritter, small, stocky and mean as a caged cougar, smiled and said, "I sure am, Charlie. I sure am."

The logging site was what Ritter expected, a wasteland of flooded ground and scattered wreckage. The great steam saws stood in water but had no visible damage. Ritter dismounted and inspected them closely. He was not an engineer but it looked to him that they could be salvaged. Everything else

340

was wrecked. Even the steam launch that had so recently terrified the swamp dwellers lay on its side, its boiler, furnace and yards of copper and brass pipes spilled into mud like the guts of a savaged animal.

Ritter walked to the edge of the swamp. It looked surprisingly serene in the morning mist and apart from the stumps of the already sawn cypress revealed no damage. Ritter smiled. All that would change when the lumber operation began again. He was about to go back to his horse when he caught movement out of the corner of his eye.

A canoe, a woman paddling at the stern, had emerged from the mist. She stopped, leaned over the side and picked up a dripping piece of canvas. She made a face and dropped it into the bottom of the pirogue.

Ritter recognized her as the woman who'd been with the Indians during the attack on the camp. She wore a tight corset over a white shirt and a long black skirt. She had fingerless leather gloves on her hands and wore a shiny black top hat.

She was an enemy and Ritter saw no reason why he shouldn't enjoy her before he killed her.

He drew his Colt and fired a round into the water inches from the prow of the canoe. Evangeline turned and Ritter saw recognition in her eyes. "Bring that scow over here, lady, or the next shot scatters your brains," he said. Ritter's next bullet knocked the top hat off Evangeline's head. "That's the only chance you get."

Evangeline accepted the inevitable and paddled to the swamp's edge. She hiked her skirt up as she climbed out of the canoe and onto drier land.

"Come here," Ritter said. "Come slow."

"Mister, I know what you want," Evangeline said.

"Well, that makes it easier, doesn't it?" Ritter said. The woman's perfume filled his head and he studied the swell of her breasts above the corset.

"You're name is Brewster Ritter and you always get what you want, don't you?"

"That's right, little lady. And now I want you."

"Suppose I say you can't have me?"

"What you say doesn't matter a damn. I take what I want."

"You didn't get the swamp," Evangeline said.

"But I'll get it eventually," Ritter said. "Now, enough talk. Get over here and lie down. Over there on the grass will do."

Evangeline said, "Now you'll die like all

the rest, Ritter. And like Mathias Cobb you'll die screaming."

The man's face changed from grin to grimace. "What the hell are you talking about?"

"Behind you. His name is Basilisk and for as long as I'm alive he's my protector."

Ritter would normally have dismissed that as an old trick that no one fell for any longer, but he read something in Evangeline's eyes that scared him. He swung around and got a shot off before the monster was on him. Screaming, shrieking, screeching, Ritter hung from the alligator's jaws as Basilisk dragged him to the swamp. For a moment his terrified eyes turned on Evangeline, but she watched impassively as Ritter died a more terrible but mercifully quicker death than Cobb.

Basilisk was not to be trusted. Having removed a danger to Evangeline he might decide to then go after her.

She hurried to her canoe, scrambled inside and paddled away from the churning, scarlet water that marked Ritter's death throes.

Unlike the debris from the storm, Basilisk would not leave enough of Ritter to untidy the swamp.

Chapter Fifty-Two

As he'd done so many times in the past, Sam Flintlock scratched the word *FLINT-LOCK* on the wall of his cell. "O'Hara, you want your name up here?" he said.

"If it's all the same to you, Sammy, I'll pass."

Flintlock stepped down from his bunk and said, "What did that lawyer feller mean when he talked about bank robbery being a hanging offense in Austin?"

"He was just blowing smoke, Sam," O'Hara said.

"I don't know about that. He had sneaky eyes."

"You can't become a lawyer unless you have sneaky eyes," O'Hara said. "Everybody knows that."

"Before now I never heard of a man getting hung for bank robbery," Flintlock said. "Hell, one time I saw a man get hung for being a damned nuisance, but I never saw one get stretched for robbing a bank."

"He was blowing smoke, that lawyer, Sammy, all gurgle and no guts."

A key clanked in the cell's iron lock and a Ranger stepped inside. "You boys come with me," he said.

"You can't hang us," O'Hara said. "We haven't had a trial yet."

"Come with me," the Ranger said.

Flintlock and O'Hara were led outside to a stone wall that stood by itself in the middle of the exercise yard. The wall was about ten foot high and thirty foot long. Two buckets of whitewash and couple of brushes stood at its base.

"I want that wall whitewashed on both sides," the Ranger said. "We got important visitors coming soon and want the place looking nice."

"It's a jail," Flintlock said. "You can't make a jail look nice."

"Then do your best," the Ranger said. He carried a Winchester and wore a belt gun, and his gray eyes were as hard as chipped flint.

"See, what you don't understand, Ranger —"

"Smith."

"Is that Sergeant Box told us we'd get a cushy job in jail while we wait for our trial,

Ranger Smith," Flintlock said.

The Ranger nodded. "Yeah, I know all about that. This is a cushy job, or would you rather clean out the outhouses?"

"We'll whitewash the wall," O'Hara said.

"Thought you might," Ranger Smith said.

At first Flintlock thought that the deserted yard might hold opportunities for escape, but a Ranger with a white beard down to his belt buckle carried out a chair, a yellow parasol and a Greener shotgun. He sat in the chair, opened the parasol above his head and laid the scattergun across his knees. He then lit his pipe and from behind a cloud of smoke said, "Carry on, boys."

"The whole wall?" Flintlock said.

"Yup. Both sides. And after it's done you'll get supper."

"This will take all damned day," Flintlock said.

"Then you'd better get started," the Ranger said.

"And suppose I don't want to?" Flintlock said, irritated.

"Well, under those circumstance I reckon a barrel of birdshot up the ass would make you change your tune right sharpish," the Ranger said. He stared at the glowing coals in his pipe. "It sure as hell would me."

O'Hara said, "You fit Comanches, didn't you?"

"Yes, son, I certainly did."

"They rubbed off on you," O'Hara said. He picked up his bucket and brush. "Let's get to work, Sammy," he said.

Flintlock did the same and then said, "I've run across some mean jaspers in my day, but there's nothing meaner than a Texas Ranger with a scattergun."

"And that's a natural fact, son," the old Ranger said. He adjusted the angle of his parasol and said, "Seems like we're in for a hot one."

Sam Flintlock and O'Hara looked like a couple of ghosts as they stood at dusk in the jailhouse yard covered from head to toe in whitewash.

"Damn it, we could have finished the last few feet of the damned wall tomorrow," Flintlock said.

"Yup, you could have," the old Ranger said. "But my orders was to make sure you finished all of it." He waved a hand to the two skinny black men who'd carried a couple of buckets of water and some rags. "This here is Cyrus and Maxwell. They're serving ten days for being drunk and disorderly. They'll help get you cleaned up."

"Well, let's get it done," Flintlock said. "I'm hungry for supper."

"Too late fer supper, sonny," the Ranger said. "But you'll get a nice early breakfast."

Flintlock opened his mouth to object but Cyrus threw a bucket of water over his head and began to scrub him with a rag that felt like a roll of barbed wire.

Sam Flintlock lay in the dark cell with his hands locked behind his head and said, "For the first time in my life I feel like a prisoner."

"Me too," O'Hara said. "And we haven't even been found guilty yet."

"You think we'll be found guilty?"

"Of course we will, Sammy. We've got nobody to give evidence on our behalf. Ritter and that bank manager feller will put our heads in a noose."

"What about me saving the Ranger's life? That's got to count for something."

"Sure it will. The judge will call you a real stout fellow and true blue and take two years off your twenty-five-year sentence."

"All right, then we have to find some way to escape," Flintlock said. "We'll break out of here and make our way to the Arizona Territory."

"Without horses?"

"We'll have to steal back our own."

348

"From the Texas Rangers?" O'Hara said. "You're dreaming."

"Damn it all, O'Hara, you've got to be the most depressing Injun I ever met."

"Go to sleep, Sammy," O'Hara said.

"Hell, we'll have twenty-five years to sleep," Flintlock said.

"I'll have twenty-five, you'll only have twenty-three," O'Hara said.

"Maybe when we get to Huntsville we can dig a tunnel," Flintlock said.

But O'Hara made no answer. He was already asleep, or pretending to be.

CHAPTER FIFTY-THREE

United States Senator Jeffrey Boatwright watched nervously as his new Rapide steam car was unloaded from his private train. Beside him and equally nervous, Evangeline and Cornelius shouted advice to the six laborers who eased the automobile down the ramp from the flatcar.

Finally, to everyone's relief, the Rapide reached solid ground unharmed. Boatwright, at considerable risk, had lit the boiler while the train was still in motion and by the time it reached Budville the steam car was ready to go.

Designed by Amédée Bollée of Le Mans, the boiler was mounted behind the passenger compartment with the engine at the front of the vehicle, driving the differential through a shaft with chain drive to the rear wheels. The driver sat behind the engine and steered by means of a wheel mounted on a vertical shaft.

Everyone who set eyes on the Rapide declared it was a wonderful machine and Senator Boatwright confidently predicted that all horse-drawn vehicles would be obsolete by the year 1900, replaced by steam cars.

Boatwright, a distinguished-looking man who bore more than a passing resemblance to Andrew Jackson, encouraged that comparison by his thick mane of white hair and lofty stature. Like Cornelius he wore a cream-colored motoring coat, trimmed at the lapels and pockets with tan leather. A large floppy cap, goggles above the brim, and a pair of English riding boots completed his attire. Evangeline wore the same type of coat but her headwear was a broad-brimmed straw hat held in place by a white chiffon scarf that tied under her chin. She wore high-heeled ankle boots and carried a parasol. The fourth car passenger was a little cock sparrow of a man wearing a brown tailcoat and a bowler hat of the same color. He was afflicted by a permanent head cold, and a pair of pince-nez perched at the tip of his red nose. Despite his unprepossessing appearance, Lucas Bardwell was one of the federal government's top accountants, and his evidence had helped put the head of the notorious swindler and wife murderer

Reverend Hugh Lowe into a noose.

Bardwell was a bloodless, prying, tenacious little man with no friends and no known vices except for the occasional pinch of snuff. He made a bad enemy.

"Well, shall we drive to the bank?" Senator Boatwright said. "Yes, I think so. The day is too hot for walking. All aboard!"

Evangeline settled into the front seat beside Boatwright and Cornelius and Bardwell climbed into the rear. The Rapide lurched into motion and the senator yelled above the racket of the chain drive, "Mr. Cornelius, do those fellows look like Texas Rangers to you?"

Cornelius peered through his goggles and saw two tall, lanky men with big mustaches standing beside their horses outside the bank. Each carried a belted Colt and a Winchester rifle. At that time in the West Rangers didn't wear a star, but they were unmistakably lawmen.

"That would be my guess, Senator," Cornelius said.

"Good, excellent," Boatwright said. "One can always depend on the Texas Rangers. That's what I always say. What do you say, Miss Evangeline? Good, I knew you'd agree with me."

Boatwright braked the Rapide to a steam-

ing, hissing halt and said, "Everyone out."
And then to Evangeline, "But not you, my
dear. I myself will assist you to alight."

As the senator helped Evangeline onto the
dusty road one of the tall men approached
him and said, "Senator Boatwright?"

"Indeed, I am He," the politician said,
managing to put an uppercase on the *h* by
tone alone.

"Name's Sergeant Box and this here is
Ranger Clover. We were sent here to make
an arrest."

"Indeed you were, my stalwart, steadfast
sons of the Frontier Battalion. And there
will be work for you to do ere this day is
done, I'll be bound. This gentleman here is
Mr. Lucas Bardwell, accountant, you will
stay near him at all times lest there be
desperadoes at hand."

Box said, "Howdy," and Boatwright said,
"These young friends of mine are Miz
Evangeline and her husband, Mr. Cornelius." He placed a hand on Cornelius's
shoulder. "This is the gallant who saved the
life of President Grant, and although we
can't see it, the golden wreath of hero
encircles his noble head. But more of that
later. Mr. Bardwell, shall we step into the
breach and be damned to the cannon fire?"

Bardwell settled his pincenez onto his little

beak of a nose and produced a steel pen from his pocket. "The pen is mightier than the sword, Senator."

"Yes, yes, indeed it is, well said. Ho, you there, boy! Yes you, the urchin with the bare feet. Guard this car well and when I come out of the bank I'll give you two bits."

"Sure, mister," the boy said. "But I ain't gonna guard that thing too close. It looks like it's gettin' ready to blow us all to kingdom come."

"What a disagreeable child," Boatwright said to Sergeant Box as they entered the bank. "Thanks to our magnanimous government the poorer classes are now able to buy butcher's meat, and that has been their undoing."

"The assets of this bank will not cover the amount of deposits," Lucas Bardwell said. "There's in excess of fifty thousand dollars of customers' money unaccounted for, Mr. Crowhurst. In short, your books are a disgrace."

"There was the bank robbery . . ." the manager said. His Adam's apple bobbed in his throat.

"Ten thousand dollars that was returned to you. Where was it entered in the ledgers? I don't see it."

"When Mr. Ritter gets back he can explain everything. You see, he borrowed money from Mr. Cobb for a logging operation that was destroyed in the recent storm. I'm sure Mr. Ritter plans to replace the fifty thousand he borrowed."

"Where is this Mr. Ritter?" Bardwell said.

"He's dead," Evangeline said. "The same alligator that killed Cobb also killed Ritter. That speaks well of the reptile's sense of justice, but not its palate."

Crowhurst was stunned and held on to the corner of a desk for support. "Ritter . . . is . . . dead?"

"I'm afraid so," Evangeline said. "The alligator carried his body into the swamp."

"Oh God," Crowhurst said. He buried his face in his hands. "Oh my God, I am undone."

"Where is the missing ten thousand dollars?" Bardwell said, an unfeeling, relentless inquisitor.

"Mr. Ritter took it," Crowhurst said.

"He didn't have it when he tried to rape me," Evangeline said.

"A terrible ordeal, dear lady," Boatwright said. "And to see a man die like that . . . horrible."

"Where is the ten thousand, Mr. Crowhurst?" Bardwell said.

"I don't know. Mr. Ritter may have hidden it somewhere, even buried it."

"You were a willing accomplice to all this chicanery, Mr. Crowhurst. You and Mathias Cobb walked hand in hand and swindled many people out of their hard-earned money. There is no way this sorry excuse for a bank can cover fifty thousand dollars. Those deposits are lost forever. I warn you, Mr. Crowhurst, you are facing trial and imprisonment."

"Wait, wait, let me show you something," Crowhurst said. "It's a letter, a letter from Mr. Cobb that will clear my name."

"Where is it?" Bardwell said.

"It's in my desk. I'll go get it."

"Yes, go bring it," Bardwell said.

The Rangers didn't go with Crowhurst. In their minds he was just a cowed little man and he'd nowhere to run. But they'd made a big mistake.

A couple of moments later a shot rang out. The Rangers hurried into the manager's office and found Crowhurst sitting slumped in his chair, a gun in his hand and a bloody hole in his right temple.

"Killed himself, by God," Senator Boatwright said, stating the obvious. "Damned lily-livered coward couldn't face the music."

"He's helped ruin a lot of people in this

town," Lucas Bardwell said. "I have no sympathy for him."

Sergeant Box said, "Budville will die now. People will move out, trying to restore their fortune elsewhere. I've seen it before after a bank goes broke. Towns just give up the will to survive and pretty soon become ghosts."

"Let's hope it doesn't happen here," Senator Boatwright said. "I will assure this fair city that the federal government will do all in its power to help its citizens survive this disaster. What's the name of this burg again?"

"Budville," Box said.

"Yes. I will pledge on my word of honor that Budville . . . will . . . survive!"

Boatwright frowned. "Unfortunately we have to get back to the train and set out for Austin. But Ranger Box, tell the folks that I will return soon. Tell them that our government never breaks a promise to its citizens. They can depend on that."

CHAPTER FIFTY-FOUR

Evangeline toyed with the boiled trout on her plate and then laid down her fork and said, "Senator Boatwright, I don't think that I've thanked you enough for taking an interest in Sam Flintlock and O'Hara."

Boatwright had stuck a huge white napkin into his shirt collar that was already stained with gravy from the roast beef he was devouring.

"Think nothing of it, my dear. The president was most insistent that I do all in my power to help the friends of you and your husband. Cornelius is quite the hero in Washington, you know, and his book — what is it called again?"

"The Flora and Fauna of the Texas and Louisiana Swamps," Evangeline said.

"Ah yes, that is it. Well, it's very popular in some circles, though I'm very much a city animal myself. Penny dreadfuls are my meat, and the bloodier the better. Ah, this roast is very rare, the way I like it."

"About Sam Flintlock, Senator, he is accused of robbing the Budville bank, but he was trying to make Mathias Cobb break his cover."

"And he returned the money," Cornelius said.

Boatwright nodded and studied his plate. "The advantage of having one's own dining car is that one can set the menu. Meat and potatoes are what I'm all about, and plenty of gravy. Gravy is a must in any civilized society. Cornelius, please set your mind at rest. I've ordered a full government investigation into what happened in the swamp, and the cypress trees have been placed under the protection of the great state of Texas." He poked his fork in the other man's direction. "There were many redskin deaths and the Bureau of Indian Affairs is deeply concerned."

"And what about Flintlock?" Evangeline said.

"He and what's-his-name will be freed pending the result of my investigation. Since that might take years, eventually no one will even remember Flintlock's involvement."

"He'll be free to go?" Evangeline said.

"Yes, just as soon as I speak to the authorities in Austin."

"We can't thank you enough, Senator," Evangeline said.

"Think nothing of it. Cornelius, are you going to eat that meat you left on your plate?"

"No, sir. I've had enough."

"Then scrape it onto my plate, man. We can't let good beef go to waste."

The train journey to Austin was uneventful though Senator Boatwright checked on his steam car often and his cook became concerned at Evangeline's lack of appetite. "I swear, child, what you eat couldn't keep a bird alive."

After the car was unloaded at the Austin station, Evangeline and Cornelius read magazines and newspapers in the waiting room while the boiler built up steam. Lucas Bardwell had elected to return to Washington and had left the train earlier.

"Look at this," Evangeline said, handing Cornelius a newspaper she'd folded to reveal only a single column under the headline:

Miss Ivy Dinwiddie's News of the Courts

And then:

Samuel Flint, a well-known *desperado* around these parts, and his *partner in crime,* **O'Halloran**, a half-breed of the most *savage* aspect, are slated to stand trial for bank robbery on September 7th. We say to our *brave* TEXAS RANGERS, *"Keep bringing 'em back alive, boys!"*

"Miss Ivy didn't get the names right," Cornelius said.

"No, she didn't, but it seems like we got here just in time," Evangeline said. "September seventh is tomorrow."

"We'd better tell Senator Boatwright," Cornelius said. "There's not a moment to lose."

CHAPTER FIFTY-FIVE

Sam Flintlock thought that the first meeting between Senator Jeffrey Boatwright and resident jurist Judge Jeptha Hyde went very well. They had served in the 5th U.S. Cavalry during the war, and both had been wounded at Gaines Mills. They greeted one another like old friends.

Hyde, a solemn, gray-haired man with a saber scar on his left cheek, listened in silence, his eyes straying now and then to savor Evangeline's dazzling beauty. The story, told in episodes from Evangeline, Cornelius and Boatwright with asides from Flintlock and O'Hara, was long in the telling.

Finally Judge Hyde seized on one point. "The same alligator killed both Cobb and Ritter?"

"Yes, his name is Basilisk and he looks out for me," Evangeline said. "At least that explains his attack on Ritter. Why he decided to kill Cobb I don't know."

"How can a cold-blooded creature look out for you? It defies logic."

"I know it does. But I shot him once and now he plans to kill me," Evangeline said. "I believe he saw Ritter as a threat and got rid of him. Basilisk wants me for himself."

Hyde shivered then said, "Young lady, if I were you I'd stay away from the swamp."

"I'm needed there, your honor, and in fifty years Basilisk will be dead."

Hyde's face revealed that he saw no logic in that statement either, but he let it go. "Major Boatwright — I'm sorry, Senator Boatwright — you've given me a great deal to think about," he said. "Perhaps you and Mr. and Mrs. Cornelius would care to dine with me tonight and I'll give you my decision then."

"I'd be honored." The senator smiled. "Captain Hyde."

This occasioned mirth and both Boatwright and Hyde grinned as they left the judge's chambers. A frowning Flintlock was taken back to his cell in chains.

"Well, what do you think, Sam?" O'Hara said.

The Rangers, much addicted to the smoking habit, had supplied Flintlock with tobacco and papers and now he carefully built a cigarette, concentrating on not spilling a single shred.

He lit the smoke and said, "I don't know. But Hyde sure looks like a hanging judge."

"Hard man to read," O'Hara said.

"You're right there. His face isn't exactly an open book."

"Well, as you said, Sammy, we can always escape from Huntsville."

"Wes Hardin is still there. He tried to escape, got his ribs kicked in and landed in solitary. When he gets out of prison he won't be half the man he was and somebody will put a bullet in his back. Pity, I knew none faster than Wes with a Colt's gun."

"You went after him once, didn't you?"

"Yeah, I went after the reward on his head. On the trail he rode rings around me, shot my horse, put a bullet in me and then gave me ten dollars to pay for a doctor." Smoke trailed from Flintlock's mouth. "Say what you want about Wes, but he was true blue, a white man."

"Did you get a shot off?" O'Hara said.

"Sure I did. I missed and he didn't."

"Think he'll recognize you when we get to Huntsville?"

"O'Hara, be damned to you for a wet-blanket Injun. We're not going to Huntsville.

I'm surprised how much influence Cornelius has in Washington. Hell, he's on first-name terms with the president. Why —"

The key clanked in the cell lock and the door screeched open. The old Ranger with the shotgun stepped inside. "You boys come with me," he said.

"What for?" Flintlock said.

"I don't know, but sure as hell you two are going to help me find out."

"Listen, after whitewashing your damned wall we don't like you much," Flintlock said. "In other words, we're not inclined to be helpful."

"You're all I got," the old man said.

Flintlock read something in the Ranger's face, a vulnerability that hadn't been there before. "What do you want us to do? If it's cleaning outhouses we're not interested."

"Right now there's only three prisoners in the jail," the Ranger said. "You boys and August Bambara. Tell you something?"

"Tells me you got a mighty dangerous outlaw on your hands," Flintlock said.

O'Hara said, "Is he the one who wiped out a settlement on the Brazos that time?"

"He sure is, sonny," the Ranger said. "Killed every man and half-grown boy in the town so he and his gang could rob the bank and outrage the woman at leisure.

That was back in eighty-two and he's done a sight worse since. Now come with me. We got work to do."

"What kind of work?" Flintlock said.

"I think his gang plans to bust him out of jail tonight. And I'm the only Ranger on duty. One thing you two should know — Bambara doesn't leave any witnesses behind.

Chapter Fifty-Six

"Name's Coon Grogan, by the way." The Ranger handed Flintlock and O'Hara a couple of Henry rifles he took from the gun rack by the front door. "They're loaded, but if I see you boys make a fancy move, I'll gun you both. Now douse that oil lamp there."

Once the office was dark, Grogan motioned Flintlock to come stand by him at the window. "Look over there," he said. "See them shadows moving over there by the corral?"

Flintlock said, "Yeah, I do. Hell, there must be a couple dozen of them working themselves up to attack us. Where are the other Rangers?"

"Out on the trail of outlaws, sonny, where they should be."

"Well, they've left us to buck some mighty long odds here, Coon," Flintlock said.

"Seems like," the Ranger said. "Ol' August

has a big gang. But it all might come to nothing. I'll go out and see if I can talk some sense into them."

"Yeah, and get your head blown off, old man," Flintlock said.

"It's my duty, sonny," Grogan said. "I knew there would be times like this when I signed on. Well, wish me luck, boys."

"Git back here," Flintlock said. "They haven't even stated their intentions."

"I know what their intentions are. They want to spring their boss and then shoot any witnesses left behind. That's their intentions, all right."

Flintlock took time to glance out the window. A single lantern at the side of a barn cast a dull orange glow on the open ground in front of the corral. The outlaws had shaken themselves out into a line and stared at the jail. All twenty of them carried rifles.

"I'm not letting you go out there, Coon," Flintlock said.

"Sonny, I done palavered with Comanche, Apache and outlaws afore you were born," Grogan said. "Now stand aside and give me the road."

"You walk to your destiny, old warrior," O'Hara said.

Grogan nodded. "Maybe so, sonny. Maybe so."

The old Ranger opened the door and stepped outside. "You boys hold up," he yelled to the outlaws. "This here is Texas Ranger Coon Grogan and I want to talk with you."

Grogan took a step toward the outlaws . . . then another . . .

"We'll talk this thing through," he said.

The old man's body looked as though it was being torn apart by the volley of lead that punched great holes though him. He teetered for a moment on rag-doll legs and then fell flat on his face.

Flintlock watched the old Ranger fall and his rage flared. He threw open the door and worked the Henry from his shoulder. One of the outlaws dropped and the rest scattered. But they soon settled down and returned a steady fire. Bullets thudded into the door and splintered wood. Windows shattered under the hail of lead and O'Hara yanked Flintlock back and kicked the heavy oak door shut.

"Are you crazy?" he said. "We got to find a back door out of here."

"No," Flintlock said. "I can hold them for a few minutes. Go find Bambara and bring him here. Hurry!"

"I don't have a key to his cell," O'Hara said.

"Then find it!"

Flintlock fired a couple of fast shots out a broken window, then ducked as bullets drove past him and crashed into lamps, chairs and desks, shattered shards of glass and wood exploding around him.

A glance out the window told him all the bad news he needed to know. Wary of his rifle fire, the outlaws advanced slowly, firing as they came, and were now only twenty yards away.

Flintlock fired, fired again. But again a hail of shot forced him to the ground. He cursed under his breath. *Where is that damned Injun?*

He moved back in the smoke-streaked gloom to the potbellied stove that stood in a corner and squeezed behind it. The stove was small and didn't offer much cover, but cast iron would deflect at least some of the rifle bullets. Flintlock hefted the Henry and prepared to charge a high price for his life.

Moments later the door opened slowly, creaking on its hinges. The corner where Flintlock forted up lay in darkness, but the part of the room near the door and windows was bathed in faint light. He reckoned he could get three or four of them before they found him and killed him. Flintlock smiled. He was no bargain.

The door pushed open again. Then stopped. And then silence.

Flintlock waited for long seconds and then left the shelter of the stove and walked slowly in the direction of the door. With every wary step a floorboard creaked and his big Texas spurs chimed. Then, from outside, a babble of raised voices. He moved to the window, stood a ways back in shadow and listened into the night.

"Are you all right, boss?" a man yelled.

And then an answering cry, "Hell, no, I'm not all right. I'm on the roof with a rope around my neck and a man's boot ready to push my ass off a ledge."

"What do you want us to do, boss? We can't even see the son of a bitch."

"He's a crazy Indian and he's right behind me, damn it. He wants you to mount up and clear out, all of you."

"You want us to do that?"

"Damn it, yes. If you don't he'll stretch my neck."

"Should we call his bluff, boss?"

Now Bambara's voice rose in a screech. "Nooo, you fool. He'll kill me. Just get the hell out of Austin."

But the man, whoever he was, wouldn't

quit. "Hey, you up there. Injun."

"What the hell do you want?" O'Hara's voice.

"Let Bambara go and you got five hundred dollars coming. That's enough to keep you in firewater and split-nose squaws for a six-month."

"Go to hell," O'Hara said. "Now you can watch this piece of human garbage swing."

"No!" Bambara yelled. "Do as he says, Evans. Get out of here."

Flintlock watched as the man who'd been doing all the talking conferred with the others. After a couple of minutes he looked up at the roof and said, "All right. We're going. But we'll be back."

The shooting had begun to attract a crowd and now armed men stood in the shadows, trying to puzzle out what was happening. One townsman, quicker on the uptake than the rest, cut loose with a probing revolver shot. The outlaw named Evans took that as his cue to leave and he and his men mounted up and rode away in a hurry.

Only the bodies of Ranger Grogan and two of the outlaws lay in the open ground, barely visible and still as stones in death.

Flintlock stumbled around in the dark for a spell and finally found a stairway that led to the second story, one large room the

Rangers used for storage. Here and there iron staples were bolted to the floor to secure chained criminals in an emergency. Despite the darkness, Flintlock knew this because he painfully stubbed his toe on two of them.

At the far end of the room a set of pine steps led to a trapdoor that opened onto the roof. Flintlock took the stairway and discovered what had caused all the yelling among the outlaws. August Bambara, a tall, slim mulatto dressed in the finery of a Mexican vaquero, stood on a ledge, a noose around his neck. The other end of the rope was tied to a steel lightning rod fastened to a wall. The rod was an inch thick and well enough secured to take a man's weight. O'Hara stood behind Bambara, the muzzle of his Colt pressed into the man's lower back. When the outlaw heard the chime of spurs he turned his head, saw Flintlock and said, "You! Get this lunatic Indian off me."

"You're August Bambara, ain't you?" Flintlock said, his voice pitched low, menacing.

"I am Bambara. Now get me down from here."

"Can you see the ground? Of course you can't," Flintlock said. "Well, let me tell you about it. A Texas Ranger lies dead down there. In his day he fit Comanches, Apaches and lowlife scum like you. I didn't like him much, but I respected him."

"What the hell do I care?" Bambara said. "I know my rights, so get that Indian away from me and get me off this damned ledge."

"What rights did Texas Ranger Coon Grogan have?" Flintlock said.

He stepped to Bambara and said, "Mister, you should have been hung a long time ago."

A gentle, one-fingered push and the mulatto screamed. The rope went taut and then vibrated like a fiddle string as Bambara kicked his legs as he strangled to death.

When it was over, Flintlock said to O'Hara, "He took a nasty fall, didn't he?"

"I think he jumped," O'Hara said. "Killed himself. That's what I think."

"Maybe so," Flintlock said. "You got your knife?"

"Coon Grogan took it. But I saw an axe knife in the storeroom."

"You'd better get it, O'Hara, and we'll cut him down. He makes the place look untidy hanging there."

CHAPTER FIFTY-SEVEN

"It is my opinion that August Bambara committed suicide rather than face a legal hanging," Judge Jeptha Hyde said. "I very much regret the death of Ranger Coon Grogan, a fine officer of the law, but I commend Mr. Flintlock and Mr. O'Hara for their gallant defense of the jail against overwhelming odds, as has been already noted by this court. When the vile monster August Bambara swung from a rope justice was done and was seen to be done. I will therefore order the immediate release of Mr. Flintlock and Mr. O'Hara into the custody of that fine statesman and gallant soldier Senator Jeffrey Boatwright."

This brought a mild round of applause, but Judge Hyde rapped his gavel and looked around his well-attended court with the piercing hazel eyes of a hawk. "Do I hear any objections to my decision? No? Then what about you, Captain Fleet?"

The Ranger shook his head. "No objection, your honor. Them two boys did well."

"Then it's settled," Hyde said. He banged his gavel. "This court is dismissed."

As Flintlock and O'Hara received congratulations from Senator Boatwright, Evangeline and Cornelius, Hyde tapped Flintlock on the shoulder and took him aside. "It's too bad that August Bambara missed a legal execution, but a hanging is a hanging. Of course we'll never know for sure if he fell, jumped or was pushed. Will we?"

"I guess not, Judge," Flintlock said.

"Then will you do me a favor, Mr. Flintlock?"

"I sure will, your honor. Just mention it."

"At the earliest opportunity I want and you and O'Hara to leave Texas. Will you do that for me?"

"We're headed for the Arizona Territory," Flintlock said.

"Glad to hear it. We don't want your kind in our great state." Judge Hyde smiled. "By the way, Mr. Flintlock, I think Bambara was pushed."

Senator Boatwright insisted on a celebratory dinner at the best restaurant in Austin. Since appropriate dress was required a tailor was summoned to the hotel and off-the-peg suits were quickly altered to fit Flintlock and O'Hara.

Stiff and uncomfortable in a high-button suit, Flintlock wore a celluloid collar to conceal his tattoo that bit into his neck like a blunt razor. O'Hara tied back his hair and suffered every bit as much as Flintlock did.

But every eye in the restaurant was turned to Evangeline. She wore a ball gown of iridescent gold taffeta, gathered at the front, a steel-boned corset of the same color accented with leather straps and gold buckles and around her neck a thin gold chain with a cameo of Hera, the Greek goddess of womankind. He swept-up hair was adorned with a cascade of gold ribbons. She was the most beautiful woman in the restaurant that evening and probably in the whole state of Texas.

Like his collar, Flintlock's pants were too tight, his broken ribs ached and the handle of his Colt gouged into his belly. He'd just finished an appetizer of poached trout when Senator Boatwright said, "Evangeline has some good news to impart."

"Indeed I have," Evangeline said. She'd just eaten a little of the trout and now delicately dabbed her mouth with her napkin. "Sam, do you remember Lady Esther Carlisle telling us about the treasure hidden in the swamp by Vera Scobey? The one her husband hunted for all his life?"

Despite his discomfort Flintlock smiled and said, "Yes, Vera Scobey, the pirate called the Blue Fox. She stole a treasure from the British after the Battle of New Orleans and hid it in the swamp."

Evangeline smiled. "It's been recovered, or at least some of it. The storm uncovered the chest but broke it into pieces and most of the coins were lost in the swamp. But here is something wonderful. Lady Esther found it, she and Ahmed! Isn't that just too exquisite?"

The combination of looking into Evangeline's beautiful eyes and his crucifying collar made Flintlock even more uncomfortable. But he managed, "That is real great. It's just a pity all those golden guineas were lost."

"Not all of them, Sam," Cornelius said. He looked cool, comfortable and handsome in black broadcloth and frilled linen. "Ahmed recovered enough to pay an excellent team of lawyers should anyone like Ritter again try to cut down the cypress."

"And he'd also have the federal government down on him in a trice," Senator Boatwright said. "Washington always stands eager to help."

Evangeline raised her champagne glass. "Here's a toast to Lady Carlisle." After the "hear hears" had died away, she again raised her glass. "And a toast to the two bravest, most enduring men I have ever had the honor to know. I give you Sam Flintlock and O'Hara."

A few of the diners had been in the courtroom earlier and they joined in the applause with Senator Boatwright and Cornelius.

To his surprise Flintlock realized he could still blush, and O'Hara looked as though he was about to dive under the table at any moment.

There were more toasts, to Evangeline, to the senator and to Cornelius. Flintlock, deciding he was quite good at it, even toasted O'Hara, who withdrew his head into his collar like a turtle and squirmed. He would later tell Flintlock that if he ever toasted him again in front of a roomful of people he'd shoot him dead on the spot.

Chapter Fifty-Eight

Sam Flintlock decided to make the next morning's farewells as short as possible. He knew parting from Evangeline would tear his heart out, and when the moment came she seemed to understand how he felt.

Kisses were exchanged and Flintlock vowed to come back one day and visit the swamp. It was an empty promise and Evangeline knew it, but she and Flintlock went through the pretense that this was not goodbye but a mere "so long for now."

Then the men shook hands and it was over.

Evangeline and Cornelius were returning to Washington with Senator Boatwright for a series of receptions, and then she and her husband planned to visit Salem, Massachusetts, where Evangeline had relatives.

The senator's parting words to Flintlock were, "Remember, Sam, you're now my ward, so let me hear nothing but good of you."

"That meant don't rob any more banks, Sammy," O'Hara said.

"I'm done with that," Flintlock said, his eyes on the steam car as it headed for the railroad station. "Right now I feel like I'm done with everything."

"You'll get over her," O'Hara said. "There will be other women."

"None like Evangeline," Flintlock said.

"You're right about that," O'Hara said. "None of them will ever be like Evangeline."

Flintlock, restored to his buckskin shirt, baggy pants, battered hat and scuffed boots, had been told by the Ranger captain that he and O'Hara should drop by the jail and collect their guns and horses.

As they turned to head in that direction, a desk clerk hurried out of the hotel, something dark blue in his hand. "Mr. Flintlock, hold up," he said.

Flintlock stopped and the clerk said, "Mrs. Cornelius left this for you."

"What is it?"

"Well, sir, it looks like a silk scarf to me. And there's a note with it."

The clerk shoved the scarf and note into Flintlock's hand and hurried back to the hotel. He read the note first:

Sam, this is so you never have to wear that dreadful collar ever again.

Flintlock smiled and put the scarf to his nose. "It smells like an angel wore this." He placed the scarf around his neck, the fringed ends falling over his chest. "Evangeline wore it."

O'Hara said, "Sure ain't an angel wearing it now." Then, "Don't you think a silk scarf is a tad dainty on a man, Sammy?"

"Any ranny who calls me dainty will get a bullet," Flintlock said. "I ain't mentioning names, but that includes a certain Injun feller standing close."

O'Hara smiled. "I'll never mention it again."

"Yes, you will because that's the way you are, O'Hara. You get jealous about stuff. Now let's go see that Ranger."

Captain Fleet gave Flintlock his Hawken and Colt and O'Hara got his knife and gun rig. "I think you should have this," Fleet said to Flintlock. "It's Ranger Grogan's Winchester."

"Captain Fleet, I think his rifle should stay with the Rangers," Flintlock said.

"We all have Winchesters. You don't. I know Coon would want you to have it."

"I'm not too sure about that," Flintlock said. But he accepted the well-worn Winchester and said, "Thank you, Captain, I surely do appreciate it and I'll treasure this gun. I don't know what else to say."

"Well, I got something to say," Fleet said. "Don't disgrace that rifle. Don't surrender it to an enemy. Don't ever use it to kill an unarmed man. Don't use it to scare anyone weaker than yourself and I include women and children in that. And whatever you do, don't fail to live every day of your life with courage, like Ranger Grogan did." Fleet smiled. "Think you can handle that?"

"That's pretty much how I try to live my life, Captain," Flintlock said. "I'll do my best to live up to Coon's example."

"And there's one more thing, Flintlock," Fleet said. "Quit robbing the banks, will ya?"

"O'Hara already told me that this very morning."

"Then he's one wise Indian," Captain Fleet said. "Heed his advice."

O'Hara led both horses out of the barn and told Flintlock he'd saddle them. Old Barnabas took advantage of his absence and called Flintlock over to an empty stall. He still wore his top hat and goggles but this time he held a cannonball as big as a man's head in his hands.

"You-know-who is ordering us to make these now," he said. "They're the best cannonballs ever made. Perfectly round and cast from the finest iron to be found in Hell's fire."

"You don't need cannonballs in Hell, old man," Flintlock said.

"I know, but we give them to the Chinese, drop them out of the sky, like. The Celestials appreciate fine workmanship in cannonballs and they're mighty grateful." Barnabas tossed the ball into the air and caught it. Then he said, "Headed for the Arizony Territory, huh? Going to find your ma and have her give you your rightful name. Ain't that so?"

"It's the general idea, Barnabas," Flintlock said.

"Well, you ain't gonna get there anytime soon, sonny boy."

"How come?"

"Because you're an idiot and get involved with all kinds of folks. There are some mighty bad times lying ahead of you, Sam, lay to that. Here, catch!"

The ball hurtled toward Flintlock with so much speed it was as though he stood at a cannon's mouth. But at the last moment the heavy iron ball popped like a soap bubble and vanished.

Suddenly angry, all his pent-up frustration coming to the fore, Flintlock yelled, "Next time I see you, Barnabas, I'll . . . I'll . . ."

"Hollering at your old grandpappy, huh?" O'Hara said.

"If that old coot could die all over again, I'd like to put a bullet into him," Flintlock said.

O'Hara nodded. "Yeah, well I can understand that. But you got to admit, Barnabas sure makes a fine cannonball."

CHAPTER FIFTY-NINE

"No! You're crazy, Sammy," O'Hara said. "Hell, we're not going back to that damned swamp."

"He's still alive," Flintlock said. "He will always be a danger to Evangeline unless we kill him."

"Damn it, Sam, he's too smart for us. The Great Spirit appointed the alligators and the crocodiles to be the keepers and protectors of all knowledge. Basilisk is probably two hundred years old and he's learned a lot more in that time."

"He means to kill Evangeline one day. I can't let that stand."

"What about your ma? What about Arizona?"

"That can wait. We can ride the rails from here to Budville. It won't take too much time."

"How do you plan to find him?"

"He'll find us."

"Damn right he will."

Flintlock swung into the saddle. "I have enough money for two fares, O'Hara. But if you're not willing to go with me I'll understand."

O'Hara shook his head. "I was once told that Great Spirit made all white men crazy, now I believe it. The white half of me wants to go kill an alligator because it's just as crazy as you are."

"Well? State your intention."

"The white half of me wins every time."

Flintlock nodded. "And that's how it should be. Now let's go catch a train."

There was still a place on the map named Budville, but people lend a soul to every settlement, be it a hamlet or a great city, and when the people leave the town dies and only its ghost remains.

Budville wasn't yet dead but the death shadows were gathering when Flintlock and O'Hara rode into the town. The doors of the *Budville Democrat* were closed and shackled with iron padlocks and the saloon had put up a FOR SALE sign, bleak omens of what was to come.

It was still early in the morning and Flintlock decided not to linger. He and O'Hara rode directly for the swamp under a black sky, the smell of an approaching thunderstorm sharp in the air. By the time they reached the landing rain was falling and out in the Gulf the thunderstorm gathered its strength for its trek northward.

They found a place on dry ground to tether their horses and O'Hara said, "As you also say, Sammy . . . state your intentions."

"See any sign of Basilisk?" Flintlock said.

"Hell, no. We just got here."

"Do alligators like rain?"

"I don't know."

"I think maybe they do. Grab your rifle and we'll find a spot to stake out the bayou."

"And Basilisk, as obliging as you please, will swim right past us."

"Maybe so. Got a better idea?"

"Yeah, let's head back to Budville."

"We're not leaving here until we kill him, O'Hara. Damn, but you're a complaining Injun. And remember, you're not doing this for me, you're doing it for Evangeline. Now let's go."

Flintlock turned west, away from the landing, then swung through the trees until they found a patch of dry land overlooking the bayou. They got behind the cover of some willows and waited . . . and waited . . .

After an hour O'Hara said, "He ain't going to show, Sammy."

Rain ticked through the pines and fell heavily on the water. Thunder rumbled and every now and then the bayou glimmered white in the lightning flashes. There was no sign of a V-shaped ripple on the surface that would denote the passage of an alligator, large or small.

"Damn him," Flintlock said. "He knows we're here."

"I told you Basilisk was smarter than us," O'Hara said.

"This is his ground. He has an advantage over us."

"We're getting mighty wet."

"Wait just a while longer. If he doesn't show we'll come back tomorrow in better weather."

"Maybe we'd do better in a canoe," O'Hara said.

"If Basilisk is as smart as you say he'd know we were hunting him. He'd bite a canoe in half and us along with it. We'll stay where we are for another hour or so."

"Be really wet by then," O'Hara said, a comment that Flintlock chose to ignore. But he said, "I could sure use some of Evangeline's fried fish and cornbread, and then maybe some honey spread thick on the cornbread for dessert."

"Dessert? Where did you pick up that ten-dollar word?" O'Hara said.

"At dinner last night. The flunky said, 'Would sir care for dessert?' I said I would, not knowing what the hell he was talking about. Then he put a slice of steamed pudding in front of me with sweet yellow stuff all over it and I knew what the word *dessert* meant. Cornelius said the pudding was called spotted dick and that it was Queen Vic's favorite."

"Why do they call it spotted dick?"

"Because it's got raisins in it."

"Oh," O'Hara said. Then, suddenly alert, "What was that?"

"What was what?"

"I thought I heard something rustle."

"Must have been the wind," Flintlock said. Thunder roared, closer now, and lightning glittered and he thought he caught the sound of a sapling breaking. He did. And it was right behind him.

The monstrous form of Basilisk crashed through the undergrowth among the pines and charged directly at Flintlock and O'Hara. Among the confines of the slender willows he looked as big as a steam locomotive and as fast.

Flintlock dived to his left, rolled and

fetched his head up hard against a pine trunk, losing his rifle in the process. He heard O'Hara roar in pain, followed by a shout. "Sam!"

Rising groggily to his feet, Flintlock pulled his Colt from his waistband. He staggered toward O'Hara in time to see the man's left arm in the alligator's jaws. Basilisk, his reptilian eyes emotionless, dragged O'Hara toward the swamp. At a range of just a few feet, Flintlock emptied his Colt into the alligator's side. Basilisk bellowed and thrashed and released O'Hara. But then the alligator swung toward Flintlock, its jaws gaping. Flintlock stumbled back, fell and immediately with incredibly savage violence Basilisk clamped onto his booted right ankle. The crushing pain made Flintlock cry out and he felt himself being dragged toward the swamp. He reached out for his fallen Winchester but both his hand and the rifle were wet and muddy and it slipped through his fingers.

Then he was in the water and the alligator went into its death roll. Flintlock turned with Basilisk, but even so it felt as though his leg was about to be wrenched from his body. He steeled himself for some moments of tearing, searing agony and hoped that his death would be quick.

But then . . . nothing.

Basilisk, as huge around as a cypress trunk, lay on his back, his white belly turned to the rain and black sky. Blood stained the water around him. Flintlock heard a splash and then strong hands grabbed him and pulled him back to shore. O'Hara looked down on him, his face close. "How bad are you hurt?" he said.

"Bad," Flintlock said.

"Me too," O'Hara said. "Can you walk?"

"I don't know."

"Then try."

"I killed him, O'Hara," Flintlock said. "I got five shots into him."

"Next time bring a bigger gun," O'Hara said. "He could have torn you apart before he died. Now, let's see if I can help you get to your feet."

"He got your arm," Flintlock said.

O'Hara looked down at his shredded and bloody left arm. "Seems like," he said.

"Does it hurt?"

"Of course it damn well hurts. Are you crazy?"

"Sorry," Flintlock said. He checked to make sure that Evangeline's scarf was still in place and then climbed to his feet. He couldn't put any weight on his mangled ankle. "I don't think I can make it to my horse."

"You'd better. I'm sure as hell not carrying you and I'm not bringing the horses over here. I'd make it once, maybe, but not twice."

Flintlock turned his face to the pounding rain. Then he sighed deeply and said, "All right, let's try."

"I got a bottle of Old Crow in my saddlebags," O'Hara said. "It's yours when you get there. A prize for being brave."

"Where the hell did you get that?"

"I stole it from the hotel kitchen before we left."

"Damn it, O'Hara, sometimes you act the white man and make me real proud of you," Flintlock said. "Shall we proceed?"

"We'd better," O'Hara said. "When them little alligators get through eating the big alligator they might look at us as dessert."

Flintlock groaned as he took a step, then said, "You like that word, don't you, O'Hara?"

"Sure do. It's the kind of word can take a man far, help him make a name for himself and be somebody." Flintlock cursed his pain and O'Hara said, "But he won't get real far with that word, Sammy."

"Well, I only want that word to get me as

393

far as my horse," Flintlock said. He grimaced. "Now you're gonna hear some more of them words. Air out your lungs, O'Hara, we'll have at it together."

The two bloody, battered men turned the air around them blue with string after string of curses . . . it took them a while, but they made it to their horses.

The storm hadn't yet played out its string. In crashing thunder and pounding rain, Flintlock and O'Hara found shelter of sorts in a hole created by the roots of a toppled pine. They passed the whiskey bottle back and forth and gradually began to feel better, but O'Hara's tattered arm streamed blood and rain and Flintlock's ankle swelled inside his tooth-scarred boot, causing him considerable suffering.

"That's got to come off, Sammy," O'Hara said.

"I tried to pull it off but it's impossible. Hurts like hell."

"I'll cut it off," O'Hara said.

"It's the only boot I own."

"You got a second one."

"Damn it, O'Hara, it's on my other foot."

"It's got to come off, let your ankle swell," O'Hara said. "Besides, you may have wounds that need cleaned."

"You'll need to cut it. Damn, I've had that there boot for years."

"Seems like," O'Hara said, his face straight.

It took a lot of pain, a lot of cursing and a lot of wild accusations from Flintlock that O'Hara was an Apache in disguise and a lot of desperate swigs from the Old Crow bottle, but the boot finally came off. "Broke, I think," O'Hara said.

"Broke, I know," Flintlock said. "And you made it worse. Look at the size of the swelling. Hell, how's your arm, O'Hara? Your blood is all over me."

Thunder crashed and O'Hara waited until the sound rolled away and then said, "We both need a doctor, Sammy. Once the storm passes we'll mount up."

"That's going to be a sight to see," Flintlock said.

CHAPTER SIXTY

"Well, that's a sight to see," Dr. Oliver D. Toler said. "Mr. O'Hara, you're lucky you still have your arm."

"Will you look at my ankle, Doc?" Flintlock said.

"I can stitch it up, but there is some tissue loss and you may never have your full strength in this arm again," Dr. Toler said. "And I'm afraid there will be scarring. It's a large wound."

"It was a large alligator," O'Hara said.

"What about my ankle, Doc?" Flintlock said.

"Nurse Meadows, clean up Mr. O'Hara's arm, please. I want to get started on it right away."

"Anybody going to look at my ankle, Doc?" Flintlock said.

"Mr. Flintlock, it's a bad sprain," the doctor said. "I'll bind it up for you later. Now tell me, in the name of God, how can someone escape the jaws of an alligator and suffer only a sprain?"

"I'd already shot it, Doc," Flintlock said. "Maybe it wasn't feeling too good."

"I don't agree with killing animals," Nurse Millie Meadows said. She was a tall thin woman, with a little steel purse of a mouth that snapped open and shut and slightly protruding blue eyes. She carried a brown bottle and a swab.

"You would have agreed with killing Basilisk," Flintlock said. "He'd been a man-eater for two hundred years and maybe longer."

"We're all God's creatures, Mr. Flintlock." Then to O'Hara, "This stuff stings like crazy, so you must be a brave little soldier."

Flintlock watched the nurse start to clean up O'Hara's arm. "Does it sting?" he said.

"Like crazy," O'Hara said, his mouth tight.

"You're next, Mr. Flintlock," Nurse Meadows said. "Let's hope you're as brave a little soldier as your friend."

"Tough to be brave when the nurse from Hell is bandaging up a broken ankle," Flintlock said.

"It's only sprained," O'Hara said.

"It felt like it was broke."

"Yeah, well my arm felt as though he was

sawing it off at the elbow," O'Hara said. "Ah, here's the restaurant, Ma's Kitchen. And Doc Toler was right. They are looking for a dishwasher."

Flintlock glanced at the sign in the window and said, "I say we ride on out of here. Look at this town, there's hardly enough people left to dirty dishes."

"Sam, you heard what the doc said — we need to stay in town for a few weeks to make sure my arm doesn't get infected," O'Hara said. "Besides, we're broke. How are we going to reach the Arizona Territory without a grubstake?"

Flintlock had a borrowed crutch under his arm, a fat bandage on his foot, and O'Hara's arm was in a sling.

"And you need boots," O'Hara said.

"I can't stand on a bad ankle and wash dishes," Flintlock said.

"I reckon they'll give you a chair, Sammy. And Doc says Ma is paying fifty cents a day. That's good money around these parts."

"O'Hara, maybe I could gun an outlaw along the trail and claim the reward," Flintlock said. "It's time I went back to practicing my old profession anyhow. I'd say it's a plan that beats dishwashing."

"Too thin, Sam. We need fifty cents a day to survive while my wounds heal. You heard what Dr. Toler said about gangrene. I could lose my arm."

Flintlock's shoulders slumped. "All right," he said, "I got no other choice but to put my head in the noose."

A couple of men were eating a late lunch when Flintlock stepped into the restaurant. "Take a seat," a large woman said. "God knows there's enough of them." Then, after looking Flintlock up and down from the tattoo on his throat to his bandaged ankle, she said, "What the hell are you?"

"I'm a dishwasher," Flintlock said.

"No, he ain't, Ma." One of the diners stood. "He's the ranny that robbed the bank."

"I gave the money back," Flintlock said.

"It was Mathias Cobb who was the real robber, Elmer," Ma said. "He's the one who destroyed this town."

"You can't trust that outlaw, Ma," the man called Elmer said. "He'll rob you blind."

"Hell, I got nothing much left to rob," Ma said. "And I need a dishwasher. Kitchen's that way, mister, and the wage is fifty cents a day and grub. You can bed down in the kitchen if you got nowhere else to live and by the look of you, you don't."

Flintlock touched his hat. "I'm much

obliged, ma'am. Name's —"

"I don't care what your name is. You can call me Ma. I'll get you a chair so you can sit at the sink. Well? Get started."

When Flintlock stepped into the kitchen he was appalled. His predecessor must have quit a while back because there were teetering pillars of dirty plates, mountains of pots and pans and tangled masses of silverware.

Flintlock found an apron and started in to earn his fifty cents.

Six weeks later Ma closed her kitchen for lack of customers. She said she was moving to Philadelphia to live with her widowed sister. By then O'Hara's arm was healing nicely and Sam Flintlock's ankle was back to normal. Ma, impressed by Flintlock's efforts, told him he was a credit to the dishwashing profession and she filled a couple of sacks with leftover grub for the trail. "I hope you find your ma, Sam," she said as she closed the restaurant door for the last time.

Three days later Dr. Toler took down his shingle and moved on with Nurse Meadows, who was now his bride, and the saloon closed the very same day. Flintlock and O'Hara had kept their horses at the abandoned livery and the animals had gone through all the hay and oats that had been left behind and were in fine shape for the trail.

Matthew Garry, the general store owner, sold his entire stock "at below cost," and Flintlock and O'Hara were able to outfit themselves for the coming winter cheaply.

As they rode out of Budville under a clear fall sky, O'Hara said, "I'm looking forward to a peaceful trail, Sammy, shooting my own grub along the way and sleeping on dry land under the stars."

"That makes two of us," Flintlock said. "You know, I've been thinking. I believe I could prosper in the restaurant business."

"Why not? Ma gave you some good dish-washing experience and that's all it takes, experience."

"Well, I'll find my ma and then decide," Flintlock said. "Just plain home cooking, mind, steaks and eggs and pork chops. Nothing fancy."

"Why, the more I think on it, the more I feel it's a crackerjack idea, Sammy," O'Hara said. "I'd like to throw in with you."

"Sure," Flintlock said. He extended his hand. "It's a deal."

"What are we going to call our place?"

"The Evangeline," Flintlock said.

And O'Hara said, "Crackerjack!"

Chapter Sixty-One:
Afterward

Sam Flintlock and his half-breed sidekick O'Hara found the town of Bearsden by accident. It was an ill-starred discovery that they very soon would have cause to regret.

They were twenty miles south of the New Mexico Territory and a few miles east of the southernmost ridges of the Guadalupe Mountains in the rugged Delaware Basin country when Flintlock said he smelled a pig on a spit.

"Wind's blowing from the north, so it's got to be just ahead of us," he said. "Man, I could eat some of that."

"I smell it too, but I never heard tell of any settlement around this part of the country," O'Hara said.

"Well, maybe it's a ranch cookout or even a hunting party," Flintlock said. "I sure aim to find out."

The vast bulk of the Guadalupe looked like a great monolithic wall through the desert erected by a giant race of men in times past. But that was deceptive. Within the wall lay dramatic canyons, hanging valleys and shady glades surrounded by desert scrub and a profusion of wildlife.

Flintlock said, "Why not build a town around here? It's as good a place as any."

O'Hara nodded. "There's something not setting right with me, Sam. I have the feeling we're riding into —"

"Danger?"

"I don't know. Something . . . bad."

"That's the Injun in you talking, O'Hara. Injuns reckon there's evil spirits and such just around every bend of the trail."

O'Hara shook his head, his long black hair moving across his shoulders. "I can't shake it, Sam. I say we ride on."

"Look!" Flintlock said, pointing. "See how wrong you are? It's a town all right and I bet they're roasting a pig."

Ahead of them lay a one-street town like thousands of others in the West, dusty, dry and barely clinging to life. But for two hungry and thirsty men it was an oasis in the desert, as bright and beckoning as any big city back east.

"Grin, O'Hara. Look, stretch your mouth wide like me."

"Why?" O'Hara was always inclined to

surliness when something troubled him.

"Because we're flat broke and we're depending on the generosity of others. Now grin, like we're visiting kinfolk."

O'Hara tried, but his grin came off as a grimace. It didn't really matter because when they rode into the street Flintlock's own grin vanished like frost in sunlight. A gallows, hung with red, white and blue bunting, had been erected at the entrance to the town and a booted man hung from a hemp noose. His neck was twisted to one side, his tongue lolled out of his mouth and his eyes, bulging out of his head, were wide open. But he'd ceased to see anything hours before when his neck broke.

A sign on the gallows said, WELCOME TO BEARSDEN.

But there was no one around to form a welcoming committee. The street was deserted.

Tables laden with food, fried chicken, great haunches of beef, cakes, pies and even a melting tub of ice cream lined the boardwalk. The pig Flintlock had smelled was spiked on a spit but since there was no one to turn the handle the huge hog had begun to char and dripped fat into the flames of the fire. All the stores were bright with bunting, their doors wide open, and inside the empty saloon a player piano tinkled the tune, " 'Tis the Last Rose of Summer."

Flintlock drew rein and said to O'Hara, "Where the hell is everybody? Hell, I don't even see a horse around or a even a dog."

"Sammy, I don't like this," O'Hara said. "Let's get out of here."

"With all this grub around and a wide-open saloon? Are you nuts?"

The crash of a rifle shot shattered the quiet, followed by a scream. "It came from the livery stable," Flintlock said. He kicked his horse into motion, O'Hara, his Winchester in his hands, close behind him.

Flintlock reined in his horse, pulled his Colt from his waistband and warily stepped from bright sun into the gloom of the stable. Gun smoke hung in the air . . . but the place was deserted.

O'Hara stepped beside Flintlock and said, "Sam, this is a bad luck town and there's evil around. We got to get out of here now."

"I think we're already way too late," Sam Flintlock said.

J. A. JOHNSTONE ON WILLIAM W. JOHNSTONE
"PRINT THE LEGEND"

William W. Johnstone was born in southern Missouri, the youngest of four children. He was raised with strong moral and family values by his minister father, and tutored by his schoolteacher mother. Despite this, he quit school at age fifteen.

"I have the highest respect for education," he says, "but such is the folly of youth, and wanting to see the world beyond the four walls and the blackboard."

True to this vow, Bill attempted to enlist in the French Foreign Legion ("I saw Gary Cooper in *Beau Geste* when I was a kid and I thought the French Foreign Legion would be fun") but was rejected, thankfully, for being underage. Instead, he joined a traveling carnival and did all kinds of odd jobs. It was listening to the veteran carny folk, some of whom had been on the circuit since the late 1800s, telling amazing tales about their experiences, that planted the storytelling seed in Bill's imagination.

"They were mostly honest people, despite the bad reputation traveling carny shows had back then," Bill remembers. "Of course, there were exceptions. There was one guy named Picky, who got that name because he was a master pickpocket. He could steal a man's socks right off his feet without him knowing. Believe me, Picky got us chased out of more than a few towns."

After a few months of this grueling existence, Bill returned home and finished high school. Next came stints as a deputy sheriff in the Tallulah, Louisiana, Sheriff's Department, followed by a hitch in the U.S. Army. Then he began a career in radio broadcasting at KTLD in Tallulah, which would last sixteen years. It was there that he fine-tuned his storytelling skills. He turned to writing in 1970, but it wouldn't be until 1979 that his first novel, *The Devil's Kiss,* was published. Thus began the full-time writing career of William W. Johnstone. He wrote horror (*The Uninvited*), thrillers (*The Last of the Dog Team*), even a romance novel or two. Then, in February 1983, *Out of the Ashes* was published. Searching for his missing family in a postapocalyptic America, rebel mercenary and patriot Ben Raines is united with the civilians of the Resistance forces and moves to the forefront of a revolution for the nation's future.

Out of the Ashes was a smash. The series would continue for the next twenty years, winning Bill three generations of fans all over the world. The series was often imitated but never duplicated. "We all tried to copy the Ashes series," said one publishing executive, "but Bill's uncanny ability, both then and now, to predict in which direction the political winds were blowing brought a certain immediacy to the table no one else could capture." The Ashes series would end its run with more than thirty-four books and twenty million copies in print, making it one of the most successful men's action series in American book publishing. (The Ashes series also, Bill notes with a touch of pride, got him on the FBI's Watch List for its less than flattering portrayal of spineless politicians and the growing power of big government over our lives, among other things. In that respect, I often find myself saying, "Bill was years ahead of his time.")

Always steps ahead of the political curve, Bill's recent thrillers, written with myself, include *Vengeance Is Mine, Invasion USA, Border War, Jackknife, Remember the Alamo, Home Invasion, Phoenix Rising, The Blood of Patriots, The Bleeding Edge,* and the upcoming *Suicide Mission.*

It is with the western, though, that Bill found his greatest success. His westerns propelled him onto both the *USA Today* and the *New York Times* bestseller lists.

Bill's western series include *Matt Jensen, the Last Mountain Man, Preacher, the First Mountain Man, The Family Jensen, Luke Jensen, Bounty Hunter, Eagles, MacCallister* (an Eagles spin-off), *Sidewinders, The Brothers O'Brien, Sixkiller, Blood Bond, The Last Gunfighter,* and the new series *Flintlock* and *The Trail West.* May 2013 saw the hardcover western *Butch Cassidy: The Lost Years.*

"The western," Bill says, "is one of the few true art forms that is one hundred percent American. I liken the western to America's version of England's Arthurian legends, like the Knights of the Round Table, or Robin Hood and his Merry Men. Starting with the 1902 publication of *The Virginian* by Owen Wister, and followed by the greats like Zane Grey, Max Brand, Ernest Haycox, and of course Louis L'Amour, the western has helped to shape the cultural landscape of America.

"I'm no goggle-eyed college academic, so when my fans ask me why the western is as popular now as it was a century ago, I don't offer a 200-page thesis. Instead, I can only offer this: The western is honest. In this great country, which is suffering under the yoke of political correctness, the western harks back to an era when justice was sure and swift. Steal a man's horse, rustle his cattle, rob a bank, a stagecoach, or a train, you were hunted down and fitted with a hangman's noose. One size fit all.

"Sure, we westerners are prone to a little embellishment and exaggeration and, I admit it, occasionally play a little fast and loose with the facts. But we do so for a very good reason — to enhance the enjoyment of readers.

"It was Owen Wister, in *The Virginian,* who first coined the phrase 'When you call me that, smile.' Legend has it that Wister actually heard those words spoken by a deputy sheriff in Medicine Bow, Wyoming, when another poker player called him a son of a bitch.

"Did it really happen, or is it one of those myths that have passed down from one generation to the next? I honestly don't know. But there's a line in one of my favorite westerns of all time, *The Man Who Shot Liberty Valance,* where the newspaper editor tells the young reporter, 'When the truth becomes legend, print the legend.'

"These are the words I live by."